A Place to Stand

Meg Farrell

A Place to Stand

Copyright ©2014, M. Farrell

Farrell Writes, LLC

ALL RIGHTS RESERVED. This book contains material protected under International and Federal Copyright Laws and Treaties. Any unauthorized reprint or use of this material is prohibited. No part of this book may be reproduced or transmitted in any form or by any means, electronic or mechanical, including photocopying, recording, or by any information storage and retrieval system without express written permission from the author/publisher.

ISBN: 1500493791

ISBN-13: 978-1500493790

Dedication

To the best husband ever.
My best friend and life-partner.

I could not have done this without you
constantly saying, "you can do it!"

A Place to Stand

Mea Farrell

Acknowledgements

Cover design: Marisa Wesley of Cover Me Darling
http://covermedarling.com

Editor: Victoria Miller
http://www.victoriamillerartist.com

Formatting: Bridgette O'Hare of Wit & Whimsy Designs

A Place to Stand

1
Worst Case

There I was. It happened. The worst-case scenario you'd never think of. It happened to me. My world shattered in unimaginable ways. The person I loved most in this world is gone. In a flash. Just a moment is all it took. Gone. Never coming back. Never smiling at me again. Never chuckling at my insipid humor. Never nodding in agreement with my sarcastic, cynical rants. No more lustful smiles. Never seeing the look in his eyes that could reach me wherever I was and let me know I am loved. I have to stop listing all the things I'll miss.

You never think about what it will be like when they're gone. You fall in love and you build a life together. You suffer through heartache and rejoice in life's miracles. You never, ever, think that you will, one day, go on living without the person who completed the other half of your soul. It's not something I ever thought of it. The day I met Ryan, I knew he was my other half. I have always been fiercely independent. To the dismay of my parents, I made life choices when they felt right, even if logic said my choices were wrong. I sometimes think it scared them that I fell so hopelessly in love with Ryan and how fast I fell for him. And now... now here I am. Mourning him.

Maybe it was all too fast. The candle burned too bright and couldn't last. Had we loved each other too much? What happened was an accident. A moment in time. Wrong place, right time? Right time, wrong place? Only a moment.

The moment that would forever change my life is always on repeat in my mind. Like historic moments shared throughout the world. Where were you when Kennedy was killed? What were you doing when you heard about the World Trade Center attacks? In my own personal world, I would always know where I was when I heard. I would forever remember the details I drilled out of the messenger who bore the worst news I would ever experience. My life ended in that moment. I wish it had ended, anyway. I don't know how I am supposed to move on with life. I always thought that when death parted us we would be nearly one hundred years old. That if we parted by death, I wouldn't be far behind him or him far behind me.

I want everything to end. Essentially it has, but here I am. Still breathing. Living in the physical sense of the word. My heart beats. My lungs process oxygen into my bloodstream. My eyes see. My ears hear. Living. Just barely. My body takes in air, so essentially, I'm breathing. Why does it feel like my chest has permanently caved in? Why do my hands and legs feel numb all the time? Why is my head foggy? All the functions of my body work, yet nothing works. Life goes on. The sun rises and sets. Time passes. Why can't I follow where he went?

Why do I think this way? Would he want me to think this way? *No.* I know the answer to that one question. The only thing Ryan would have wanted was for me to be happy. He would have told me to live. Go on with life. Be happy. But he didn't get that chance. We didn't get to talk about any of this before it happened. I know—*knew*—him. I know his mind; he knew mine. *"Live. Be happy."* It would have been a very serious face he gave me when he meant what he was saying. I could almost visualize the small half-grin he would give after being so serious. He would wait for that recognition in my face that let him know I took his point to heart, then would come that half-grin. *Yes. There it is.* If I close my eyes, I can see it. I can see his face.

God, I don't know what I'll do if there comes a time when I can't see that face. When I close my eyes and dig deep, I can see that smile and hear that laugh. He is alive. He is alive and holding me in a warm embrace. What happens to me when I can't feel his arms around me anymore? I shiver as tears begin rolling down my cheeks.

"Sweetie?"

I sigh. I don't want to look away from him. If I open my eyes to look at my sister, he'll fade away.

"Rhae. Honey. Take this."

Damn. I'm going to have open my eyes. It is real. I'm really sitting in this room. Slowly, I look up at my sister. The long, black, curls of her hair are tickling my nose. Why is she so close?

"Do you need a pill? I can get you a shot of something in this tea. Whatever you want, just tell me."

I chuckle. It feels wrong but necessary. People stare at me. This is how we always get through tough times. Every funeral or family reunion, we had Percocet, Xanax and/or whiskey or vodka. We were always such a mess when it came to emotional dealings. Of course she would be here for this time in my life. Holding me up and taping me together with pills and liquor. Honestly, it was all I wanted. Numb. I needed to be numb.

"Hey. Thanks. Yes. Put something in my tea, and bring me whatever you have in your purse." I try to give a smile of gratitude. I'm not sure it comes across that way. It just feels awkward.

She always had a good hookup. Jess worked at the local casinos. Either serving or tending bar. She loves it. She is an amazing server. All the other bartenders and dealers had the hookups on pills. Whatever you needed, they could get it. I'm not sure if they needed it to get through all the crazy hours they worked or to relax at the end of their shifts. I'm pretty sure that doctor they dragged me to see a few days ago gave her a stash of something to keep me even.

She leaves me holding the tea and then goes to get her purse. Relatives stopping her on the way. They look from her to me and back. She shakes her head and keeps moving. Whatever she said to them, makes their expressions change and they stare with such sadness before moving back to their personal discussions. I hate it. Why do they have to show so much pity? Fake bitches. I can smell the fake a mile away. I hate these things. This was no ordinary gathering, though. No. It is a visitation for my dead husband's funeral. Five years of marriage. Gone.

Someone calls my name, and I turn to see a coworker slowly approaching. I hate her. Rage and panic start to swell in my gut. *Why is she here?* I need to get out of here. My breathing quickens. She raises her arms to hug me. I don't know what else to do. I drop the tea cup and run. I push through the crowd, knocking into old people—I have no idea who. I just run. Bursting through the doors at the back of the funeral home, I skid to a stop in the late afternoon sun. I have to cover my eyes. It has been so long since I saw daylight that it hurts. I feel the tears again. They are hot lava running down my face and dripping cold on my chest. Maybe there's snot mixed in. I can't tell. I stand there, sucking air into my mouth, to make it stop. I hate crying. I hate how this is making me feel. I want to be numb or dead. Either would suit me fine. I have no idea where I'm going. I just can't go back in there.

"Rhae, honey! Come here." Jess is grabbing at me. She hugs me, and I feel my knees buckle. I collapse to the ground and damn if that doesn't hurt. My knees grind into the concrete. Probably tore my hose. Probably cut my knees. I'm always graceful like that. *Why did I wear a dress and hose?* I shake my head and chuckle. Poor Jess is on the ground with me. I can be such an ox sometimes.

"Sorry."

Jess holds me back from her, "Don't be sorry. Here, put this in your mouth. Drink this. Swallow." She orders me, and I respond like a robot or a small child. I don't ask questions. I just take what she hands me. All the while laughing like I have lost my mind. I collapse in her arms again. This is good. I think I'll just stay here a while. I try to rest my head against her chest for a few minutes when I hear more some shuffling, doors opening and closing.

"You got her, baby?" My dad comes out looking for us.

"Yeah, Dad. I got her."

"Take her home. I'll handle the rest of the visitation. Get her to bed. She can't take this."

Did his voice crack? My dad is breaking down, too. God, why couldn't I be strong through this for him? It hasn't been that long since

Mama passed. I guess about four years. He had been strong through that. I didn't see him cry. He never lost his composure. He certainly never freaked out and ran away. Even in this moment, he does an amazing job of living since she died. It hasn't occurred to me, until now, that Dad had been close to Ryan. My poor father had three girls. No sons. His first "son" was Ryan. Dad would call Ryan when he had technology questions, including how to use his cell phone. They spent a lot of time together doing what men do in work sheds. I always thought it was mostly drinking beer and trash talking about the women in our family. We are a hard-headed bunch. Demanding and particular, we could drive people insane, quickly. I laugh just thinking about it.

I hear Jess whisper something to her husband, who I hadn't realized was standing there. Then he's gone. That man is stealthy! I would have to remember to ask Jess about it one day. She and Dad finish talking. The desire to curl into a ball and lay on the concrete for a while is all consuming. Everything feels cold despite the heat. July in Mississippi is ridiculous. It's hot in the shade. It's hot sitting in a pool of ice. I have seen people stand in the heat long enough to start melting the soles of their shoes. Clichés about cooking eggs on pavement come to mind. Hell, today we could throw down some bacon and get a sizzle.

My thoughts are fuzzy, and I realize that whatever Jess had given to me is starting to take effect. I want to get up and hug my dad for being so strong for me when Mom died and even stronger now that I'm a...what am I? A widow? The opportunity passes while I'm lost in my thoughts. I look around and see dad walking back inside anyway. I haven't embarrassed him. That feeling doesn't last long. Definitely that pill working. I have no idea what Jess gave me, but it is lovely. Numbness is slowly creeping through my body. I sigh, hoping to relax long enough to let it.

"Bitch! Get off the damn ground! Your knees are bleeding through your hose. Get the fuck up."

I snap my eyes open. *Who? Dammit, Elizabeth made it. God love her.* I start laughing.

"Guess, I am a mess. When did you get here?" She shakes her head and helps me get on my feet.

"In plenty of time to see you bust up out of that sad-as-hell room. Let's get you home. Let's get you drunk. I'll crawl in the bed and cuddle you if you need it."

"I need it." Before I know it, my knees are buckling again.

"Oh, bitch! No, you don't. I can't hold your ass up. Walk. Move one foot then the other. We're leaving." Jess and Liz are laughing together. Sometimes I guess laughing is all you have left. It feels better to be laughing.

At that moment, my brother-in-law pulls up. He comes around the front of the truck to help Jess and Liz. Jess moves out of the way, passing me to Connor. He helps me into his jacked, redneck truck. Connor is such a good guy. He and Ryan were as close as brothers. They had jacked up Ryan's Jeep Wrangler together last summer. Ryan didn't know much about cars. Okay, so he knew nothing about cars. Connor taught him everything. It's the biggest reason I can't look at Connor right now. If I do, I will see the pain he feels from losing his friend. I lost more but seeing that pain in others isn't something I can handle.

"Rhae! Help us get your big ass in the truck!" Liz is fussing. I'm wrapped up in my head again and frozen my progress as I focus on not looking at Connor's face. He has the truck running and the air conditioning going for me. Probably so my ass wouldn't stick to the vinyl seats. *Gross Mississippi heat.* I start moving again. My knees hurt like hell. *I guess I really did land on them bad when I ran away from the funeral home.*

Jess climbs in behind me. Liz and Jess talk for a minute, and then we're off. I fade in and out of consciousness as we drive. Jess is rubbing my arms and squeezing me every time I make any kind of noise. The ride is smooth except on the highway. Geez, we have potholes that can swallow a Volkswagen. Still, the rhythm of the ride lets me rest in my numb state just a little while longer.

Sometime after we get to Jess's house, I'm led to a bed and left alone for a few minutes. I crawl to the middle and sit staring blankly at the wall. I'm thankful they didn't take me back to our house. The thought of being in the bedroom I had shared with my husband isn't appealing. Although, the more I think about it, I can almost smell our sheets. I can almost hear his snoring. That man could snore. Tornados did less damage to windows than his snoring. Closing my eyes, I'm lost in memories of watching him sleep. I chuckle out loud as Jess and Liz come back through the door.

They exchange a look with each other and then side-eye me. "Okay, what is it? What were you thinking about?" Liz asks. I start to answer but my laughs turn to sobs. They both sit on the bed with me, trying to hold me, stroking my hair and wiping tears from my face. I push them back.

"Stop. Please. Just stop." I nearly scream at them.

"Right. Here. Drink this." Jess is pushing more booze.

I take the glass gratefully and gulp down whatever she handed me. It burns my throat, and I have to hold my breath to swallow it all. "More."

Jess nods and leaves to get me more liquor. When she returns, I decide to sip this glass. She and Liz start to banter back and forth. I really don't have anything to contribute to the conversation, so I just listen and sip. Liz is older than us by about five or six years. I can't remember what our actual age difference is. I do remember when we lived across the street from her. She was our babysitter. My mom worked nights, my dad worked all the time, and her mom didn't work. She was a teenager while we were still in elementary school. I always smile like a goof when I think back to those days.

We were such little dorks. We did everything she said. She was the coolest thing ever. We count her as one of the sisters. My parents had so many more daughters than they knew about. We adopted anyone that stuck around and showed any hint of loyalty. I actually have two real sisters, but I hadn't lasted at the visitation long enough to see if Marie had shown up. We haven't spoken in about a year since she got remarried. That situation is also upsetting, and I can't think about it right now.

I shake my head and laugh. "Bitch!" I look between Jess and Liz.

They are looking at me like I have lost my mind. Again. I laugh, "Sorry. I was just thinking about Marie and all that bullshit."

The girls keep feeding me drinks until I don't have taste buds left. My throat is scorched from all the liquor. I just drink whatever they hand me.

"You numb yet?" Jess asks.

"Pretty sure I can't feel my nose, teeth or lips anymore." My voice sounds foreign and slurry.

Liz laughs. "Great. Now it's time for 'deal with this shit' therapy."

I groan, "Do I have to? Can't I just enjoy being numb?"

Jess shoots her a look. "Yes. We have enough chemical support to get you to a happy place. A place in your little mind where you can deal with all the fake, crying, hugging bitches at the funeral tomorrow." Jess is a mind reader. She knows exactly what I think about people at funerals. Sure, they are friends, family and coworkers, but I despise the way people change and act at funerals.

"Where do we start?"

"Music." God love Jess. She always knows what I need. She turns on the iPod and I freeze up.

"What the hell, Jess!" Country music is pouring around the room. She and Liz jump up and start spinning each other. I have no idea if this is the schottische or the freaking "Cotton-eyed Joe." Mississippi's best rednecks probably couldn't tell. These two are probably as numb as I am at this point. Somewhere in the back of my mind I hope Connor is downstairs, sober. These sweet idiots don't need to drive or be near an open flame. Plus, my niece, Jillian, doesn't need to see any of this. I hope some family member is watching her, but I have no idea where all the kids ended up. This is always my role. I'm the overly responsible adult in this group. I have looked after these two on more than one occasion when porch perchin' had turned to porch dancin' or a late-night run to Sonic.

Somehow, I can't help myself. I start laughing so hard there are tears rolling down my face. Surely, I'm going to run out of tears soon. *Just run dry already. Damn it.* It's about that time Jess hits the floor. She can't spin herself or stand any longer. Connor bursts in to see what's wrong. Just the look on his face is priceless. He helps Jess off the floor, then sits down by me on the bed and starts laughing at his drunk wife. I hear more than a few "yee haws" and "woo hoos." For a while, I don't think about Ryan. I don't think about my responsibilities. I can't think about what comes next. I just want to forget for a while.

"For crying out loud! What the hell are you doing to her?" Jess stops mid-spin and starts laughing.

Another one of our adopted sisters, Red, has arrived. Red is really Amber. We have called her Red for forever on account of that hair. She keeps it short. Almost pixie-like. I have known Red since I was thirteen years old. She is my rock when Jess and Liz got into this country shit. I'm such a rock girl. Red is only slightly older than me. She took me under her wing and taught me what great music there was in the 80s. I mean, Red gave me The Smiths, Elvis Costello, The Cure—the good stuff. My parents raised me on the 60s' greatest hits.

Later Red and I would discover 90s' alternative rock together. She always got a kick out of Ryan and I, too. She enjoyed that he had introduced me to 70s' classic rock, and progressive rock from every generation. I never heard Pink Floyd or Led Zeppelin before Ryan. Then there was Rush; his absolute favorite band. He was a guitarist and loved every technical aspect of playing progressive rock. He was so good at it too. He had magical fingers. I sigh. Before I can start feeling anything again, I turn my attention to the sisters.

"Country's greatest, Jess? Really? As if she isn't going through enough, you torture her with this shit." Red is displaying faux frustration with her hands on her hips and fighting a smile.

Jess can only laugh. Liz and Jess are three sheets to the wind. They are beyond caring what Red's saying.

They all continued to trash-talk each other for a long time. I suspect that some of it is forced for my benefit. The longer they can keep me numb and distracted the better, and they know it. Surrounded by their laughter and shitty banter, I lay back on the bed and fall asleep.

2
Funeral

I wake the next morning spooned against Jess's back. I tilt my body to try and stretch when I bump into Liz. "Bitch," she murmurs in her sleepy stupor. Lord, it's her favorite word. Everyone is a bitch. *Bitch* is a multi-functional word for her. It is a noun, pronoun, proper noun, verb, adverb... you name the part of grammar, she uses it in that context. I love her for it, too. That girl has been looking after us for nearly fifteen years and she's still here. Cuddling me through this pain like she said she would.

I look over and see Red passed out in an arm chair. She is small enough to ball her whole body up in the damn thing. I wish I was a petite, feisty red-head. She is so fun. No one gives her shit. She hands people their asses and is my mentor in sarcasm. I take in the scene around me and know I can't ask for better people to see me through this. Sisters all around me. Every last one of us. But where is Marie? I have a momentary ache of concern. I sigh in resignation and shake the thought.

Very carefully, I inch toward the end of the bed, sliding out of the middle. Jess flops on to her back and stretches, while Liz does the same on her tummy. I grin and make my way to the bathroom. I have to pee so bad I think my bladder is going to jump out. I am washing my hands and consider using Jess's toothbrush when I accidentally look up into the mirror. I freeze. I don't recognize myself. My eyes are puffy and bloodshot. Dark circles reach deep under my eyes. I'm ghostly pale, yet my nose is bright red. My hair is sticking out in every direction possible. I am a hot damn mess.

I decide to take a shower even though I don't have clean clothes. I run the shower and get in. The water is hot enough to melt skin. I wash my hair and soap my body. Then I stand under the water letting the heat numb me again. That is all I want, numbness. I don't want to feel or deal with anything. Can't Jess and Liz sign papers and make phone calls? Red can certainly deal with life insurance and payoffs on stuff. They can get the death certificate.

Death certificate. Yeah. I have to have that now, too. There is actual documentation that certifies Ryan is gone. Dead. Somehow, I slide down to the tub and rest on my aching knees. I guess that sting is all the scrapes from yesterday. Then I remember how southern people handle death. People are going to be coming over all day. I shake my head and try to forget that part. I really dislike people, in general. At some point I start crying as I'm thinking through all the details of the coming days. Ryan always did the right, social things. He always held me up, an arm around my waist, and helped me do the right things. I was always so awkward in a crowd of people. He was a superstar. People loved him. He was warm and genuine. Just laid back all the time. Easy going.

My throat aches and my back hurts. I'm shaking all over. I don't notice the water is running cold. I have no idea how long I sit under the cold streams crying when they're finally turned off. I look up and Jess is holding open a bath robe. I stand and wrap it around me. I try to wipe the tears and water from my face. Maybe she can't see the tears.

"I'm sorry. I'll help pay the water bill."

"Are you crazy? Don't worry about that. Let's get your hair combed out before it knots up."

My hair is the same as hers—long, black, curly. It knots up easily. Jess sits me on a stool at her vanity. She is a classic southern belle in some respects. She has her vanity and her tools of torture…I mean brushes and combs. I'm sure, if I dig around, I'll find the flask she keeps in her bra at social events. Not to mention the piles and piles of makeup she is so adept at applying. Compared to her, I am a plain girl. I don't get so much into the aspects of being presentable and beautiful at all times. Ryan had loved me anyway. I was just his type of "no fuss" girl. *God, I miss him*. He would have laughed endlessly at her primping me the way she does.

She decides the heat is just too much. Flat-ironing my hair would look amazing at the funeral, but she decides against it. Sweat is worse for forced-flat hair than humidity. I sit still like a child. She oils my hair, combs through it as gently as possible for her, which isn't gentle at all, turns out. I can't look in the mirror while she works. We look so much alike that seeing us together in that mirror would reinforce just how horrible I look and feel right now. I just sit with my eyes closed and focus on not thinking. When she finishes, I know better than to mess up her work, but I can't help the desire I have to climb back in bed. Once I'm there, I become aware that Liz is gone, and Red isn't in the chair.

"Where's Liz?"

"Making breakfast. You scared us when you got up like that."

"Where's Red?"

"She and Connor went to get your car from the funeral home."

I nod, and then something she said comes back to me. "Scared you?"

"Yeah. I'm not saying you're not capable, but you don't know how to live without him. We are seriously concerned. Don't be mad, but that's why we all slept here last night. You needed us, but we needed to be sure you wouldn't do anything...drastic."

Ouch. That hurts. It's just Jess being Jess. Honest and straightforward. That's her way. "True. You can trust me. I'm not stupid. I couldn't do that to you or dad."

"You can't. Do you hear me?" She lowers herself until she's eye level with me. Nose to nose. "We can get you through this. But you have to agree to keep living." I stare into her emerald eyes; they are just like Mama's. Her worry is evident.

"I know. Didn't your dumb ass hear the shower running? That should have let you know where I was, and that I was okay." I try to lighten the mood.

"I did, but that doesn't mean you didn't... You could have...never mind..."

I absorb her words. It's shocking that she thinks I could do that. "Jess, promise me one thing."

"Anything." She is rubbing my back now; a sure-fire way to put me to sleep quickly.

Sleepily and through a yawn, I manage to make my one request. "Don't let me feel anything. Okay? Promise?"

She doesn't answer immediately. Finally, she says, "Promise."

I can count on Jess to hold up her end of the deal. She will be my buffer. She can get me through this. We have always gotten each other through the tough stuff.

When Mom was sick, my sisters and I learned to lean on each other pretty hard. Two long years of watching her health decline. We promised each other not to cry in front of our dad. There were a lot of tag team walks when one of us just couldn't handle anymore. Jess and I were always the strongest together. Marie isn't as strong as us; she always wears her emotions in plain sight. She never understood why Jess and I didn't. How could we? How would we get Dad through that if we did? I'm overly competitive and sarcastic. My voice carries for miles when I'm talking or laughing. I can't whisper.

Once, my mother had been called to the school to see the principal because they were concerned about my hearing. My mother gave them permission to test me. Turns out I could hear fine. My mother eventually explained, "She's a middle child and competes for attention." After that, I was left alone and only reminded to use my inside voice. My mother was fantastic.

She died at home after declining dialysis and requesting hospice care. I never saw her body before the cremation. In my mind, she is alive somewhere; still breathing, still making jokes, still laughing. The same way Ryan is in my mind. I never went to see him in the hospital morgue. My dad and Ryan's mom did the identification. Plus, he had his driver's license in his wallet. I don't understand why someone had to go do that. I think Ryan has good company up in heaven. *Hopefully Mama is showing him the ropes.*

I didn't even make decisions at the funeral home. My dad and Jess picked the casket, the plot, the order of service, and called our friend, a pastor, to lead the services. I heard all the whispers about me losing it because I was *the* decision maker. Always. I knew what was supposed to happen and when. I lived by an agenda down to the fifteen-minute mark. In this, I couldn't. I was losing it. I did shut down. No one seemed to believe I was capable of a shutdown. I wouldn't have believed it either. It was like my mind was doing self-preservation and shut itself down.

The more I think about my sisters and immediate family, I'm glad Jess is the one getting me through this. One day I would have to remember to let her know how appreciative I am for everything she's doing for me now. It isn't over. There's so much to get through.

"Did I hear Marie downstairs?"

"Yeah. She got here a couple hours ago. She's fielding visitors and accepting casseroles." Damn. Southern women try to feed every emotion.

"No Jell-O salads, please."

"You know Mrs. Virginia brought a damn Jell-O salad."

"Gross. Tell Marie 'Thank You' for me. I know we haven't been getting along, and I know she can't handle things like a normal human, but I appreciate her being the one to handle all these people for me."

"Honey, she was built for that shit. She can handle those fake bitches better than you or I can. She knows how to thank them and send them on their way without letting them up here. It is her greatest skill. Southern hospitality."

"At least one of us got that trait."

Jess laughs at me and rubs my back until I'm nearly falling asleep again. The only thing I'm worried about is my hair being a knotty mess when I wake up. I'm glad that is what's going through my head. I can't think about Ryan anymore, or my poor lonely daddy, or the mother I'm still grieving four years later. I need to keep things surface-level for the duration of at least one nap. I can deal with everything else when I wake up. Whenever that is. *If I wake up.* I can't care.

"Are you awake?"

"Hmmmmm, no... should I be?"

He slowly wraps his arm around my waist. He snuggles into my back and tugs me into his body. I feel a wave of aggravation because he stole half my pillow. I groan and turn my head until I can see his face.

Smiling, I ask, "Any reason you want me to be awake right now?"

"Well, I have to go meet Connor. We're re-wiring the cables in their house to improve their Wi-Fi performance on DSL to the stereo system in the living room." I shut him up by kissing him. Boy, when he gets on a roll with that stuff. Don't get me wrong, it's hot, but irritating sometimes.

"...And...?" I ask as I let go of him.

"And... I was hoping you might want to see me off." I can hear his smile as he runs his nose down my neck.

"Mmmm, are you going to make it worth my while?"

"I can try."

"There is no try, only do." I smile at him and he laughs.

I roll over and look directly at his sweet face. Ryan's eyes are a very light green with a touch of blue. Not your typical emerald green. Oh, and he smells delicious. I just want to sniff his neck all day. I lean in to nuzzle him.

"I'll take that as a yes." he laughs lightly.

"Yes. Mmmm, yes." I kiss around his throat and down to his chest.

He wraps me snuggly in his arms and trails his hands over my body. I kiss up his neck then tug on his earlobe, and he lets out a groan. I know that's one of his things. He slides my tank top off and kisses down my chest between my breasts. He moves one hand to my left breast and his other to squeeze my rear end. I throw my head back, enjoying his explorations of my body. Ryan kisses down my body, leaving a heated trail of tingling goosebumps from my breast down to my hip. I lift off the bed in an arch as he kisses my inner thigh. "Ryan! Don't... Oh, my...yes." I hear him laugh. Oh, he loves doing that.

I look down to see him, determined to stop him so I can get a few more kisses in. I see his light brown hair and reach down to find the edge of his jaw with my fingertips. "Wait, up here," I try to stammer out, and then try to tug at him to get his attention. When he looks up at me, all I can see is blood. It is dripping down his face. There's a gash on his forehead. I look, and it is everywhere. It is on my body and smeared across our sheets.

"Help me, Rhae." He reaches his hand out to me. I try to grab it and it slips away from me. I try over and over again, but I can't seem to get a grip on him. He's slipping away from me. His skin is gray and sickly. "Ryan! Oh my God! Ryan!" I'm screaming and trying to grab him again, but he is gone.

"Rhae. Rhae... Rhae! Wake up. Stop screaming."

Jess? "What?"

"Are you okay? You with me?"

I can't seem to shake that dream. The tremors seem worse now that I'm awake. I look around the room, searching for Ryan. Where is he? He was just here, where did he go? I grab a pillow and pull it to my face. The tears come fast. I sob until I hurt all over. Jess smooths my hair down. Then she apologizes. "I'm sorry I had to wake you up. Were you dreaming?"

"Something—" *Sniff.* "—like that."

"Nightmare?"

I thought about it for a moment. "No. Definitely dream. Well, mostly. Until the end."

"Want to tell me about it?"

"It was the last time we…" I stop.

The corners of her mouth turn down into a frown before she says, "Oh, you're still not comfortable talking about sex with me? You have been married for five years, but won't talk about sex?"

I smile at her. She knows me so well. I just have no idea how to have that conversation with someone. It feels like I'm betraying a private moment with Ryan if I do. "I could tell you, but I'm not sure what would happen. Would you get grossed out? Would I laugh? Would I...break...down..." I am breaking down. I can't even joke with her about it right now. "Jess… I can't do this," I say through sobs. It feels like I'm drowning. I can't catch my breath despite the anger I feel for letting anyone see me like this. I know it's Jess, and she promised to take care of me.

"Rhae, breathe honey. Deep breaths. Close your eyes. You are okay and strong enough to get through this. I promised to get you through this, and I will. Try to calm down. Get in the shower. Wash your hair again. I'll be back in a minute. You've had a nice nap, but we have to get you ready."

She's right. I know she's right. I take deep breaths; each one feels like it's stretching my ribcage. Finally, I start to feel myself calm, and I make it to the bathroom to do what she told me to do. *What time is it? What day is it? How long have I been asleep?* I avoid the mirror and get undressed and into the shower. I run my hands through my hair. I haven't been asleep long. Just long enough for it to dry looking crazy. A shower is a good thing. I try tune out all emotions and feelings. I try not to think. I just wash like a robot and get back out. When I step into the bedroom, I see that Red, Liz, and—*oh shit!*—Marie are here.

"Hey. Where's Jess?"

"Right here," she calls as she comes back up the stairs. "Here. Take this. Drink. Sit down at the vanity. Red, go into her bag and get her something to wear to the funeral."

When did I get a bag? Damn. Today is the funeral. I don't want to do this. As I think through what Jess is saying, I feel the panic rising in the back of my throat. I feel her stroke my hair. Styling me. I know she can tell I'm shaking and breathing crazy again, but she just lets me work through it on my own. Continuing to give orders, I hear her tell Marie to bring me something to eat. She gives very specific instructions, "Bring her something with protein but will sit light on her stomach. Only bring enough to keep her from passing out." Marie hurries out of the room to execute Jess's orders.

Liz sits on the bed and starts to make jokes about casseroles and crazy ass southern women trying to feed everyone until it goes away. "It's why we're all overweight. Bad habits handed down by many generations."

I think she has a great point, but Jess tells her to shut up anyway. Who cares about being fat today? It is what it is. God love Jess; always practical and just taking care of what has to be done in the current moment.

"Okay, babe. Stand up and get dressed." Jess is ordering me now, I realize.

I stand and turn to see a black dress in Red's hands. "No."

"What? You have to go."

"I'm going, but I'm not wearing a dress, and I'm not wearing hose. No heels, either. I can't do that today."

Jess looks to the others for support, and then asks, "What do you want to wear?"

I take a minute to think about what my options might be. Finally, I say, "My sleeveless green V-neck top and gray dress pants."

"Hon, you sure about that?" Red looks at me, puzzled. "People will talk. You should at least wear..."

"No," I cut her off. "I'm sure. Ryan loved that outfit. He picked it out for me. I also need all my silver jewelry."

Liz nods. "I'm on it. Back in twenty minutes."

"Liz. Flats. I can't wear heels today." I repeat for emphasis.

"Yes, ma'am. I can do it. Give me the keys to your house."

Jess speaks up, "They are in her purse by the front door."

With that, Liz is gone. Marie comes back and sets a tray in front of me as I lower myself into the chair Red had been sleeping in last night. I don't even look as Jess starts to feed me pieces of food like a toddler in a high chair. I mechanically open my mouth and eat what she gives me. Salty, sweet... has to be a piece of ham. As I chew and swallow a few bites, something wakes me up, and I am suddenly very hungry. Taking over from Jess, I force down some ham, macaroni, and a roll. Lord, thank you for sweet, fake, southern women trying to feed everyone. I drink a little iced tea—thank God that Marie knows I like it unsweetened—and then I sit back. I sigh, slightly content, and then look over at Red, Jess and Marie sitting in a line on the bed. They are talking to each other and not really paying attention to me anymore.

It makes me think of when we were young girls and Mom would dress us for church. She would line all three of us up according to age. We had the same hair, matching dresses, white gloves, slips and hose. No matter how hot it was, we dressed right for church. She meant business when it came to proper appearances. She would be frustrated with my choice in outfits today.

I laugh out loud a little bit. The girls look over, and I guess my smile is a little out of place. They make concerned faces at me. I can't share with them what they look like. They would definitely believe I had lost it. A familiar numb feeling crawls through my fingers into my chest and down to my toes. *Ah, thanks, Jess. Thanks for keeping your promise.* The feelings are fading. Before I know it, Liz is back with the outfit I requested.

The girls leave me alone to get dressed. I still don't look in the mirror. Going by feel, I ensure my pants are zipped and my top sits right on top of my hips. I check the ladies to be sure there is no bra sticking out, and that the ladies are sitting properly with no excess skin exposed. I slip my shoes on and head to the door. I put my hand on the bannister and make my way down the stairs. I find the girls in the kitchen. I'm stunned at what I see. *Holy Lord! There are a lot of casseroles.* The girls are discussing what to do with all of the food. Marie has already put my favorites in the freezer for later, but the freezer is full. These women are serious about feeding grief.

"Take some home. Everyone. Good Lord, that's a lot of food." All four of my caretakers start laughing at me.

"Yep. Bitch is numb again!" Jess declares with an evil grin.

"Are you guys ready to go? What time are we supposed to be there?" I ask.

Marie approaches me slowly. "The funeral home is sending a car. We are going to ride together if that's all right."

"Sure. Sure. I wouldn't have it any other way. Where's Connor?"

"He already headed out. He's going to help your dad make sure everything is ready and happens on schedule. We know how you get about that stuff. Just a little built-in stress reducer," Red explains.

We decide to sit in the kitchen until the car arrives. It is far too quiet. I really hate sitting in a silence that turns awkward. They are trying hard not to make things awkward for me, but there really is no helping it. I, myself, tend to be very awkward. I get lost in my own thoughts, and before I realize it, the car is there. The driver is an older man, I vaguely remember meeting him at the funeral home during the visitation. He has on a black suit and nods to me. He makes me uncomfortable with the nod. I give him a small smile and dutifully get in the car.

Our drive to the funeral home is quiet. The silence is unnerving. It isn't until we arrive that the others seem to come alive. Everyone helps check the others' makeup and ensure no one is near any type of wardrobe malfunction. Everyone gets out of the car except Jess and me. She holds me back to talk, and she starts off with a hug. This is weird; she must have something prepared to say.

"I promised not to let you feel anything. But this is a goodbye you don't get to do over again. This is like saying goodbye to Mom, only ten times harder. You need to say goodbye to Ryan. It will eat you alive if you don't."

I consider what she is saying and what she isn't. "Okay."

"Do you know what I'm telling you? I can't keep you numb once we get out of the car. You need to feel some of this. Okay?"

"Okay."

She puts her hands on my shoulders, and looks at me sternly, "Okay. That's it? You're ready?"

"Yep. Let's go."

We step out into the July heat. I can smell rain. Usually rain is so scarce this time of year, and the change in atmosphere has a distinct smell. I turn my head to the sun and close my eyes. I think—in some ways—I'm taking in the sun, letting it warm me, and in other ways, I'm just buying time to stabilize my knees so I can walk. Jess notices but doesn't say anything. She puts her arm around my waist and lets me lean on her for a minute. Dad comes out the back door and over to us. He hugs Jess, then me.

I don't want to, but I look into his eyes. "Hey, Daddy."

"Hey, Rhae. You ready?"

"As I'll ever be." I try to smile and come up with a half-smile, just the corner turning up a little bit. My eyes feel so heavy, and I blink back more tears.

"Let's go say goodbye."

He gives me his elbow. I straighten my back and force strength into my legs. I take his arm just like I had five years ago when I married Ryan. I think his words then were, "Let's go get your husband." The symmetry of these moments is almost overwhelming. Thank God the pill Jess had given me earlier is still working, somewhat. Pushing the emotions back down, I let my dad lead me to a room that has two small sliding doors with inset stained glass. Jess, who had been walking with us, drops back. I see her over my shoulder, the other girls standing with her. My girls are all shoulder to shoulder watching Dad walk me into that room.

I take a deep breath and face forward. I hold Dad's elbow a little tighter. He reaches over and puts his other hand on top of mine. We stop, and the doors are closed behind us. Dad faces me, and tenderly wipes tears off my face. He starts to lead me to the open casket at the far side of the room. Panic bubbles up in my throat and I stop walking. I can't see Ryan like this. Lifeless. Motionless. Painted up so his skin doesn't look gray. I know his light tan will look horrible. His hair won't be shiny, and I won't be able to see his amazing eyes. *No. I'm not doing this.* Why do people want to view their loved ones this way?

"Daddy. I can't. I just can't do this." I start pulling back from him. Digging my heels in like a two-year-old throwing a tantrum.

He looks torn. His eyes soften. "I understand, baby. The doctor thinks it will help you have closure if you can see him now."

I continue trying to pull away from him. "I can't!"

"Stop pulling, honey. I won't make you go over there if you don't want to. Just don't hurt yourself pulling on me."

"In my head, he's alive. Warm. Moving. His eyes and hair shine. His skin is tan. He is full of life." I start crying again.

My dad pulls me to him in a tight hug. "Screw the doctor. I agree with you. This doesn't do you any good. Let's go."

He walks me to the main area of the funeral home. We sit on the front pew with my sisters. People are still coming in and talking with each other. Marie goes to man the door as the family representative. My dad keeps his arm around me the entire time. At some point my mother-in-law arrives. Liz scoots down to make room for her by me in the pew. I reach over and take her hand. The three of us sit like a connected puzzle until everyone is seated.

Ryan's casket is rolled in. The guest of honor has arrived. The first song played is "Bravado" by Rush. His favorite. I'm glad Jess remembered the CD when we came to the funeral home. My guess is Connor knew to tell Jess about this song.

Then the pastor begins, "Ryan Walker Wells. Born September 13, 1983. Survived by his wife of five years, Rhae." I cringe and squeeze my dad's hand. A tissue is placed in my other hand. Gwen, my mother-in-law, tries to find a smile for me. She is fighting crying too hard for it to work, though. I pat her hand and give her a sincere smile.

"Thank you." Is all I can squeak out. She nods and holds my hand again. She is such a tender, sweet lady. I haven't stopped stewing in my own misery long enough to consider hers. Her only son is gone. I don't have children with Ryan, not for lack of trying. But I have my sisters, and if something happened to me, my dad would still have them. Gwen lost Ryan's dad when Ryan was a teenager. Now she has lost Ryan too. I don't know how she is able to function. I am such a mess. Why haven't I been thoughtful enough to reach out to her before today?

Again, lost in my own thoughts, I don't hear the rest of what the pastor says. A lady from Ryan's work sings "Amazing Grace." No doubt that one would be played; so predictable. I sigh. Ryan's childhood friend stands at the front of the room and plays an acoustic version of a song they had written together. There are other people to speak. There are other songs. The stress exhausts me so completely that I fall asleep leaning against my dad. He is so comforting to me right now. Next thing I know, he is helping me to stand and walking me to the car at the back door.

I look up at him sleepily. "I'm sorry, Daddy. I didn't mean to..."

"Don't be sorry. I'm glad you found enough peace to sleep for a minute." He hugs me and whispers in my ear, "We are going to the graveside now. Let's get in the car."

I nod numbly and do as I'm told. Liz hands me a drink. I toss it back. I'm just handing the glass back when Jess sits down and scowls at the girls. I reach over and hug her before she can roast them for feeding me alcohol. I lay my head on her shoulder. Marie and Dad slide in beside me.

Thankfully the graveside portion of the service is fast. It starts raining. I knew it would; I could smell it coming. Mama taught me that. Plus, I think my dad told the funeral director to stop dragging it out. While we sit at the service, people walk by, pulling roses off the casket arrangement, and hand them to me. I have more in my arms than I can carry. When we get back to Jess's house, we put them in a couple different vases and place them around the house. I stumble my way upstairs to put on pajamas, brush my teeth, and fall into bed. It is all I want, and I do it unceremoniously and without grace.

A Place to Stand

3
The Last Day

As I lay in the bed, I begin to think through the details of the accident. The moment that changed everything is replaying again. I think about that entire day, actually. I close my eyes, hoping for a glimpse of Ryan.

Ryan and I are making love. It is always so good. He looks at me with such love and adoration. It's like I'm his whole world. It makes pride burst in my chest because he is my whole world. I hope I convey my love through the look I'm giving him now. I could feel his love for me down to my toes. It always made me think of my insane coworker, Nancy. She would see us together and say, "That man loves your dirty drawers. Know that." I know it. I really do.

We cuddle for a long time after; maybe an hour or so. I don't always take note of time like I should, I guess. He kisses my forehead and gets up to shower. I am not a morning person. I roll over, wrapping the best bits of me in a sheet, but leave my legs hanging out where the ceiling fan and box fan can circulate some air. The heat is so bad, especially for this early in the day. I fall back asleep. After a while, I feel Ryan sit on the edge of the bed. God that man smells so good. My sleepy body somehow manages to sit itself up and nuzzle into his shoulder while he hugs me.

"Go back to sleep. I'll see you this afternoon."

"Okay. Be careful, please. And don't be too late we are meeting Reese and Carrie for dinner."

He groans and rolls his eyes. "Sure. Sure. Not too late. If I'm late you can kill Connor."

"I won't have to. I'll get Jess to do it. Just one phone call."

"Geez, you and your sister are vicious. I'll see you later."

I flop back on the bed. Within a few minutes, I'm too hot to lay there. Sucks to have central air conditioning and two fans blowing, but still be hot enough to sweat. It's the last Saturday in June. The really hot season here isn't until August. Why the hell is it so hot so early in the season? I consider my options for the day. I could go grab Jess while the boys worked. We could go shopping or swimming. Ugh.

Shopping sounds hot. Maybe I could lay naked under a fan and read for a while first. Yep. That's what I want to do. Read, then call the girls and see if they want to meet for drinks and swimming. Liz is the best hostess with a pool. Then we can call the boys to bring dinner and we could hang out all night. Reese and Carrie won't mind changing dinner plans to pool plans. That's just the kinds of friends I have. Flexible. We have to be to live in this heat like we do. I send Carrie a text.

I grab a T-shirt and some underwear. I can't bring myself to lay around naked without Ryan being involved. I make sure the fans are on their highest speed and head into the kitchen. Ice water. Lots of ice water. On my way back into the bedroom, I grab a well-worn book off the shelf and then lie on the bed. It is nice. I start reading. This is one of my favorite romances.

I read until well after two p.m. My cell phone breaks my concentration with a "quack, quack, quack." Shit. Jess changed my ringtone again. I roll my eyes and answer it.

"Hey, Red."

"Let's call Liz and go swimming."

"You read my mind. You call Jess. I'll get dressed."

"Got it. Bring the left-over beer in your fridge."

"Got it."

I haul my butt off the bed and get a quick shower. I always feel better after a shower. Who cares that we were headed swimming? At least I won't put more scuzz in the pool. I dress in my bathing suit and cut off shorts. I use one of Ryan's white undershirts as a cover for my bathing suit and slide into a pair of sandals. I grab my SPF 100 sunblock, the beer and head out.

It takes me about thirty minutes to get to Liz's house. She lives in the middle of nowhere. She doesn't even live inside city limits. She is in an unincorporated part of the county. Her property is surrounded by old shade trees, and it is comforting to be out in the woods with her. Liz and Jess are out by the pool already when I get there. They have a cooler of beer, wine coolers, and watermelon with them. I can almost taste the watermelon the instant I see it. I bound up the steps of the deck and settle my beer contribution in the ice with theirs.

Looking over the yard and taking a deep breath, I see Liz's kids swinging on the tree swing. They are happy as larks swinging and laughing with wild abandon. I wonder what they're talking about. My sisters and I used to make up all kinds of stories to make time pass. Laurie and Cooper were the spitting image of their mama. Lean with dark brown hair, and tall for their ages. I had been there when they were born, and I love being a babysitter for them from time to time.

"Hey, bitch," Liz drawls. She sounds like she's almost asleep on the lounger.

"What's up? Hey, Jess. Where are the boys?"

Jess scoffs. "Ryan is teaching Connor something technical. He'll probably only remember enough to be dangerous to the routers and shit. Is Red coming?"

"Yeah. She called me before I left. She should be here soon."

I slide out of my shirt and shorts, and slather on the sunblock to Liz's amusement. "I'm telling you! Just burn and get it over with. You'll tan after."

"The hell she will. She burns for a few days, and then she's ghostly white again." Jess jumps in to defend my sunblock regimen.

I laugh at them both. Jess is right as usual. I do burn easily, and then I'm Casper-the-ghost pale again. No point in hurting and getting skin cancer.

I lay back on the pool chair and enjoy the sun with a slight cool breeze. It feels so good. Somehow cooler than the air conditioning at home. I need to tell Ryan to get a guy out to check it when we got home tonight. I take a brief nap laying there sunning. Eventually Red arrives, and we jump in the pool. Jess and Liz want no part of it yet. Those bitches are too busy browning nicely. Red and I are always jealous of them. Oh well. Swimming is fun. We do laps, flips, and float. You would think we were kids again. Eventually, we conspire to splash the others. It is hilarious. Liz and Jess cuss us so bad all we can do is laugh until we are crying.

It is nearly dark when I realize the boys aren't here yet. Jess is on it. She calls Connor. He is on his way after stopping to pick up some chicken. No one wants to cook, and cold fried chicken is as good as anything else.

"Jess! Find out where Ryan is," I call to her from the water.

She waves her hand at me and goes back to talking. I assume either Connor has volunteered the information, or she plans to ask herself. I go back to floating while she wraps up the phone call. I drift around until I get to the edge. Jess is standing there, looking down into the water.

"What?" I ask.

"Call Ryan. He left our house around four p.m. He should be here by now."

"I'm sure he went home and got wrapped up in a video game/guitar/project thing. Hand me my phone." I pop myself out of the water and sit on the side with my feet dangling.

She hands me a towel first. I dry my face and hands, then reach for the phone. I call Ryan, and it rings through to voicemail. That's odd. I try again. Maybe he's playing guitar and can't hear it.

Connor arrives and kisses Jess. He puts ice and beer in the cooler. They are talking about the day, and I am redialing Ryan's phone. This is the fourth try. I am starting to get worried. Even playing a psychedelic riff that blends into a twenty-five-minute song wouldn't take him this long to answer the phone.

"Hey, Connor, where was Ryan going when he left your place?"

"Uh, I think he said he was headed home. Why? Can't get him to answer? Maybe his phone died."

"I don't know. Ryan is really good about keeping his phone charged. I'll wait a little longer and try him again."

We settle into our various perches on the porch. Reese and Carrie show up a little while later. They brought sandwich stuff, so we have an alternative to Connor's cold fried chicken. We laugh, drink, and talk forever. I can't shake this really bad vibe, though. Where is Ryan? I can't shake it. I try to call him again.

"Hello?"

I pull the phone away from my ear and check the display. It says 'Ryan,' so I didn't mistakenly call someone else. "Hello. Who is this?"

"This is Officer Thomas with Bell Hills police."

A hollowness of fear starts to burn in my chest. "Okay, Officer Thomas. May I speak with Ryan?"

"Who is calling?" Okay this is getting very weird. It must show on my face because all discussion around me has slowly stopped.

"This is Rhae Wells. Ryan is my husband. Why are you answering his phone and asking me questions?"

The officer clears his throat and takes a breath before saying, "Mrs. Wells, where are you? Give me an address. We need to speak with you." My hands start shaking, and I calmly give Liz's address. We hang up, and I look around to find Jess and Liz. Connor is pacing. I shrug.

"Rhae, what's going on?" Liz asks.

"A cop answered Ryan's phone. He won't tell me what's going on. He asked where I was, and I gave him your address."

"Okay, honey. Whatever is going on, we'll get through this. Just stay calm." Jess made an effort to move closer and soothe me.

I hop off the chair and start pacing with Connor. He grabs me by my shoulders and says, "It's probably nothing. DUI is the worst that could be going on." Connor is so good. I manage a weak smile for him. He lets me go and we pace in circles until blue lights reflect off the trees surrounding Liz's place. Jess goes to the front and guides the police to the back porch. Connor has his hand on my back guiding me to sit. Liz sidles up next to me and puts her hand on my knee. I look over at sweet Carrie cuddled into Reese's arms. She looks at me with a mix of apprehension and pity. It's like she is terrified for me.

"Mrs. Wells?" The officer approaches me slowly.

"Yes. That's me. What is going on?"

"Ma'am. There was a car accident on Cypress right outside of Bell Hills. Another driver saw the wreck after it happened and called it in. We just finished working the scene."

"Was it Ryan? What hospital is he in?" I am always a cool customer in the face of panic. Just get the facts and take care of business.

"The driver of the vehicle did not survive the accident. The driver was a male. He had ID in his wallet, but we need a positive identification."

The burning feeling in my chest starts to spread. I hear what the officer is saying, but it's not clicking. My heart is starting to ache. "What are you telling me?"

"Ma'am, we strongly believe the driver of the vehicle to be Ryan Wells. However, he was unrecognizable compared to the photo on his license."

I ignore the request for identification. "What kind of vehicle was it?"

"It was a green Jeep wrangler. It was raised with big tires."

"Oh my God." I can't breathe. The reality of what's happening starts to sink into my mind. "How?"

"We are doing some diagrams. It might not have been a single car accident. Likely a hit and run. The Jeep flipped several times. The doctor at the emergency room thinks he was killed instantly. As you know, there were no doors or top on the Jeep, and he was thrown from the vehicle mid-flip, as best as we can tell." He is speaking slowly. I can sense he is trying to be gentle but giving me the information I'm asking for. Everyone else is asking questions and starting to cry. I look around at all of their faces.

Everything starts to spin. Connor is holding me. Jess is holding me around my waist, her head on my shoulder. I feel like I'm falling. The officer backs away from the group. He is talking to Jess and Connor, then turns to leave. Liz walks with him to the front. I'm not sure what else is said, or what else can be said. That's it.

That is the moment when everything changed. Why they still wanted someone to come ID him was beyond me. I told Jess to call Dad.

I guess she did. I don't even know how I got to Jess's house that night. I handed her my cell phone and told her to call everyone. She was crying. I tried to soothe her and told her all our friends and family were good people, easy to talk to. She could totally handle it. It never occurred to me why she was crying. It wasn't hard for her to call people. No big deal.

In retrospect, I guess the worst thing for her was my being calm and not crying. She was worried. It wasn't long before I was a sobbing mess in the rear parking lot of the funeral home. So, she had nothing to worry about anyway.

Actually, the only thing I did think about in the days between Ryan's accident and the visitation at the funeral home was, "Where did he go?" The accident happened around five-thirty p.m. based on the police investigation. He left Connor's around four. Plus, Cypress, the direction he was headed, was on the way out of Bell Hills—the opposite direction of our house. The thought process baffled me then. It was just too much grief to consider at that point, but now? Now that I am past the funeral and falling asleep in Jess's bedroom, it is coming back to me. *Where was he going when this happened? Why didn't he called me after he left Connor's?*

Maybe when I wake up and I'm capable of coherent thought, I'll try to figure out what was going on in that sweet man's beautiful head. I wonder for a while what I would have done differently that day, if I had known it was our last.

Would I have made him stay home? Would I have tried to stop the series of events leading up to that deadly accident? Is there anything I could have done to stop what happened? In the end, sleep was pulling at me hard. I decide that God has a plan, and I won't ever know the answer to the "what if" questions. It is just not possible to know. I give into sleep, praying I won't dream.

A Place to Stand

4
Going Home

I set my feet on the floor. The hardwood is cool and feels nice against my toes. It is too hot to sleep very well. Still, I need to get my head moving this morning. I stumble into the bathroom. Carefully running my fingers through my knotted hair and pulling it into a high ponytail that lets the ends tickle the back of my neck. I wash my face and brush my teeth. Steeling myself for what I might see, I look up into the mirror.

Not so bad. I think I have been getting a little better every day. My tears ran dry a few days ago. Minor remnants of dark circles are under my eyes. My body is slowly recovering from the ache of crying so much. The aches have given me something to focus on instead of using pills or liquor to numb myself. This is a good thing. I didn't need to chemically numb for too long. I dress in a familiar pair of cut off shorts, and a newish tank top.

Tip-toeing down the stairs, careful not to wake my niece Jillian, or Jess and Connor, I make it to the kitchen and start a pot of coffee. Having a routine keeps me going every day. It's automatic. I don't need to think to do it. Brew coffee. Make a bagel with strawberry cream cheese. Make very large cup of coffee with half & half, and no-cal sweetener. Sit on back porch to eat. That's my routine and has been for the month or so I've been living with Jess.

Settling myself into a chair at the patio table, I fold my feet under my butt. The sun isn't up yet, but I look forward to watching it rise. The beauty of a peach, pink, and blue sky, scattered with a fringe of white clouds reminds me of the joy this world can hold. I need the reminder.

Cradling my coffee cup in both hands, I let the warmth sink into my skin. Taking a tentative sip, the creamy goodness spreads across my tongue. I let out a ragged sigh. This is a good life. All pain and misery aside, I could live like this. Couldn't I? Jess and Connor would let me stay forever, right?

Who am I kidding? I could stay here another six months and not be ready to go back home. Fact is, I need to be out on my own. I take a bite of bagel and chew over my food with my thoughts. The toasty flavor makes me remember how I introduced Ryan to my favorite breakfast. Well, second favorite. Mama's eggs, bacon, grits, and biscuits would always hold number one in my book. Ryan had never eaten a bagel before we met. He was a little boy in his food choices. I always did my best to improve his options.

"Aunt Rhae?" says a small, sleepy voice. I turn to see little Miss Jillian stepping through the patio doorway.

"Hey, sweet girl, what are you doing up?"

"I smelled breakfast. I can have some?" Oh, that smile. She is the sweetest, freckle-faced little girl in a pink nightgown anywhere.

"Of course. Come here." I bring her up on my lap and let her have a drink of my coffee first. "Did you have good dreams, baby girl?" I ask as I sweep her little bangs to the side and tuck them behind her ear.

"I did! It was so pretty. I love swimmin' with my friends. I dreamed we were done swimmin' and runnin' through the field and playin' on the tree swing." No doubt, she dreamed of playing with Liz's kids, Laurie and Cooper.

"Who's your favorite?"

"Hmmm, that's hard. I love them both. Laurie does my hair and teaches me to play ball. Coop does whatever I say. Him is so sweet to me." Her face lights up every time she talks about Coop.

"That's okay. It's good you don't have a favorite. That means you love them both." I snuggle her closer for a hug.

"Ughhhh, Aunt Rhae! Can't breathe!"

"Sorry, sweet pea. I just love squeezing you! Why don't you go in and get dressed? It will make Mommy so proud to see you being a big girl."

"Okay! Save me coffee!"

She slides off my lap and runs to the patio door and right into Jess who is joining us for coffee. They exchange good mornings and hugs. Jillian goes in to dress while Jess sits down in the chair opposite me at the table.

"Hey, kid. You're up early. Sun isn't even up yet. How you feeling today?"

"I'm good. I guess," I answer with a sigh.

She stares into her cup as if the coffee is doing something extraordinary. Finally, she says, "So. Moving back to your house today. Are you sure you're ready for this?"

"Yeah. I think I can do it. I have to eventually. Plus, Red said she'll come help me get my junk and stay with me to handle all of Ryan's things."

"You don't have to do anything right away. Just deal with being back in the house first. Everything else will get handled over time."

"I know." I immediately start running down a mental list of all the work we need to do this week. What Jess doesn't know is that it does have to be this week. Today if possible. I can't move on until I finish addressing everything left on my list. I can't let this drag out any longer.

I'm going to need to make a run to Goodwill or get the AMVETS truck to come out for all of his clothes. Maybe I can keep some T-shirts and sell the CDs or give them away to friends. I could consign his guitars to the music store but keep the red acoustic. I know his Taylor is a family heirloom, so I need to call my mother-in-law and see what she wants to do with it. Then there is the matter of all the pictures. I'll just box those up in the attic. I can't look around our house and see him every day. I'll just keep one out in a non-so-conspicuous place. That way I can see him when I need to without being overwhelmed.

Closing my eyes while I run through my to-do list, I imagine Ryan's sweet smile. He's laughing at me, as he does—did—so often. He's holding open his arms so I can sit between his legs on the beach. We could sit on that beach, cuddled up watching the ocean for hours. We were on vacation, last summer, at Daytona Beach. We would laugh and sing on the way to the beach from his cousin's house. "A1A Beach Front Avenue..." Vanilla Ice was good for a chuckle as we would remember dancing like dorks and singing along at high school dances. It was always a good trip for us. We would stay with Clea and Stephen, Ryan's cousin and his wife. Vacations were extra special because of Clea.

She and I hit it off the moment we met. We graduated from school the same year. Only difference is she's from Texas. I wish I had gone to school with her. Something about her sweet nature and keen sense of fashion would have balanced out my dorky band geekiness. I always felt like a toe sticking out of a holey sock at my high school, but she never made me feel like that. I remember when she and Stephen got married, Ryan and I had gone down to be attendants in the wedding. Clea and I got stuck making decorations and cleaning house while the boys went out for wings. Conveniently, it was one of those places where all the servers wore shorts that let their ass cheeks hang out. Never mind the tank tops stretched beyond capacity. Yep, they went there because the wings were so good and the beer was so cold. Right.

Clea and I ended up at a diner, tanking coffee and eating horrible food. It was a riot. I love that girl to pieces. I know they were at the funeral, but I don't remember much beyond my circle of sisters. I can't believe I was such a horrible hostess. Hostess? Is that what I was? It was a funeral. What do you call a funeral hostess? I don't remember if I hugged them. I don't remember if I saw them at all. Chemical numbness was a necessary evil. I need to call her and take a trip to see her soon. Maybe that would give me a reason not to be in the house for a little while. She and Stephen have a new place so there wouldn't be many Ryan memories there.

"Rhae, honey, where'd you go over there?"

"Sorry. I checked out again, didn't I?"

"You do that a lot lately. You okay?"

"I was thinking about Ryan. We were on the beach at Daytona."

Timidly she asks, "Are you sure you are ready to go back home? You can stay as long as you need. Jilly loves having you here, and Connor doesn't mind you cooking either."

Swallowing a lump in my throat, I manage to force a small smile for her, "I need to go. And I'm sure Connor can't wait to get back in the bedroom with you. I mean, seriously. We've been sharing the bed. The man deserves to sleep in his bed and jump his wife whenever he wants."

Jess lets out a hearty laugh and shakes her head. "Fair enough."

We finish our coffee in relative silence. Jillian eventually makes an appearance, long enough to tell Jess she's going to swing on her tire swing. I head upstairs to finish packing my meager collection of belongings. Little by little, my friends were bringing my things to Jess's while I refused to go back home.

Don't get me wrong, I love our little place. Just two bedrooms, about one thousand square feet in total. It was in bad shape when we bought it. Got it for a steal because it had been abandoned and foreclosed on by the bank from the previous owners. We fixed it up together. It is a little white clapboard with a wide front porch. I always wanted the porch to wrap around, but Ryan hadn't mastered general construction yet. He did his best to learn from my dad and Connor as we worked through the many house projects together. But he also knew the limits facing our motley crew of construction workers. He paid to have a tin roof installed when the traditional shingled roof failed us the same year we bought it. Ryan knew there was no proper way for our crew to install a new roof together. I love that tin roof. The sounds it makes when the rain hits it is like a lullaby for me.

My favorite thing is taking care of the yard and flowerbeds. Ryan always complained that I should keep the beds simple, so we could easily maintain them. I had agreed to use perennials to keep from replanting every year. I think my favorite is the climbing confederate Jasmine we planted by the front steps. Ryan had built arbors for the unruly vines to climb on. They put on small white flowers every spring with a smell that keeps the entire house full of a sweet enchantment every time the front door is opened.

Otherwise, we have an assortment of irises, day lilies, a planter full of lavender, a few hostas in the shady places, and columbine in the sunny places. In the back, he let me have a folk-art mecca. All my friends insist I'm a crazy lady, but who wouldn't want a claw foot tub full of colorful flowers? My yard tub has sweet potato vine, moss roses, fountain grass, and lantana. We also have our haint tree. Actually, most people call them bottle trees. Just an iron frame that we sunk in the ground, then began to fill the branches with bottles. Our friends contributed blue beer bottles.

Other friends came over and drank wine with us, so we could put the bottle on the tree. I always wanted some red bottles, but Ryan said buying bottles was cheating. The people who thought the concept of the bottle tree was insane had to read the lore for themselves. I always laughed and told them, "Ain't no evil spirit getting in my back door." I don't care how it sounds, but Southern Baptists are the ones who are easiest to offend with that. They just don't understand that Mama raised us with a solid foundation in Christianity and a respect for the other belief systems. Yes, there is a touch of voodoo belief in the bottle tree, but not enough to cause any harm.

Realization hits me, I miss my home. My plants keep me close to Mama, among other things. I really need to submerge myself in the memories held there. I think it will do me a world of good. I know it's pushing harder than I should. I mean, everyone says give yourself time to grieve. It's only been a week, but I'm not like other people. If I wallow in this misery any longer, I might get stuck.

I call down to Jess, "I'm ready to go home."

When I pull up to the driveway, I see Red's car parked out front. Always on time, meaning early.

"Here we are! Aren't you glad to be home?" Red is always so enthusiastic. Although, compared to the others, I would rather have her with me than anyone else. If I cried, she would just let me without questions or opinions.

"Yep. Let's do this." I grab my duffel bag and sack of dirty laundry out of the back seat. Red takes my keys and goes up to unlock my front door.

Taking each step with caution, I start to think I may not be ready for this after all. Ryan's things and memories of him fill this house. We drop my stuff in the entry. It needs to be sorted out anyway. Inhaling a deep breath, I hope it'll make me feel settled as I look around. I'm struck by how everything seems stale. Then I realize stale is probably the wrong word. Putrid is more like it.

"What the hell is that smell?" I grab my nose and step backward and bump into Red who is also holding her nose.

Red is moving quickly to get the windows open. "Smells like something went bad in the fridge."

"Lord help me! That is awful. C'mon, let's get some gloves and bleach water made."

"I'm miles ahead of you!" Red hands me a pair of latex gloves from under the sink.

We both pull our T-shirts over our noses. Then we carefully approach the refrigerator and open the door. We jump backward and grab onto each other as if something might jump out. Nothing does, thankfully. There are leftovers containers growing like science projects. Really? All these people looking after me and no one wanted to come

A Place to Stand

check my house? I shake my head at the thought.

"The fridge doesn't feel very cold." Red points out.

I check by placing my hand against the wall inside. Sure enough, it's room temperature, if not warmer. "Good call. Guess I need Connor to come over and check it. Just what I needed."

"I'm not washing that," Red says pointing to a container which once held spaghetti sauce. "I'm not even opening it long enough to scrape it out, so the dishwasher can wash it." She looks like she's about to gag.

"Toss it. Toss all of it. I'll get new containers." I shake my head, again. Seems like that's all I've got.

She starts throwing things away and taking the trash out back for me while I start scrubbing the fridge with the bleach water. Then I move on to mopping the floor for good measure. Red starts dusting. I guess the house is stale to her too. Next, we gather laundry to start a load. While the laundry runs, we head to my bedroom. Standing in the doorway of my bedroom, I'm paralyzed. I can't even form a thought, Red brushes past me and starts pulling the sheets off the bed, and I'm thankful she does. Overwhelming memories of Ryan and I there on the day he died swim through my mind. My chest aches and butterflies fill my stomach. I'm afraid I might start crying, so I start swallowing huge gulps of air to abate the tears.

Red gathers the sheets and some towels out of the bathroom. As we head back to the laundry room, there is a knock. Red and I exchange a look. I shrug, and she returns it. She passes me the dirty laundry and heads to see who's at the door.

"Hey, bitch!" Red says when she opens the door. I peek around the corner from the kitchen to see who it might be.

"Same to you. What are you doing here?" Liz answers.

I walk toward the front door.

"I brought a little pick-me-up for our girl." Liz steps in and Red closes the door behind her. Liz looks at me and a devilish grin spreads across her face. "You ready?"

"What should I be ready for again?"

"Your 'Welcome Home' bash. Duh. Let me guess, Jess didn't say anything?"

A small chuckle escapes as I shake my head, "No, she didn't. I guess she'll be here any minute."

"And you know this. Now, what can I do to help freshen up the house?"

I direct her to vacuum the living room carpet, and then water my house plants. The poor schefflera is looking ill. Liz jumps right in—after putting the vodka in the freezer. Jess blows in and starts by cleaning my ceiling fans and straightening my bookcases. When we cross paths, she grabs my arm and pulls me aside from the others.

"Listen, you need to know, Marie is coming over. She has casseroles from her freezer to drop off. I don't want you to be mean to her."

My mouth drops open at the implication. "Jess, really? Mean? I'm cold, maybe impersonal, but not mean."

"You're mean when you don't realize it. She's sorry about what happened, but she won't apologize. She just thinks your hard-headed ass will just drop it. Will you?"

"No. I won't. But I will be polite. Will that work?"

"I can't ask more than that, I guess."

I shrug, "Anyway, my fridge is broken. If she brings those casseroles over, someone has to take them home."

Jess groans and fishes out her cell phone. She calls her husband to come look at the fridge.

We keep working through the house. Taking turns rotating laundry. It really only takes another hour to scrub everything. Marie arrives shortly after we finish working.

We decide it's time to have some dinner. The five of us worked in my tiny kitchen to reheat a casserole, make rolls, a gallon of unsweetened tea, and dessert. Before we can sit down to eat, Connor walks in with a toolbox and a big grin. He sets to work as we go out to sit on my back porch for a while.

We pass the evening eating and laughing. It seems everyone is forcing the conversation around the elephant in the room. Ryan. While I can appreciate their concern, and willingness to avoid he subject, my mind won't let me. I feel the mental separation from my group of friends as I think back to our anniversary, which we celebrated on this very porch.

I text Ryan. "Hey hot stuff."

He replies quickly, as usual, "Hey yourself. Whatcha doin'?"

"What else? Working."

"Awww, sorry baby. Happy Anniversary!"

"Happy Anniversary to you! Listen, today sucks. Would you mind if we don't cook tonight? Maybe we can go out somewhere." I was hoping for a steak dinner somewhere.

"Sure. Just let me know what you want to do. I already have post-dinner plans."

My breath catches, and I start grinning like a maniac, reading his response. Feeling devilish, I write him back, "Really? Can you share? ;)"

"I could, but it would make work a little tougher for you."

"Oh?"

"Yeah, I would think you couldn't sit still if I started outlining my plans."

I am already having a tough time focusing. "You're right. I'll see you tonight. Love you!"

"Love you too!!"

When I get home, he is nowhere to be seen. "Ryan! Where are you? Should I change clothes? Where are we eating?" There is no answer. I start walking room to room, looking for him. Maybe he was in his studio/man-cave working on something. I peek inside. No Ryan. Where the hell could he be? I kick off my shoes and pad toward the back door. I step out and lights came on.

"What is this?" I look around slowly at the paper lanterns and white Christmas lights strung across the porch and down to the huge oak in the back yard. It is like he made a faux gazebo out of the lights. Before I can take it all in, he slides his arms around my waist and kisses my neck.

"What did you do?"

He laughs. "You like it?"

"Of course I like it! Who did it?" I look over my shoulder, so I can see his face.

He slides his hands up to my shoulders and starts rubbing the tension out of my neck. He smiles and feigns offense. "Uh, I did it."

"No, really. Who did it? You had to work today."

He laughs louder. "I did it. I took a vacation day. Our anniversary is too important to mess up. With you having a sucky day, I asked for a day off and came home to do this for you. I have dinner too."

"I have to say, sir, I'm shocked. Pleased. Surprised. Shocked. I love it!"

He kisses me, then clicks on the porch radio. Pink Floyd's **Dark Side of the Moon** fills the tiny space. He pulls me into his arms and we begin to dance; although, he's never been much of a dancer. Ryan knows I always wanted to be twirled around like they did in old black and white movies. For my benefit, he would try from time to time.

Back when I left to go to college, he gave me a remastered version of this CD. Little did he know I had also stolen one of his flannel shirts. I wrapped the shirt around the pillow and would fall asleep cuddling it while listening to the CD. It was almost enough to make living in the dorms bearable. It was a long semester being away from him. We ran up crazy phone bills trying to talk every day. In the end, I had given up and moved home to attend college at a campus closer to him. Maybe it wasn't a smart decision to base my life choices on the guy I was dating, but I just *knew we would end up together in the end.*

After we dance, we eat. After that, we fall into our bed and worship each other with an enthusiastic appreciation. Ryan's hands sear and his lips scorch as he explores my body. Years together and still it always feels new when he makes love to me. Like it is his first time looking at my body or touching me, every time.

I'm pulled from my thoughts by a shrill squeal. Bewildered, and looking around I see Liz has Marie pinned, and is tickling her in the middle of the porch. Contagious laughter breaks out as we are laughing so hard we are tearing up. As the party winds down, I start yawning. Red notices.

"Okay, ladies. Our girl is tired. Let's clean up and get out of here so she can get to bed," Red announces, taking charge, as usual.

Everyone mumbles and shuffles around picking up plates and glasses. We wash dishes and fold all the laundry we washed earlier. One by one, they start leaving. Red is the last one in the house with me. We put fresh linens on my bed. I have to turn off all thought just to get through that chore. Apparently, she notices that too. She's so observant lately.

"I'm staying with you tonight."

"No. That isn't necessary. Go home. I've got this under control."

"What? You don't like having me over for sleepovers anymore?" She smirks with mock offense.

I smile knowingly, "Of course I like having you here. You're welcome to stay as long as we can fall in this bed in the next ten minutes and sleep late tomorrow. You should also know, if you stay, I'm putting your ass to work tomorrow."

Her eyebrows draw in as the corners of her mouth turn down. "Okay, what are we doing?" She smooths the comforter and walks around to make sure it is even on all sides.

"Jess thinks I should stretch this out as long as possible, but I'm cleaning out Ryan's things tomorrow. I have to."

"You'll get no arguments from me. Just tell me what we're doing, and I'll be happy to help."

"Thanks. I knew I could count on you."

It feels like we literally fall into the bed. It's not long before I hear Red snoring. Yikes. I probably shouldn't tell anyone she snores like that. It is highly unladylike. I laugh to myself. I'm actually starting to get jealous; I can't seem to sleep. Sleep and I aren't on the best of terms these days. I mean, while I was at Jess's, I slept okay, but now I'm not sleeping at all. I'm sure it's all the anxiety and busyness from moving back into the house. Plus, I'm not chemically numbing myself anymore. There must be some residual effect from all of that. Then again, I'm not exhausting my body crying myself to sleep either.

I think back to when I was a kid and couldn't sleep. My dad would tell me to close my eyes and imagine a blind being drawn over a window. "Just picture it. A blind comes down and blacks out the entire room. No light. No sound. Just you in the dark. Breathing deeply. Breathe in the sleep, breathe out the stress." It has never failed. So, as I lay next to Red and stare at the ceiling fan, I repeat my dad's words to myself. Over and over, I say them. Hoping to dull my mind into sleep. My dad's sure-fire sleep plan fails me.

I sigh and get out of bed, carefully, so I don't disturb Red. I tip-toe into the living room, avoiding all the noisy creaks in our floor. I grab a glass of water and pull a book off the shelf. I have read this one many times, but I'm hopeful it can calm my mind and distract me enough to help me sleep.

It seems like I just sat down when I see sunlight peeking through the windows on the front of the house. I'm nearly done with the book. Crap. Tons of things to do today and no sleep. I take a deep breath, stretch, and then put the book back on my shelf. I head to the kitchen and start making us breakfast. I think we'll have coffee, eggs, and bacon. Red wanders in as I get the bacon going.

"Mmmm, smells great. I thought we were sleeping in this morning?"

I shrug and roll my eyes. "Yeah, that would require being able to sleep. You're welcome to go back to bed if you want."

"Nah, I'll start the grits for you."

"Thanks."

We finish making breakfast together. As we eat, I outline everything we needed to get done today. She nods along as I run down my list. It is a lot, but I need to finish laying Ryan to rest in every possible way, so I can move on with life. What moving on means? I'm not really sure. I just know what I needs to be done today. Tomorrow will tell me what needs to happen tomorrow. I can only get through one day at a time. I also need to call work at some point.

This isn't going to be fun. I love my job, but I'm still so unsure of facing all the sympathetic, gossiping, fake faces at work. Red and I finish eating in companionable silence. We clean the kitchen and start on my to-do list for the day.

5
Visitors

    Two months, eight weeks, have passed since Ryan died. I haven't returned to work yet. I did call Dee, my boss, and she granted me some more time off after having the inevitable, "Take all the time you need," discussion. Sympathy and I'm sorry talks drive me insane. Having exhausted all the time Dee granted me, and wanting to avoid any further discussions about everything, I have decided to return to work tomorrow.

    Sitting in my recliner, drinking coffee, I take in all the empty spaces around me. Ripping down pictures and mementos had left an unmistakable mark of loneliness. I had no idea it would look and feel this empty. I hope the CDs don't turn into puddles of plastic under the heat in the attic. I planned to give them away or have a yard sale, but I just didn't feel like it yet. Giving things away meant I would have to face more of Ryan's family and friends. It's still too soon.

    The YMCA was happy to get all the sports equipment I donated. Honestly, I never paid attention to how much the man loved playing sports. Not that he was exceptional at any of them, but he did like getting together with friends and trying to play. One part of me thinks I should feel guilty for getting rid of all of Ryan's things, but I don't feel bad about my donations since I'll never use those things. It's been years since I played on the church softball team. Turns out I am not cut out for church league anyway. I am far too competitive. It never ended well when the game didn't go my way. I laugh just thinking about the last game we played together. Ryan had to pick me up and take me off the field. I give *poor loser* a whole new meaning.

I study my little notepad as I drink my coffee. I'm a list maker. There, I said it. I have lists for everything. It doesn't make me a control freak. Okay, yeah, it does. Today's list is all about what needs to happen, so I can successfully return to work tomorrow. On the one hand, I'm looking forward to normal. On the other, I'm going to have to face my coworkers and my least favorite of all, the Dragon Lady. I never look forward to seeing her.

I need to call Jess to see if she has any updates from the insurance company. Ryan had a hefty life insurance policy with his employer. We never planned on dying, but since it was in his benefits package, he had signed up. Jess said the HR lady from his job told her he had a 401k with them. Ryan listed me as the beneficiary on that too. Just add this to the list of things about Ryan that I never knew.

Adding to my list, I need to figure out what I'm wearing to work tomorrow. I'm sure I've either lost or gained weight with all that's been happening, and I'll need to try on my work clothes. It occurs to me that I should be bright, but not perky. I should be grieving, but not depressed. I should be a little sad, but not enough to draw more sympathy. I definitely shouldn't appear to be too over the whole situation so soon. *What is the appropriate grieving period?* In the old days, they would grieve for like a year, I think. I can't imagine Ryan, or anyone, would really want me to grieve him for that long. Am I not supposed to be getting on with my life? I mean, I didn't die. He did. Why do people think there is some magical mold that someone who is grieving, after a death, is supposed to fit into? I have never fit any mold. Why would this be different?

If they think badly of me or judge me, that's their problem. It shouldn't even be a concern. I should wear the brightest, happiest outfit I own. A yellow dress with a full skirt that Ryan loved. That'll get them talking for sure. They don't know how I'm dealing with all of this. *"That's my girl."* I could hear Ryan's voice just beaming in the back of my mind. *"Always so tough."* I'm grinning and laughing to myself when my cell phone starts going off. I look at the phone's display before answering. It's Jess calling. I guess she has an update for me after all. I cross calling Jess off my list. "Hey! What's up?"

"Hey. I talked to the insurance agent, and they are sending you a check. It's coming FedEx, requires a signature, and should be in around Thursday."

"That's great. Thanks for handling that for me. I have no idea what I would say to an insurance person, and I might screw up. Are you okay? How's Jilly?"

"Well, she misses you, and she talks about Ryan every day." She sighs and hesitates for a moment. "We're having a hard time getting her to understand he won't be around anymore."

I take a deep, shaky breath. Talking about him hurts. I always feel a sharp, stinging ache in the middle of my chest at the mention of his name. She must have sensed my distress.

"Oh God, Rhae! I'm so sorry. I didn't mean that to sound so... casual."

"No. It's fine. I have to get used to this at some point."

"I know, but I'm still sorry. Connor and I decided to stop talking to her about him. We figure, at her age, she'll eventually stop. Plus, we can always explain everything to her when she's older."

"True. I'm sorry she has to deal with all of this too."

"Me too. I'm sorry you're dealing with it. Want a girl's day next Saturday? We can get breakfast and go shopping."

"I'd like that."

We wrap up our phone call shortly after that. She's on her way to see Dad. Apparently, he's dealing better than anyone. Still, I feel guilty. I need to be better about calling him. He and I are just so much alike. He thinks, if he calls me, he'll be interrupting or bothering me. I keep thinking that he's out fishing and carrying on with his friends, and that I'd be bothering him. Plus, every time we do call each other, Jess calls him. He handles this by hanging up on me to answer her. I can't be sure if he doesn't know how to work his cell phone, or if he's just in a hurry to talk to her. The bottom line is our inability to change is causing a gap between us, and *that*, I don't like.

    I take another long tug on my coffee and decide that my funky ass needs to shower. My hair has more build up than an oil slick right now. I rinse my coffee cup and put it in the sink. I can always load the dishwasher later. The doorbell rings. I stare at it, willing my x-ray vision to kick in and show me who's out there because I'm not expecting anyone today. In fact, I had put everyone on notice. "*Leave me alone.*" I need some time to myself. I make my way to the door and see the outline of a woman standing on my porch. Glancing down at my jammies, I shrug, and decide I look decent enough to answer the door. Hell, I know women who wear this style of outfit to the Wal-Mart.

    Slowly I crack it open. "Hello?"

The woman looks terrified and confused. She's a cute blonde, shorter than I am. Curvy and pretty. She might be my age, if not a little younger. "Hello? Can I help you with something?" I ask again, trying to be direct.

    "Uh, I wanted to see Rhae Wells."

    "You're talking to her. Who are you?"

    "My name is Melody. Melody Richards."

    "Hi, Melody. I hate to seem impatient, but was there something you needed?"

    "I wanted to talk to you about Ryan."

    I purse my lips and cock my head to the side. She wants to talk to me about Ryan? "Did you know him from work?"

    "No. I knew him from..." she trails off and looks like she's about to cry. "Can I come in? I don't want to talk through your front door."

    The hair on the back of my neck stands up and heat floods my face. Something about this is wrong. This is not going to be pleasant for me. I always assume the negative, so I take a deep breath and swallow my apprehension.

"Come in. Do you mind if I run and change real quick? Would you like some coffee?"

"That would be really nice. Thank you."

"Okay, well make yourself at home. I'll be out soon."

I grab my cell phone as I breeze through the living room on my way to my bedroom. I call Jess and try to whisper as I say, "A strange girl just showed up on my front porch. She says she knows Ryan and wants to talk."

"What the fuck?"

"Yeah, I know. I was headed to shower when she got here. I let her in and left her sitting at the kitchen table while I change clothes."

"What is wrong with you?" Jess sounds exasperated. "You are going to end up slaughtered!"

"I think she's okay. I don't know what she has to say to me, but I'm trying to overcome my knee-jerk negative reaction to everyone I meet."

"Okay, well, I'm on standby if you need me."

"Do you remember meeting a blonde at the funeral? A friend of Ryan's, little shorter than I am. Curvy thing."

"Not ringing any bells. She know him from work?

"She says she's not from his work."

"That's weird."

"I know. I'll call you back."

I dress like my hair is on fire. Stepping out of my room, I apologize for taking so long. I make myself another cup of coffee and one for Melody before sitting at the kitchen table. Drinking my coffee,

I mentally prepare for whatever this is. I would have thought, since she was the one who had something to say, she would just start talking, but she doesn't. Her demeanor lets me know this is big. She sits as still as a statue and stares out the window and slowly glances around my house. Standing slowly, she starts strolling around looking at tables, bookcases, and even the fireplace mantle.

She stops and turns to look at me. "You don't have any pictures of him."

I scowl a bit. "I do, actually. Since he passed, I needed a break from seeing him everywhere. I packed all but a few away." Just the thought ignites an old familiar ache in my chest. I take a deep breath to steady myself.

Melody nods and comes back to sit at the table with me. She doesn't start talking. She just stares at me for an uncomfortably long time. It's like she's committing my face to memory. Awkward doesn't begin to describe it. I don't want to interrupt her thoughts, so I try to be patient with her. Okay, who am I kidding? Of course, I want to interrupt her thoughts. The suspense is killing me. "So, you had something to talk to me about?"

Melody nods and looks down at her hands. "Yeah. I do."

Being patient is not something I'm really good at, but I'm trying. I want to reach across the table and shake her, and demand she start talking.

Finally, I see her take a breath, wringing her hands as she starts, "Ryan and I were dating."

I didn't hear her right. "Excuse me? Could you say that again?"

She looks up to my eyes. "Ryan and I were dating."

I think my heart just stopped beating. Panic swells into my throat, and the ache in my chest spreads to my limbs like a freezing wave. She must be mistaken. There is no way she was seeing my Ryan. I can't form a thought to ask her any questions. My stunned silence is, apparently, a cue for her to continue.

"I knew he was married. I knew about you," she clarifies. "I saw your picture in his wallet. He was..." she trails off.

"I'm sure there's some kind of mistake. Ryan didn't have it in him to cheat." I smile at her sweetly. She's probably just infatuated with him. Ryan was handsome and very compassionate. She likely took his kindness for something more than what it was.

She shakes her head and holds out her phone to me. On the screen is a picture.

What I see isn't exactly clear at first. Like a fuzzy puzzle. One of those optical illusions where you have to turn your head funny to see the different images. I stare. I study. I wish I could unsee this. It's her kissing a guy, but not any guy. It's Ryan. Not a selfie, more like someone else snapped it while they weren't looking.

"I knew you would need proof."

I just stare. Light brown hair. His jawline. Slightly tan skin. It's Ryan. My heart is still frozen. Now my lungs aren't functioning. I'm suffocating. This is not happening. He did not do this to me. I feel a familiar burn in my eyes. I'm about to cry. Waves of emotion crash in on me all at once.

Pushing the tears down, I close my eyes, swallow hard, and give the phone back to her.

"I'm sorry," she says, contrite.

"No, you aren't." I shake my head. "You said you knew he was married. You should have walked away. By the way, you weren't 'dating' Ryan. You were having an affair. Call a spade a spade, honey." I feel anger welling up behind the hurt. Anger is good. I think better when I'm angry, more so than when I'm hurt. I look up when I hear her sniffle. She's crying. *Good.* A feeling of satisfaction surges through me.

"I'm sorry, and you're right. It was an affair. I'm ashamed of myself for that."

"Is that all you have to say about it? I'm sure there is some reason you didn't just let the affair die with him. Why did you come here to tell me this?"

There's more to the story. I listen to her explain how they'd met. Ryan was a frequent customer at a restaurant on his route between work and home. Usually for lunch, but on this particular day it was a breakfast stop. Melody is a student at one of the local community colleges. She works two jobs to pay for school. Her first job is at Brown's, a southern diner-style place that's only open for breakfast and lunch. After school, she works nights at Dancin' Cowboys, a small-town watering hole. We aren't real creative with the names of businesses around here. I listen to her story as long as I can stomach it. I can't be sure how many details she provides because I'm so irritated, and I can't stop the swirl of thoughts in my mind.

She stops talking. I guess giving me a break to digest, and eventually continues, "We would meet at my dorm and go to dinner or movies. Sometimes, he would take me muddin' in his Jeep." She searches my face. I don't know if she's hoping for acceptance or understanding. She doesn't get it, and she goes on, "I know you don't want to hear all this. Listen, I know this hurts. I don't want to have to tell you about any of this. Please don't judge me."

"Maybe that thought should have crossed your mind before you carried on with him like that."

"I deserve that."

Oh honey, you deserve so much more from me. I have a white-knuckle grip on my coffee cup, which has gone cold. I can't drink it because I'm afraid I'll either spill it all over myself or throw it on her. Just another mess for me to clean up either way. Instead of spewing more ugly thoughts, I try to dig for her true motive. "Why are you telling me this? He's dead. What benefit could there possibly be for you to tell me about any of this?"

"I'm pregnant."

This just keeps getting better and better. I burst out laughing. It's a rather maniacal laugh. There's no humor. Just uncontrollable laughter because, after all of this agony I've been in, it's all I have left in me. He was having an affair and got her pregnant. "Let me guess: it's Ryan's baby and there is no possibility that it could be any other guy." The statement drips with sarcasm.

Her mouth drops open in shock. My words have her momentarily stunned, "Please don't treat me that way. I'm no angel, but I'm not a whore. He is the only one I've slept with since January." Her face is hard and sad.

"What do you want from me? Money? Hoping to cash in on that life insurance? I don't understand why you're here." I'm exasperated with this woman. I stand and start pacing because my nerves won't let me be still anymore.

"I don't really know," she says defeated. "When I stopped hearing from him, I thought he was dumping me. I planned on finding him at work. Then one day I was clipping coupons with my roommate and we saw the obituary. It was just chance that I even saw it. I mean, who sits around reading those. That was how I found out he was dead. I thought he had just been avoiding me. I didn't know what to do."

I stop pacing and turn to face her. "What do you mean? Are you saying Ryan knew you're pregnant?"

She nods slowly, wiping tears from under her eyes. "Yes. He knew."

I'm not processing this well. The whole time I feel like I'm in a room where the walls squeeze in slowly. I'm still struggling to thaw my heart, so it can keep beating. My lungs are burning because I'm not breathing right. My arms feel like they're made of lead. I manage to maintain some semblance of calm because of all the malfunctions I'm feeling at this moment. The air is thick with the silence. I can't form words. From the look of her–slumped shoulders, dark circles around her eyes, shaking hands–she's bearing a ton of guilt. Ryan is just as guilty as she is, and she's the only one left here to face the consequences.

Staring at her while she sips her coffee and figures out what she'd like to say next, I decide I don't hate her. I think under different circumstances we might have been friends. If she was my friend and was cheating with someone else's husband, I would tell her she's crazy. Married men are just that, married. Taken. Off limits. I can tell she comes from good people because of the amount of guilt I can see on her face, and I feel sorry for her. She has a baby coming, the baby Ryan and I could never have together, and no dad to help out now. Hell, did she think Ryan could go on living a double life once the baby came? How did she think he was going to manage it? All my questions bring me in a full circle.

"Melody, where do you live?"

"In Lakeview."

Holy shit. I sit as my mind starts adding things up. "When was the last time you spoke to Ryan?"

She won't look me in the eye.

"Melody, look at me. When was the last time you spoke to Ryan?" Her avoidance is her tell. I should encourage her to never play poker. She has no poker face at all.

Still refusing to look at me, she answers anyway, "It was the night he died. He called to break our date. We fought on the phone because he was dumping me to be with you at a friend's cookout. He said he was in a hurry to meet you. I was losing my mind and yelling at him. He hung up on me. That was the last time we talked."

"And?" I ask.

"And what? I was being a selfish brat. That's it."

Her body language tells me that's not the whole story. "I'm not an idiot. There's more to it. Him breaking a date wouldn't set you off like that. I can tell you are normally good people."

She hesitates, wiping fat tears off her cheeks before going on, "You're right. I told him about the baby that night. I was hoping that, if he knew about the baby, he would change his mind, and maybe it would get him to come see me instead of going with you." She starts crying harder. Sobbing. "I was using the baby to keep him from breaking up with me. I thought that since you two couldn't have kids that he'd be happy. When he refused to come see me, I went crazy thinking I was going to have to do this alone. Telling my parents, I got knocked up by a married guy and he wouldn't be around for the baby and me, well, that would not fly. But, like I said, I was going to give him some time and then find him at work. Then he died. I mean he *died*. How could he do that?"

Bitch.

The anxiety coursing through me was giving me a headache, and heat was flooding my face. He wrecked his Jeep out on that country road because he was fighting on the phone with his…his…mistress. I don't feel anything anymore. I cannot believe this. She killed him. Well, she didn't kill him. He killed himself using the phone and driving. He was just more distracted than normal because of what she told him. I hate her. I hate Ryan. "I need you to leave now." I stand and motion to the door. I'm doing all I can to keep calm until she leaves. She gets no tears from me. I refuse to give her that.

"But, I was hoping…" She's stammering to form a thought.

I don't care. There is ice in my veins. "I really could care less about what you were hoping for. The fact is you made a dumb-ass mistake by getting involved with a married man and getting pregnant. I don't know if you did that on purpose, or if it was pure accident. I'm withholding judgement right now. The other fact is that Ryan is dead. There is nothing he or I can do for you. I'm doing my best not to hate you for being young and stupid, but it's really time for you to go."

Melody looks at me like I've ripped her to shreds. Not really my goal, but I am finding it hard to feel bad for her right now. "Thank you for listening, and for the coffee. I'm leaving, but here's my number if you want to talk about it sometime. I know what I did was horrible, but since we both loved him, perhaps we can end up friends."

I take the paper she offers me and walk her to the door. I don't wait until she's safely to her car like I would a friend. No, I slam the door shut as part of an angry tantrum and lock it.

I start pacing. Walking circles until I'm numb. My phone buzzes on the table, and I see that I've missed some calls and texts on my phone. I don't look through the whole list. Apparently, my quick call to Jess earlier had resulted in the sister grapevine being activated. I turn my phone off. I don't remember time passing, but I start to feel hungry. The bagel and coffee from earlier are gone.

I warm leftover macaroni and cheese, and then pour myself a Dr. Pepper. I plop down in my recliner to eat my lunch while everything is playing over again in my mind. The only thing I keep coming back to is resentment. I resent Ryan. I resent Melody. What would make him do something like that? How could I believe he was so honorable and faithful to me? I sit there making myself miserable for hours. The questions are just piling up on me. Why do I believe her? She could just be making up the whole story. She could be lying about being pregnant, but she's not lying. I can feel it.

I vaguely hear my doorbell ring through the haze of my thoughts. Then pounding and another ringing of the bell. I don't care. "Go away!" I yell. More pounding. "Rhae, honey, let me in."

Jess.

Of course, turning off my phone and going M.I.A. for a few hours had scared her. Oh goody, she brought Red. They're both taking turns knocking on the door and calling to me. I roll my eyes. Looking around, I notice that it's gotten dark out. I have been in my chair and pacing the house all day. More knocking, and then threats. "We'll call Liz. Let us in!" Oh, that's right, they think I'm possibly suicidal. Finally, I motivate my ass out of the chair and answer the door.

They come in slowly. I can tell they're forcing themselves not to freak out on me. I guess they know if they come in here all crazy-like it would have the opposite effect of what they want. At first, they ask a million questions, but I don't want to talk, so I don't answer. Mostly, I'm embarrassed, and I'm replaying the whole conversation with Melody. The despair in her voice. The shame in her eyes. I replay how I had torn her apart. I waffle between being ashamed of my behavior toward her and feeling justified for my actions. I haven't considered how to explain all of this to my friends and family. *What does it say about me that my husband was having an affair?* I was inadequate as a wife. He wasn't satisfied. I wasn't enough for him. I wasn't important. I'm not important.

All these years together. I was seventeen when I met him, and he was the only man I had ever been with. I was an awkward teenager. Boys didn't notice me. So, when I met Ryan and he was so into me, I was in deep from the very beginning. He was my first real date, first kiss, and first make-out on Mama's couch. My first everything. *Everything.*

I feel something cold being placed in my hand. I look up and see Red has made me a drink and is forcing it into my hand. I take it as she wipes tears from my cheeks. I didn't even know I was crying. Gaining some composure, I stand and take a sip of my drink. The liquor makes my throat burn, but it's just what I need.

"Tell us what's wrong? Talk to us. Please." Jess is attempting to break through the wall I've put up.

I take another drink and clear my throat. I'm not sure where to begin. The beginning? The whole story? I blurt out the bottom line, "Ryan had an affair. He was on his way to see her when the wreck happened. Oh, and she's pregnant." I gesture wildly with my hands in a sarcastic *ta da*.

I can't look at Jess or Red. Instead, I take a huge gulp of my drink. I'm not even sure I like what I'm drinking, but it is having the desired effect. I chance a look at their stunned faces. I'm not sure how long I let them stare at me, but I finally decide to sit down and let it sink in.

I was happily married to the best guy anyone ever knew. He was faithful. He was kind. He loved me more than anything in this world, and I loved him just as much. We had an epic love story. *Didn't we?*

Red breaks the silence. "Who was it?"

I polished off my drink and hold my cup out to her. "More."

She gets me a refill, which I gulp down. As soon as I can speak, I start at the beginning. I tell them every detail of my morning revelations with Melody. I let them know that I thought she was just some dumb kid and didn't do any of this on purpose, but I can't hold back the hate and venom in my voice. Who am I kidding? They are my "sisters" and would know if I was holding back.

"Did you say she's a shorter blonde girl that works at Brown's?" Jess clarifies.

I nod.

"And works at Dancin' Cowboys at night?"

I nod. "Except Tuesdays and Thursdays. Those are the nights they…they…you know."

"Don't you worry about any of this? She won't bother you again." Red declares.

It is truly scary when she makes proclamations like that. Mafia movie levels of scary. "Red, don't do anything. Let her be. She won't come back here. I know that. What's killing me is Ryan. Why would he do this to me? Why wasn't I enough for him?" My body slides from the chair to the floor, as I drop my glass. I can't finish my rant because of the sobbing. I must sound like a big baby. Stammering and sputtering, trying to come up with a complete sentence and failing miserably. I know I am ugly crying. Slobbering and sniffling like a snot monster. I start laughing. Snot laughing. Sniffle-snort-snot-laughing. At least it's better than ugly crying.

Jess and Red sit back and let me get it all out of my system. Later, they carefully tuck me into bed. All I can think is my whole day was wasted. I never finished making my list. I never completed the tasks on it. I close my eyes and start to pray. It's been a while, and I am angry with God for all that is happening to me. I also know I'm not the best example of a Christian, but everything I know about God says he hears the cry of my heart even when I don't know what to pray for.

I start out praying for understanding, then I pray for Ryan. Eventually, I pray for Melody and her baby. Somewhere in the middle of my prayers, I fall asleep. The emotions my body has been through today leave me feeling zapped like I've a run a marathon. I've never actually run a marathon, but now I have some imagined comparison.

Maybe it's because of all the Melody-drama, but I dream of Ryan. It's a warm, sunny day, and we are out on the back porch. I'm reading a book and he is pretend sleeping, kicked back in his chair. I can feel the heat all around me like a blanket. I stare at him in the chair and wait on him to give up the facade of sleeping to talk with me. But he doesn't. He eventually lowers his sunglasses to stare at me, but we don't speak. Well, I don't. Ryan only says one thing, "I love you. Until the end of time, I love you." I start crying because I know it's not true. He might have wanted me to believe it, but it just isn't true. I know the truth now.

A Place to Stand

6
Perspective

Ryan is dead. He had an affair and got his mistress pregnant. My marriage was a sham. Is my whole life a lie? *God, I hope you have a better plan in store for me. I don't know if I can handle things getting any worse.*

Oh, my God. Please let the hammering in my head stop! What is that? Slowly, I surface from sleep and recognize the noise as the alarm on my phone. It's earlier than normal because I planned to be early for my first day back at work. I wake up with swollen eyes and my pillow is soaked. I recall the dream I had about Ryan last night. It makes me feel like there is a knife twisting in my heart. I take a deep breath and throw my legs out of the bed. Sitting on the edge, gathering my thoughts, I decide I have to start moving.

My routine allows me to get through the morning without much thought. Make the coffee. Toast a bagel. Get a shower. I wrap myself in a towel and go into the closet. I decide on the white top and gray pants. Ryan's favorite yellow dress is not an option today. In fact, I may give it away. I can't even think of things that made him happy right now. I know it's childish, and I don't care.

I brush my teeth and my hair, and style my curls with some oil and shake it out. I use a rhinestone clip to hold a back a small section. I don't bother with much make-up. Less is more today. I decide on a sterling silver chain and bracelet, then notice my wedding set is on my left hand. Sighing, I decide I don't need my rings anymore. My chest burns as I muster the willpower I need to place my rings in the jewelry box.

Honestly, I don't know what other widows do. Do they continue wearing their rings? I'm sure the answer to that would be "yes" since they have only suffered a death. I, on the other hand, have the added insult of finding out my late husband was having an affair. Shaking that thought, I dig into the closet for a pair of shoes. I choose the Iron Fist Zombie Stompers, a fantastic heel with crazy art on the sides. A punch of color in my otherwise monochromatic fashion choices today. They definitely match my current mood.

I slip on my shoes and turn to the full-body mirror on the back of my door to take in my appearance. Functional. Passable. Boring. Bereaved and yet still living. I hope no one will see through my facade. I really don't want to be around people today, but that isn't new. I need to get through today and forget about everything Melody told me. No, today, I won't think about anything except getting my work-life back on track. I don't have client meetings, as I have been missing for a while. I probably need to meet with the designers who have been working my sites since I've been off. I hope everything is documented properly. I won't worry about that before I get there. Everything in due time.

I grab my to-go coffee mug and lock the front door. The drive to work is faster than I wanted it to be. Typically, it takes me around forty minutes to get to Memphis from Bell Hills. I park my car, locate my ID badge, and get out. I lock the doors and take another deep breath, forcing strength and confidence into my limbs. I think that might be my mantra today—breathe deeply. As long as I do that, I can get through anything, can't I? If I keep the biology of living intact, maybe the emotional part will recover and join the party.

Our sweet old man of a security guard is at the desk this morning. I'm thankful for his kind smile. "Good morning, Ms. Rhae. How you been?" His standard greeting.

"I'm just fine. Thank you for asking." It is my standard answer, for today. Another part of my strategy—standard smiling responses.

Nothing too fake about that, right? I head to the elevator and then to my desk. My reports have been piling up, but other than that, nothing has changed. I'm not sure what I expected to change. I mean, just because my world has imploded doesn't mean other things had to change.

As usual, I'm the first in the office. I try to take a sip of coffee but discover my mug is empty. Only I would drink the last of something and not realize it. Smiling, and exercising today's theme of breathing, I make my way to the office coffeepot. After I make the coffee, I flip through the stacks of reports on my desk. Everything seems to be in order. So much so, it makes me wonder how necessary I am to the company. I might just be a waste of money for them. The other designers took care of my clients in top order. As I'm finishing up my initial review of what happened while I was out, others start arriving. The typical grumbles about traffic, pleasant good mornings, and complaints about a lack of sleep fill the cube-farm as more and more people arrive.

For the most part, people are kind and don't ask any questions. They gave me smiles and say things like, "Glad you're back," or "Welcome back!" Some even come up with, "How ya been?"

To which I can use my standard answers, saying, "Thanks," or "Good." My smile gets easier and easier to show off. Reluctantly, I begin to wonder what they're thinking. Are they judging me on my lack of grief or apparent grief? I mean my husband died, and here I am smiling at work. I must be a cold-hearted heifer. A small chuckle escapes involuntarily.

"Well, that is a nice sound!"

I look up to see a coworker who shares my cube quad. "Hey there. What's a nice sound?" I ask.

"You laughing. That is a nice sound. I wasn't sure I'd get to hear it again. You okay?" Mr. Bill always has a way of making me smile. He knows how to ask that question without making me cry.

"I'm good." This time my smile is genuine.

He pats me on the back and heads on to his desk. It's not ten minutes later that he hollers at me to help him remember his password. I can't help falling back into old routines, yelling, "Bill! I've been out of the office. Why do you think I can help you with your password? Maybe you reset it. Did you write it down?"

"Aww, Rhae, give me a break. IT said not to write passwords down, so I didn't."

"You know you can write them down and keep them in your wallet, right? As long as you don't leave it on your desk, you're good."

"Why didn't I think of that? You're too smart for your own good."

I head over to his desk and walk him through the self-help password reset. Too bad he's forgotten all the answers to his security questions, too! So, I help him make a call to the support desk. It's out of my hands at this point. Good thing the coffee finished because I am going to need a ton today. I grab Bill's cup and fill us both up before returning to my desk.

Just when things start to feel normal and routine in the office, I hear her. The Dragon Lady. A small ping of panic fills my chest and I start to look for a way out. What do I *need* to do that will take me away from my desk? Scrambling for anything, I see Bill walking away, shaking his head. He must be headed out to smoke. Convenient. He can't stand her either. "I swear, when I retire..." he always rants. Unfortunately, I don't smoke, so I'm stuck. She doesn't sit on our side of the building. Why in the world would she be over here? She's been lying in wait for me to return. Scary thought. That's when it happens.

"*Heeeeyyyyy Girrrlllllll!* So glad you're back. Are you okay?"

Jesus help me. The syrup dripping off her words is nauseating. I start to have a post-traumatic stress flashback. She was at the visitation. She was the one that finally put me over the edge and sent me bailing out the back door. Bernice Daigle, office gossip and fake bitch extraordinaire. I reinforce my chest with a deep breath, "Hello, Bernice. How are you? Did you need something?"

"Me?" Insert mock surprise. "I'm good. How are you? I remember when my third husband died. Girl, I couldn't come back to work for forever. I was just so depressed. I didn't know how I could go on every day, but somehow, I did. So why are you here?"

I didn't think I'd have to answer. She was off on a tangent all by herself, per her usual conversational skills. Her statements are rhetorical. She doesn't care how I am or what my answer would be. I notice she's stopped talking; I think she's waiting on my response. "Oh, well, I'm good. I had to get back to work at some point. Today is as good a day as any."

"Lord, you are so strong." She leans in, it's like one of those movie slow-motion events. I see it happening and I'm powerless to stop it. Catastrophe right here in my cubicle. *Oh God*, she's going to...she hugs me. I don't really do a lot of personal contact outside of family and seriously close friends, so this is disconcerting. My body locks up and I don't move. Perhaps if I hold still she'll let go and leave me alone. Her perfume is so strong I can taste that shit in my mouth. Why hasn't she let go yet? Oh, she might be waiting for me to hug back. I bring up my right arm and gently pat her back near her shoulder. Finally, she lets go. That was nasty.

I motion to my computer. "Lots of catching up to do. Did you need something?"

"Oh, I'm sorry. I'll let you get back to it. Let me know if I can do something to help you. I mean it. This is going to be so tough on you." There's that fake bitch sympathy smile I hate so bad. Fucking hell.

She has no idea what I'm going through. I call in my fake bitch from her bullpen and muster a smile for ol' Dragon Lady. "I will. I think most of my sites and clients were well cared for in my absence." Too well.

She walks away and wiggles her fingers in a half-wave as she goes. Thank God.

"*Sqeeaakkkkkkk!*"

I jump. What in the world was that?

"*SQUEAAAAKKkkkkk, squeak, squawwwwwkkkkkk!*"

What the hell is that sound? I stand and look over the cube wall. Bill's head pops. He is red-faced from laughing. "You like that?"

"What in the world are you doing? Have you lost your mind?" Laughing even harder now, Bill squats out of sight and holds up a large rubber chicken.

I start laughing too. I can't help myself. "Where did you get a rubber chicken?"

"You like her, don't you?"

He starts rubbing her belly and walks around to the inside of my cubicle. He perches on the edge of my desk and lays the chicken down, ever so gently. Then Bill pushes that poor chicken's belly down until it is flat against the desk. He slowly starts letting up the pressure and it seems to me he is playing that rubber chicken with a reverence that would rival a good fiddle player.

That poor chicken squawks the most God-awful sounds. I laugh until I almost pee my pants. I love this man like I love my own daddy. Our antics have drawn a crowd. Everyone is having a good belly laugh off that rubber chicken. Then he gingerly picks her up and says, to the chicken, "Let's go, baby."

I'm not sure how long I laughed. Eventually, everyone goes back to business as usual. Sitting back, I have to take deep breaths for reasons other than feeling sad or overwhelmed by fakeness. It feels good to laugh. Really laugh. Forgetting the torment my life is in, and just laugh at something because it was hilarious. I want to hug Bill's neck for that. Maybe I'll keep the pot full of fresh coffee for him. He is as big an addict as I am. Silently, I smile to myself and thank God for sending Bill over with that confounded rubber chicken.

The day wears on and on. At one point, I seriously think I'm in a time warp or that the clock is broken. I have meetings with my manager and other designers to get up to speed on everything that happened while I was out. I feel even more useless because everyone is on top of everything without me. Great, now my work feels as shattered as my personal life. Maybe not shattered, but I definitely don't fit here anymore. It's only the first day back, I remind myself. I'll stick out the week and see if it gets any better. I don't feel hopeful. I hope God has a plan in the works. Better to think there was something happening than nothing.

When my usual lunch hour approaches, I disappear to my car. Yeah, it is hot as hell, but I am so overwhelmed that I need some time to straighten out my head. I roll down my windows and open a new book on my phone. The warmth from the sun and the calming breeze coming through the windows lulls me to sleep before I can finish the second chapter. There's nothing like napping on a summer's day. I dream of Ryan, then I re-live the talk I had with Melody. She seems different in my dream. Perhaps my mind is starting to forgive her for her part in the betrayal with Ryan.

The alarm I set on my phone startles me awake at the end of my hour. Groaning, I roll up my windows and head back into the building. I have so much to decide. None of which has anything to do with Ryan. Nothing in my life is about him anymore. Realization strikes me. I'm on my own. For the first time in my life, I'm on my own.

I've lived with my parents and sisters, then my dorm roommate and shortly after that, Ryan. I have never had a place of my own. I have always made decisions based on cooperation with another person. I don't have to do that anymore. Maybe my life isn't a hot mess. Maybe I need the right perspective.

Still a little groggy from my car nap, and just a tad sweaty, I head to the HR office. This is a tiny little space in our building and only three ladies work in here. Luckily, I am blessed with finding Ms. Jimmie coming back from her lunch. She's a plump lady with rosy cheeks. I want to hug her. It's a natural instinct with her. She notices me waiting to go in the door and she smiles her sweetest for me.

"Hey, honey. I'm glad to see you. You look well."

"Thank you, Ms. Jimmie." I reach out and hug her anyway.

She squeezes me good. I feel my eyes well up while she holds me tight. I haven't felt like crying today, but now, with her squeezing like my mama would have, there it is. The feeling in my chest is like I'm going to split wide open. I force myself to take a couple of breaths as she pulls back to stare at me. Sometimes you don't know you need a hug until it happens.

"You're barely holding on, aren't you? Do you need to take some more time off?"

I shake my head. "No, ma'am. I came to change my name. I want to take my maiden name back. I think it'll help."

Her expression changes from maternal concern to all business. "Well, I can definitely take care of that for you. Come on in. Have a seat." She motions to the gray chair at the visitor's side of her desk. That thing has seen better days. Carefully tickling through pages in her drawer she pulls out a few forms.

"Fill this out for me, baby, while I get this darn computer going so I can key them in for you. You'll be back to Rhae, er, what is your maiden name?"

"Peters."

"Well, you'll be Rhae Peters again by this afternoon."

We work in silence while I ponder her kindness. It occurs to me that Ms. Jimmie is the only person, other than my family, that I feel comfortable with. She isn't fake and doesn't ask how I'm feeling.

"Ms. Jimmie?"

"You done with that form, hon?"

"Nearly, but I wanted to ask you a question. How do you know?"

She's diligent, studying her computer screen for the next place she needs to click, and asks, "Know what?"

"You don't act overly sympathetic. You don't push me to talk about...things."

Ms. Jimmie moves around her screen to look at me. "Oh. Well.

Most people don't know I lost my husband a couple years ago. It was before I started working here. We had been married for nearly thirty years. I know that you aren't doing okay. Why ask that? It never made sense to me. Being a widow is not easy." She smiles knowingly. "Going on after they're gone and all. I know you have to get back to your normal life eventually. People think you need to be sitting around at home to properly grieve your husband, but I'm here to tell you I think you are right to pull your bootstraps up and get back to living," she finishes with a wink.

I am staring at a sixty-year-old me. This lady is kind and tough as nails. I love her. I stand up and nod to her. "Thank you. For everything. For understanding how to help me without smothering me." I hand her my completed forms and return to my desk. It feels like a change in the winds. I am going back to my maiden name. I am going to live on my own. It's okay to miss Ryan or even be angry with him for the affair with Melody. But I am going on living. That's what I'm going to do—living and shit. I laugh to myself and catch the attention of the admin on this floor. She looks at me over her glasses. *Judgy, judgy.* I try to stifle my laugh, making it worse.

I start calling my clients to set up meetings for this week. Surprise, surprise: they are all happy working with the other designers and don't need to meet with me. *Well, shit.* If I felt unnecessary this morning, now I feel downright useless. Completely. The day wraps up faster than I thought possible. Before I realize what time it is, people are breezing by my desk asking things like, "Working late, huh?" or "Still catching up?" I look at the clock and it's at least an hour past my normal quitting time.

Then I hear the sweetest sound ever. "Hey, sista! You ready to go yet? We're taking you for a drink."

Looking up from my screen, I smile widely, looking at the three best friends I ever made at work. Alana, Lucy, and Jules are all smiling back at me and waiting for a response. "Ladies, I am so happy to see you! I know we didn't get to hang out today, but I need to take a raincheck. I have been drinking way too much lately."

"Fair enough, we'll take you to dinner." Lucy says, without missing a beat. She's nodding as she says it, subconsciously willing me to accept any kind of offer.

"Dinner. Just dinner?" I ask in clarification.

"Just dinner. We will totally behave." Jules confirms.

"Well, then, where are we going?"

An excited Alana declares, "Beale Street!"

"How about we steer clear of environments that encourage my terrible drinking habits? Let's go to the Arcade."

They all agree. I shut down my computer and grab my purse. We all drive since we will be going separate ways at the end of dinner. About twenty minutes later, we are seated in the back room ordering our drinks and settling in to look at the menu.

"I'm not going to ask how you are, but I am going to hug you. I love you, my Rhae Rhae," Alana says as she reaches around the corner of the table to hug me. I have to swallow hard to choke down tears. Why are hugs doing this to me today? These are my girls, the Shady Ladies. We talk about everything. Usually we go out every Friday for lunch and dish about dirty thoughts, desires, or what's going on with our lives. Sometimes we drool over book boyfriends. Why is a simple hug pushing me over the edge? I really have to get over this. Emotions are for the birds. Like me, useless.

"You do know she doesn't like emotions or being touched, right?" Jules asks Alana.

"I know. But I need her to know I love her." Alana replies as she pets my hair. Such a sweet girl.

I see Lucy reach out and rub Jules's arm. "It's okay. It's us. She knows we need to hug on her."

Before I know it, each one has taken a turn at coming around to hug me. The love these ladies have for me is almost overwhelming. It occurs to me that I have so many great people in my life that care about me deeply. After everyone has a turn at me, I smile and open the door for what I know they need, the goodies. "So, I know you want to ask, and I have to learn to talk about this stuff. Fire away."

Jules goes first. "We heard the rumors of how Ryan died. Tell us what really happened."

I didn't expect that to be the first question, but that's Jules. I take a deep breath and launch into the story of our last day together. Alana watches me with tears in her eyes as I talk about our making love that morning. Lucy shifts uncomfortably as my story approaches the visit from the police at Liz's house. Jules looks like she is committing every detail to memory. I get to the bits about the funeral, what I can remember anyway. It's funny, when I told them a coworker I hadn't expected showed up and that was the breaking straw, they all knew who it was.

"Dragon Lady showed up? You have got to be shitting me." Alana is clearly offended by the audacity of that crazy heifer.

Lucy shakes her head. "Ugh, nosey bitch loves it when people are sick or dying. That must have been right before we got there. We didn't see you, but we signed the book. So sorry she pulled that, babe."

"Thank you," I reach over and squeeze her hand. "I'm good. My sisters and dad were there to block it out. Plus, it was a great opportunity for them to get me home." I went on telling how I had spent most of my time off at Jess's house with Connor and Jillian. Then I explained how I had already done the pack and donate routine on Ryan's stuff. Finally, I was up to the hardest part of the conversation. The affair. "So that brings me up to yesterday. I was at home in my pajamas, drinking coffee, and making a list of what I needed to do for coming back to work. That's when *she* showed up. Ryan's pregnant mistress."

The girls break out in a chorus of, "What? What the fuck? His what? Back the train up." I half expected a spit-take on that one. Maybe hoped for one anyway. I never say anything funny or shocking enough to get a spit-take. Note to self: work on that. Taking another drank of tea. I nod. We are interrupted by the server, so we can place our orders. I get my favorite, the Eggs Redneck with deep fried hash browns. Thinking they'll let that story slide, I start asking how they are.

The girls will not be denied. They stare at me, expectantly.

"Fine. Fine. I'll tell you the story." When I finish telling them about my impromptu morning discussion with pregnant, college student, two-job working, cheating Melody, I was staring at the three most appalled faces I have ever seen. The silence is deafening.

Jokingly, I add, "What? Not all dead husbands have an affair hiding on the side?"

Alana sniffles like she's crying. "I'm so sorry."

"Don't feel sorry for me. I'm okay."

Jules, as practical as I am, asks, "So what are you going to do about her?"

"Do? There's nothing to do. I don't owe her anything. Ryan died. She's on her own. I hope her family helps her, but there's nothing for me to do."

"Exactly. You don't owe her shit. Why would she even come over to tell you something like that?" Lucy says.

"I have no idea. I drank a lot last night trying to get through telling my sisters. I think Red was about to go find her and kick her ass until I told her to leave that girl alone. She's made a mess that she has to live with."

Being done with this whole pity party, I deflect, "All right, catch me up. What's going on with you guys?" They take the hint and spin tales about everything I've missed. I'm actually starting to feel jealous. I mean, when I'm at work, nothing happens. I miss a few weeks and I miss everything. What's up with that? Alana reaches over and pats my knee when she notices I'm not connected to the group conversation. I am in and out of the moment, and can't pay much attention, but I do my best.

Our server eventually brings the food. We eat and talk. It is an obscene amount of food. We part a while later and after some more very necessary hugs, I drive home without even turning on the radio. I simply think over the stories shared and how blessed I feel to have these people in my life.

It's nearly dark when I get home, and I can't help thinking how happy I'll be when I get to enjoy more nighttime. I change into a tank top and shorts and start the laundry. I watch *Jeopardy* and *Wheel of Fortune*, then it occurs to me that this sucks. I should be out with my friends or something. I should be doing something. If Ryan was here, we would have found something interesting to do like going to hear a band or visiting with friends. I could always go see Jess, but I don't want her to worry. Maybe I could re-read another book, but the thought isn't exciting to me. I need to get out of this house. When I was at work, things were still on my mind, but being in this house, everything seems to pile up on my shoulders. The burden is heavy. Ryan is everywhere. His betrayal is everywhere.

I decide to go for a walk. I can walk and think. Strapping on my under-used sneakers, I try to decide which way I'll go. I don't have a destination. I don't know how far or long I plan to walk, but I feel like moving.

Starting at a leisurely pace, I head south on our little road. In just a short distance, I'm power-walking. That's right, power-walking like the little old ladies at the mall. Before I can get through a mental repeat of my conversation with Melody, I reach the massive oak tree at the intersection. I guess that's about one mile from the house. Estimating distance has never been a strong suit for me. I usually over-estimate, and I haven't gone as far as I think. If this becomes some kind of habit, I'll need to get one of those fancy fitness apps on my phone. You know, the ones that track distance, calories, blood pressure, farts, gas levels...whatever they track. Looking around, I decide one mile, give or take, isn't enough. Definitely not enough yet. I decide to keep going.

It must be the chemicals in my brain doing their thing because I decide to start running. My legs stretch to their full length for the first time in ages. It occurs to me that I shouldn't go too hard—I'm not wearing a sports bra. Yet I can't shake the feeling of how good it feels. Running away from Ryan and Melody, but toward the unknown. Exhausting my body physically. Maybe this will help the emotional fatigue I'm drowning in.

I run about mile and a half. The burn in my legs is crazy. My lungs hurt, and my throat is raw from taking in huge gulps of air. I stop abruptly and bend over, putting my hands on my knees to catch my breath. I have sweat running down my face and I'm nauseated. Still bent over, I start taking even larger gulps of air. In through my mouth, out through my nose.

"Hey." I hear a distinctly masculine voice interrupt my recovery. Being that it is after dark now, and being alone, I am not too enthused to hear it. *Great, this is where it ends.*

"Hello." I say coldly between gasps. Squinting into the dark in the direction of the voice, trying to see a face or something. My vision picks up a body stepping away from the cover of a porch. A tall body.

"It's a little late to go for a run, don't you think." Seriously? This guy is probably a rapist or murderer.

My breathing is still heavy as I stand up straight and put my hands on my hips. "I guess." *Gasp.* "Sorry I disturbed you." *Gasp.* "Think you might step into the light a little bit, creeper?" *Gasp.*

He lets out a hearty laugh. "Sure thing." He slowly steps into the light. I guess being told he was acting creepy made him more cautious as not to scare me. Jesus, he is easy on the eyes. I must be about to die. The exertion and lack of oxygen is taking a toll on my mental and visual acuity. He has to be a mirage.

I can't tell if he has dark brown hair or black hair, but I can tell it is clean cut. He is just so tall. I suddenly feel a chill run over my body. He's wearing jeans and a white, sleeveless T-shirt. A wife beater? Lord, help. Definitely a pre-death mirage.

"I'm not sure I've seen you before," I state dumbly.

"I'm visiting some family." He turns and points to the house. I start to recognize where I am. Ah, I know this house. An elderly couple Ryan used to help out lives here. Wondering if helping the elderly was his cover story for seeing Melody, I groan at the thought.

"Nice of you, I suppose."

"As I was saying, little late for a run. You aren't running away from something are you? Someone, maybe?" He starts looking around as if he expects my pursuer to come into view at any moment.

"No. Yes. Maybe. I don't know." I am an idiot. I can't even talk to a guy anymore.

He laughs again. "Okay. How about we start with names? I'm Cade, Cade Miles. And you are?"

"Rhae Wells…er…Peters."

"I'm sorry. Was it Wells or Peters?"

"Don't be. I recently went back to my maiden name, Peters. My married name was Wells. I haven't settled back into my own name yet."

He looks confused. "So, you're divorced?"

I sigh. I really shouldn't be talking to a complete stranger in the middle of the road in the dark. He might be a freaking criminal. Here I am giving him enough information to hunt me down. Still, it is refreshing to talk to someone who has no idea what I've been going through.

"No offense, but you could be a serial killer," I blurt out. I roll my eyes to myself. He can't see them anyway. "Not that I think you are; I just don't know you. So, I'm pretty sure I'm messing up by telling you so much about me."

He laughs again a little harder. It is a great laugh, too. "No, I understand. You really don't have a reason to talk to me. I saw a young woman running down a country road, by herself, at night, and thought I should be chivalrous and see if she needs help. I can see that you don't. You seem pretty tough. Would you like a drink of water? You must be thirsty running in this heat."

I start to go near him, and then stop myself. What am I doing? *Hello!* Serial killer potential. "That's probably not a…"

"You're right. Serial killer." He indicates himself and nods. "How about you come into the yard and wait here? I'll go get you a glass. I'll try to remember to leave out the date rape drugs, so you know I'm not a rapist too."

Now it's my turn to laugh. "Smart ass," I grumble, and he laughs again.

I slowly walk into the yard and lean against the tree. When I'm good and settled, he turns to go in the house. A moment later, the front porch lights come on. Definitely a home for elderly people. They have enough lights to signal airplanes. Shielding my eyes, I try to keep a watch for his return. Soon enough, he nearly runs down the stairs, a glass in each hand.

"Thought it might be less creepy if I turned on the lights." He flashes the brightest smile I have seen in a long time. No sympathy behind those pearly whites. "You are thirsty, right?" What? Of course... oh. I had zoned in on his devilish good looks and didn't notice him holding the glass of water out to me. I mean, those huge dark brown eyes. I didn't get to see them before in the darkness by the tree. My breath hitches.

"Sorry. Distracted. Thank you." It's true. I take the glass, and then a small sip. Lemon. He put lemon in my water. Just right, too. "Thanks. That's tasty. I don't know many people who like lemon in their water. I appreciate the thought."

"No problem. So, do you frequently walk or run after dark? It is awfully hot out here."

"I, uh, no, I don't. I didn't want to sit in my house, alone, anymore." I exaggerate the alone part.

"Well, do you want to sit on the swing, or do you still think I might kill you?"

"We can sit on the swing. Keep your rapey hands to yourself." The corners of my mouth turned into a sly smile as I look sideways at him.

He throws his hands up in mock offense and follows me up the porch steps. We sit on the swing and start a nice, patient rhythm of swinging. Not enough to disrupt my glass, but just enough to get a small breeze going around us. He's doing a good job with the swing, so I pull my legs up and under my rear-end, cradling the glass between my legs.

"So, divorced, huh?" Oh, we're going to have a conversation. I hoped he would skip over it. No one is giving into my childish desires to skip topics today.

"No. I'm, uh, widowed." That's the first time I had said it out loud to someone who didn't know. It hurts, but not as bad as it did at first. I always thought that was the worst title for someone to have. Now it's who I am.

Cade blinks in surprise. "Wow. I didn't mean to assume divorce. How long?"

Looking up from the glass between my legs to meet his eyes, I take a deep, shaky breath. "Recent. A couple months ago." I keep staring into his eyes, expecting the pity or sympathy so many have given me lately. There isn't any there.

"How long were you married?"

"Five years this past January."

"How old are you?" His tone is incredulous.

I laugh. "I know I got married young. I'm only twenty-five."

He smiles at me like a devil. "So...shotgun, huh?" He's confident that he has me figured out.

I frown. "What? No. We started dating when I was seventeen. We dated for a few years and got married because, well, because that's what you do. And don't waggle your eyebrows at me like that."

"Sorry." Devil grin. "I don't know about that. What was his name?"

"Don't know about what?"

"Getting married because the timeline says so."

"We were in love." *Weren't we?*

He nods like he's going to leave it alone. I take another drink of my water. He keeps the swing going, almost hypnotically. We sit in silence for a while.

"His name. You never answered that question," he reminds me.

"His name was Ryan."

"You miss him?"

"Honestly, I think I'm supposed to. For some reason, I have a greater peace about it now than I did originally." Maybe because if he was alive I would have removed his balls with an ice cream scooper for that affair bullshit. I am not about to reveal everything.

"Cade, was it?" I ask.

"Yes, Rhae. Cade Miles."

"Why am I answering all the questions here?"

"Good point. You can't be sure I'm not a serial killer-rapist, can you? What is your question, Ms. Rhae Peters?"

I smile because he's making fun of my earlier assumption. "Who are you visiting here?"

"My grandparents."

"For how long?"

"As long as necessary." He looks down, not meeting my eyes.

"What kind of answer is that? You don't have a home or something?" I grin to encourage his good-natured mood to return.

"No." He smiles sadly. "I'm not some homeless man who came to call on his grandparents. My grandfather is sick. Hospice thinks that he could pass any day now. We are on 'wait and see' status." He looks down at his feet moving the swing.

"Oh." It's the only thing I can think of to say. As torturous as it was to lose Ryan instantly, waiting around has to be worse. It *is* worse.

"That's it? Oh?"

"I hate it when people tell me they're sorry. I am, but I don't want to be a hypocrite and say what I wouldn't want to hear. I just remember what it was like when we went through a similar scenario when my mama passed a few years ago." Things have gotten a little too intense. "I think it's time for me to get home. I'll see you around Cade Miles." Standing, I walk towards the steps.

"Let me give you a ride," he offers sincerely. "I did start out talking to you to be chivalrous. I mean, that is unless you would like to run home, in which case, I can run with you." That was a mouthful.

"I guess if I turn you down, you'll follow me anyway. So, I'll take a ride home." I smile genuinely. I don't know what I was thinking earlier. I don't work out enough to be over two miles from home on foot.

Cade hops up and takes the glass from me. He sets it down on the porch railing and then grabs my hand. His skin is soft and warm, and his hand is large enough to swallow mine whole. He escorts me off the porch and around to the carport. I'm a little surprised.

"A four-wheeler?" I ask.

He grins that devil of a grin. "What? Mississippi girls don't ride four-wheelers?"

I feign offense. "Of course we do, but would you let me drive?"

It's his turn to look shocked. "I'm not one to turn down a pretty lady. After you," he says as he gestures to our ride.

"I think this works better when you get on first. Slide all the way back." I instruct.

He smiles incredulously and does as he's told. Good boy.

I have to climb on in front of him. First, I step on the running board and throw my right leg over the seat. I realize, too late, that when I get on, I'll have to shove my ass right in his face before I sit down. I try to appear confident. As I finish my climb on to the four-wheeler, Cade clears his throat.

"Feeling okay back there?" I ask.

"Yeah," he answers nervously. "Great. Let's see if you can drive this thing."

He has the same model as my dad, so I know exactly how to operate it. I crank it and look over my shoulder to see him leaning against the rear basket, balancing himself by putting his hands behind him.

"You sure that's enough support?" I ask, and he nods. "Okay, hold on." I squeeze the accelerator and the four-wheeler jumps forward. Thrown off balance, Cade grabs my waist to keep from falling off. I grin to myself. It feels great to have him wrapped around me. Geez! I don't even know him! I can't think things like that about him right now. The feel of him against my back sends chills all over me.

I am in fourth gear before we lose sight of his grandparent's house. He hugs me tighter as I shift gears. I smile big. A few minutes later, I pull into my driveway and turn off the four-wheeler. He slightly releases me, and I make a move to get off. Again with the booty-in-face action. He sits still, and I notice he's smiling too.

"What? Girls from your neck of the woods can't drive four-wheelers like that?" I make a sarcastic face as I ask.

It takes Cade so long to respond that I start to worry I have acted too tough, and then he blurts out, "Want to have lunch tomorrow?"

I narrow my eyes in suspicion, "Excuse me? I don't even know you."

"But I want to know you. Have lunch with me tomorrow."

"No." I suddenly feel self-conscious. There's no way I should even have friendly dates with men right now. I don't know how this is supposed to work.

"Please?" he asks.

I shake my head, "I-I...just...can't." I can feel panic rising in my throat.

Cade takes a step off the four-wheeler and reaches out for me. "Rhae, calm down. It's okay. How about we skip lunch tomorrow, but meet for a run tomorrow after work?"

I nod.

"Yeah?" he asks for confirmation.

"Yeah. A run tomorrow sounds good. Let's take it slow. I need to get a background on you first." I'm joking, but it's worth a thought.

He laughs and gets back on the four-wheeler. "See you at six tomorrow night." With that, he takes off.

I stand in the driveway a bit longer, and then go into the house. What happened tonight? Who is Cade Miles? This is ridiculous.

I make a glass of tea from the pitcher I keep in the refrigerator and go over to the stereo in the living room. I turn on the radio and sit down to consider what the hell happened tonight. He's being friendly, right? He would offer this to any woman he saw running alone. Poor guy is sitting around waiting for his grandfather to pass.

I start to frustrate myself and decide it's getting late. Judging by the way today went with work, I should get to bed. I lock up the house and change for bed. I put on a pair of Ryan's boxers and a T-shirt. This is the only set of his clothes I kept. I turn on my box and ceiling fans, then lay down. I run over the events of my night as I fall asleep. I can do this. I can live and move on. I didn't die with Ryan.

A Place to Stand

7
Running Buddy

My alarm goes off. I grumble and bury my head under the covers. Today is going to go just like yesterday. What choice do I have? I need to work. Begrudgingly, I get started with a shower, style my hair into a twist, and then get dressed. For a moment, I think I could wear the yellow dress. I stare at it and contemplate doing it. The longer I think about it, the angrier I get. *Fuck Ryan.* I am not wearing that dress. How long can I stay pissed at a dead man? I make my coffee and bagel and then head out to work.

Today is a little more miserable, with an obvious exception for my girls who stopped by at irregular intervals to be sure no one is irritating me. Still, more people felt comfortable coming by to talk to me. I get lots of, "Hi-how-are-ya," and "You okay?" It's miserable. I'm making a pot of coffee when I feel the Dragon Lady approach.

My back stiffens, and I turn around slowly. It's good to keep motions slow and gradual to not startle her into attack mode. "Good morning, Bernice," I manage to say politely. She looks confused for some reason. Then, after staring holes through me for a beat, she cocks her head to the side.

"You changed your name," she accuses.

"I did. I decided to go back to my maiden name. Ryan is gone, after all," I remind her.

She looks around and leans closer to me. God, please don't hug me again. "That's a little inappropriate, don't you think?" She exaggerates the last part for emphasis, then raises her eyebrows at me.

I can't help the twisted look on my face, when I respond, "Are you serious? You came over here to lecture me about propriety?"

"All I know is it ain't right for you to change your name and quit wearing your wedding rings so soon. Your husband hasn't been gone that long. You're already moving on? Had a man on the side already, didn't you?"

This conversation is not happening. This isn't happening. This crazy bitch. *Jesus, take the wheel so I don't hurt her.* "Bernice, I appreciate your concern, but it's none of your business."

She looks like someone is choking her favorite dog. "Well, I know your mama is gone. I thought *someone* should tell you what's right. I had no idea you would be so rude." She even raises her eyebrows on the word "rude." I am imagining that comedy show from long ago where they guy was dressed as a prudish old lady saying, "Isn't that special."

I take a calming breath before I respond, "Again, I thank you for your concern. This is none of your business. If you knew my mama and cared to stand in for her during this time, you would know she would tell me to put on my big girl panties and get on with life. I am. No man on the side. I'm offended you would make such a statement." Ryan had side-booty, not me. I finish that part in my head. I'm not up to sharing that with anyone else yet. I am certainly not sharing this with the Dragon Lady.

She stews on that for a moment—an uncomfortably long moment. I was just starting to feel awkward enough to apologize when Bill comes over. "Where's the coffee, Rhae?"

I look from Dragon Lady to Bill. "Making. It'll be ready before you can whine about your passwords not working."

Bill notices how close Dragon Lady is to me. "Bernice! Don't you have something to do on your side of the building? You ain't drinking

Rhae's coffee up from me. Go on." He makes a shoo motion with his hands.

She gives us both a murderous look but smiles and leaves. Why is this so important to her? This conversation is far from over, I can tell. Freaky, nosey, crazy lady. After she's out of sight, I look over at Bill, who is pounding his mouse on the desk. "Thank you."

"Yes, ma'am," he answers without looking up.

"Ma'am? Please."

He glares at me with mock sternness, "That's right. Ma'am. I was raised right; don't matter how old you aren't. What was she over here for anyway?"

"She's offended because I changed my last name and put my rings away."

"Why is that any of her business?"

I nod and sigh. "That's what I said. It really pissed her off. She thinks it's too soon. She thinks I should be more publicly grieved." I roll my eyes.

"Well, that's how you know you are living right. You keep Bernice pissed off." He laughs. "Do I need to get Ginger out of the drawer?"

"Ginger? Who's Ginger, and why is she in your drawer?" I cock my eyebrow at him.

"She's my chicken." He pulls the rubber chicken out of the drawer and lays her on the desk. "I'll leave her here in case the Dragon Lady comes back.

I laugh and walk back to my desk. "Thanks Bill," I call over my shoulder.

I get busy checking on my sites, monitoring the error logs to see that everything is working properly. The performance measurements on all my sites are fantastic. To be sure, I look at the support call log. No issues have been called in for any kind of support. Only tickets for content changes that were easy enough. Maybe I'm unnecessary to my

A Place to Stand

clients. I designed their sites so well that they are running smoothly without intervention. That feels a little better than thinking the other designers were encroaching on my clients.

Before I know it, I'm pondering my run "date." Cade is completely distracting. What does he look like in the daylight? What will he think of me in the daylight? It will probably confirm the "friends" that I assume we are becoming at this point. A running buddy. I heave a big sigh and decide to go to the ladies' room and check my face and hair. Not sleeping well is starting to take a toll on me. After some stretches in my cube, I grab my phone and slide it into my pocket as head to the bathroom.

Once in the bathroom, I stare into the full-length mirror and decide I look like hell. I do my best to adjust my top over my hips and make sure my skirt is hanging evenly. Years of being with Ryan and not being worried about my appearance is showing. I have been so complacent. Definitely carrying more in the middle than I used to. I shake my head. I could start working out. I have been thinking about that for years. Hell, having a run on the calendar with the guy down the street has to count for something.

There's nothing to be done about my figure today. At least I have boobs that kind of balance out my look. I do my best to freshen my makeup. I rub at the circles under my eyes, more evidence of my lack of sleep. Maybe I can get a box of over-the-counter sleep aids on my way home tonight. I remove the clips from my hair, shake it out, and restyle my twist. With all my curls, it's best to just start a style over instead of trying to use my fingers to tuck in stray pieces.

My phone buzzes, indicating a new e-mail coming. It's Alana, and she wants to go for lunch today. I type out a quick reply for her to meet me in the lobby at eleven a.m. This is actually a really great thing. I can bounce my Cade experience off her and see what she thinks. Which makes me wonder, does anyone else know him? I mean, his grandparents have lived here a long time, so he must have visited before. Someone must know him. Even if no one does, I need to do some Internet research to see if he is a known serial killer, rapist, graffiti artist, or whatever.

When I get back to my desk, I hit several websites and all the usual social media sites. Nothing. Not even on Facebook. Who doesn't have Facebook at our age? Definitely something I can ask him about. I can't find any criminal records locally or in any of the surrounding counties. He might not be a serial killer. I immediately start making a mental list of things that could be getting me false results on my searches. Everything from lying about his name to thinking he might not be from around the local area at all. I know he said he was visiting, but from where? I have to stop doubting everyone I meet. It is really a sickness.

When eleven a.m. rolls around, I grab my wristlet and put on my sunglasses. Bill perks up and says, "Where ya headed?"

"To eat. Can I bring you something?" I ask.

"Naw. I'm going to eat soup out of the cabinet."

"Alrighty then." I head down and meet up with Alana.

I feel extra light as we walk out into the sunshine and head for the deli. It is a quick walk, but it is a great little spot. They even have patio tables and chairs for those who may want to sit outside. I hope we can sit inside so I don't sweat all down my legs and have to deal with that the rest of the day. I get lost in the warmth of the sun on my face. We come to a stop at the crosswalk and while we wait on the light to change, I close my eyes and lift my face to the sky. I smile and breathe in the air around me.

"Hey! Let's go!" Alana pulls my arm.

"Sorry." I stumble forward and catch up to her.

"Where do you go when you do that?" she asks, almost annoyed.

"I don't know. I'm not trying to check out. It just keeps happening."

"Are you okay? And don't give me that bullshit answer you throw everyone else. I know you too well."

"I don't know. I think I might be okay, eventually. All

other...things...aside, yeah. I guess I'm better than okay." I smile at her.

"Really? Do tell!" She demands excitedly.

"There's nothing to tell."

"Yes, there is. You never smile like that. Spill."

We step into the deli and order our food. I avoid eye contact with her while we make our drinks. This conversation needs to wait until we have a table. I scan the deli for an indoor table and spot an empty booth in a corner. I settle in and place our number on the holder.

"You are not getting out of this conversation. Start talking."

"There's a lot going on, you know." I smile. "But you're right, there is more to talk about. I met someone."

"What?" she fires back, almost screaming.

I shrink back in the chair and attempt to shush her. "What is wrong with you? I thought we were talking. Nice way to get everyone in the room to stare at us."

"Sorry, but you can't drop that kind of bomb on me."

"Okay, well, shall I finish, or are you going to yell again?" I cut my eyes at her. "Right. I met someone. I was lonely last night just sitting in the house listening to the laundry, and I didn't want to call anyone or hang out anywhere. I decided to go for a walk. Before I knew it, I was running."

"Now, that *is* impressive," she laughs.

"Bitch. Anyway, I stopped to catch my breath, and there he was. Sitting on the front porch of a house. He approached me, and we talked for a while. Eventually, he got me home and asked me to lunch today. I turned him down because I felt weird, so we agreed on a running date." I look at Alana's puzzled face when I finish my ramble.

"So, running buddy? What does he look like?" she asks.

"I don't really know. It was dark. He is tall and built, I know that." I smirk and feel my face redden.

"Built? *How* do you know that?"

"Well, he gave me a ride home and let me drive the four-wheeler. He had to hug me to keep from falling off. It was awesome." I fan my face at the thought of it.

"Oh, my God. Let me dream about him for a minute. He sounds tasty. What's the problem?"

"Well, I don't know. I feel like I'm supposed to still be mourning Ryan. Like it's too soon to move on. Plus, I don't think he got a good look at me either. I know he will only want to be friends once he sees me in the daylight."

"What is wrong with you? Is your self-esteem that low? Really? I could smack you for even talking that way. Why do you think that?"

"C'mon, 'Lana. I'm overweight. I've been married five years. The only person I have ever had sex with is dead. I don't know what I'm doing here."

"Let me tell you what you're doing," she leans forward and takes a firm tone with me. "First, you are going to let him judge you for himself. Don't put words in his mouth." She takes my hand and squeezes. "Second, you are going to quit thinking you owe Ryan something because he died. You have to move on with your life. Be friends with this guy and see if it grows into something else. It's not like you are looking to remarry right now."

I nod and ultimately agree with her. He will either love me, hate me, or just want to be my friend. I mean, c'mon, fat girls are the funniest.

We finish eating and I listen about what's going on in her work world. There is always something when you've been with a company for any real time.

As we're leaving, Alana grabs my arm. "You have a mission: I want a full report after your run with tall-and-built."

I smile. "Cade."

"Cade?"

"Cade. That's his name. My running buddy."

She smiles. "I like that. Let's get back. Tell Bernice to kiss my ass when you see her."

We walk in with a few minutes to spare. I consider Alana's directive. She's right. I have to think more of myself than to assume Cade will run screaming into the night when he gets a good look at me. I take a deep breath and dive back into work. Time seems to fly today, and before I can obsess about the clock, it's time to go. I hop into the car and roll down all my windows, turn on some 90s' tunes, and blast the volume as loud as I can stand it. By the time I'm home, the sun is starting to set. I get out and stand by the car to check out the start of the evening.

A beautiful splash of orange covers the bottom half of the sky as I stare out across a field. I'm still standing by the car trying to commit the color blends to memory when I hear footsteps on my porch. I jump and turn around. There he is. Cade is standing at the top of my porch steps, with the waning light of day coloring the shadows across his face. My breath catches. I don't know what to say, so I lift my hand and wave.

He returns the gesture and then says, "Hi."

"Hi," I mutter, barely audible.

"Ready for that run?" he asks.

"Yes. Uh, no, I mean, I need to change."

He smiles and nods as if acknowledging my attire is inappropriate for running. "Fair enough. You get changed. I'll wait here."

I nod and bound up the stairs. For a few moments after I enter the house, all I can do is stand inside the door and pant. *Good Lord*. He's even better in daylight. *What the hell am I going to do? Shit! Shit! Shit!* I should call Jess. She'll know.

I grab my phone and look for her contact and then it hits me, Jess may not approve of this. No. I can't take that chance. Instead of calling Jess, I run around my room and change clothes. I go for a sports bra this time. Don't want to be held back by super-bouncy boobs. I throw on a tank and some yoga pants. I grab two bottles of water out of the fridge and then my keys as I pass the table.

I lock up and run down the stairs to where Cade is waiting, leaned against my car. He pulls his hand through dark brown, wavy hair and looks over as I'm coming down the porch steps. The man is delicious.

"Water?" I ask as I offer him a bottle.

"Sure. You ready?" he asks.

I strike a pose to highlight my change in attire. "Sure. Let's do this."

"You stretched?"

"Uh no. I thought we would just run." Stretched? Who is he kidding? Do I look like I do this very often? He might lose points for common sense on that one.

"Okay, here let me show you."

Cade proceeds to demonstrate proper stretching. I attempt to follow his example. I'm sure I look more like a wounded flamingo while he looks like a complete professional. I mentally remind myself of Alana's words. I put on a brave face and feign confidence.

We take a run down to his grandparents' house. The recovery time is a little faster this time. Well, I have to recover. Cade is a pro and is bouncing from foot to foot while I bend over and swallow as much air as I can stuff in my lungs. Everything hurts. My shins are burning, the arch of my foot has a cramp, and my lungs are on fire. Cade gives me a few minutes before he stops running and squats down so his face is level with mine.

"Don't run very often, do you?"

"How…" *Gasp.* "…can you…" *Gasp.* "…tell?"

He laughs and smiles wider, "Call it a hunch. How long have you been running?"

"This is…" *Gasp.* "…the second…" *Gasp.* "…time."

"Shut up. Last night when I saw you running was the first time?"

I nod.

"You should have told me you're a beginner. I would have taken it easy on you."

"Maybe I don't want you to take it easy on me."

He lets out a raucous laugh. I feel redness creeping into my cheeks, and I'm starting to get pissed. What the hell? I mean, it wasn't that funny. Cade is still laughing when I think I've had enough. I start walking back toward my house.

Cade runs up beside me and says, "I'm sorry. I didn't mean to laugh at you."

"You sure about that? Seemed like you got a big ol' belly laugh off me there."

"No, seriously. I'm sorry. It's just when you said that, my mind went to, well, a dirty place. Sometimes I can't help it. My mind lives in the gutter."

I stop and turn to stare at him. "Are you kidding? You heard innuendo in that?"

He looks incredulous. "You didn't?"

I consider his position and think back through what I said. Someone of the gutter-minded persuasion could take it that way. I shrug. "I see your point."

He laughs again. "Shall we?"

We walk back to my house at a leisurely pace. We talk about nothing—honeysuckle, stray dogs that follow us, my sudden interest in running.

Back home, I go inside to get us more waters, and we sit on the porch to talk for a while. I mostly listen to Cade talk about his grandparents and how much they mean to him. I really don't want to volunteer any more information than I already have. Seems a little scary to share anything more with someone I've only met twice. He might see through me and think I'm a total weirdo. What if he judges me by Ryan's death or affair? I realize I'm not really listening but staring at Cade while I run through my own thoughts. I become aware when he reaches out and grabs my hand.

"You okay over there?" he asks.

"Oh, my God. I'm sorry. I don't have as much focus as I once did. I get lost in my own thoughts. I didn't mean to check out on you."

"Maybe one day you'll include me in those thoughts." He smiles.

"No, really, my head is a dangerous place sometimes." I laugh, humorlessly.

"Well, seems like you've been through a lot. If you want to let some of those thoughts out, I'd listen. Before I go, I wanted to ask if we can do this again sometime."

"What, running? Sure. Shouldn't we take a day off in between? I mean isn't a break recommended?"

"Okay, day off tomorrow, and we'll run the day after. I'll meet you after work again."

"Sounds good. Why don't you call me if anything changes?" I offer.

"That means, Rhae Peters, that I need your phone number. You okay giving me your digits?" I feel my face heat as he unleashes that devilish grin on me.

"I can only give them to you if you promise to use them responsibly."

He nods and makes a cross over his heart. "Define responsible."

I laugh and give him my cell number.

8
Friends

Besides Cade, the only thing happening in my life is work. Bernice is on a new warpath with me. I have no idea what set her off, but she is definitely looking for any reason to get me. Good thing I'm a rule follower and that makes it hard for her. Bill is extra grumpy. Alana is hovering, waiting on our chance to debrief the run with Cade. We haven't had a chance because I've been in meetings all day. The more I think about the dishing that needs to happen with the girls, the guiltier I feel for not calling and letting Jess in on the goodies.

I'm settling into my e-mail and calendar checking routine, and drinking a cup of coffee, when my cell phone vibrates on my desk. *What the hell is this?* I think to myself as a number I don't recognize lights it up. I refuse to answer because, let's face it, I don't answer for unknown numbers. Plus, if it's anything worth my time, they'll leave a message. As I'm logging into the site maintenance system, the phone chirps to indicate voicemail has been left.

I sigh and pick it up to listen. Shit! It was Cade. Why would he call this early? I get up from my desk and run down the hall to a conference room. It's dark, so no one is planning to use it. I flick on the lights, grab a chair, and call him back.

"Hello?" he answers.

"Hi. Was someone trying to reach Rhae Peters?"

"Yes. Yes, I was. This is Cade, the running buddy down the street."

"Oh, I thought that was you. What can I do for you, running buddy?"

"Well, I have to be in Memphis today to run an errand for my grandmother. I was thinking you might want to have lunch. Is that a possibility?"

My face-splitting grin is making my cheeks hurt. "Well, I am a very busy woman. Let me check my calendar."

"Oh, come on, Rhae. We both know you checked your calendar three times since you sat down at your desk. You know your availability."

"Have not," I say, indignant. "You don't know me like that."

He chuckles. "Really? You seem like the overly prepared type. That's all."

I sigh, "Okay. You're right. We'll discuss your stalker tendencies and assumptions over lunch."

"Great. Where can I meet you?"

I give him directions to the deli we frequent. I know an outside table will be secure, as well as right up his alley. Who cares if I ate there yesterday? It happens.

I sit for a few minutes after we say goodbye. Just sitting, staring at the wall, trying to process what I agreed to. My hands are shaking at the thought of spending more time with Cade. What will people say about me having lunch with him? I need to talk to Alana. I stand to leave the conference room, and I'm met face-to-face with none other than the Dragon Lady.

"Excuse me." I force a smile and try to slide by her.

She blocks my escape. "I had this room booked for a conference call, but when I got here you were squatting to have a personal phone conversation."

"I'm really sorry. I didn't realize it was booked. I hope I didn't cause you to miss your conference call."

"You didn't. You really should be more considerate. It's unprofessional to squat in a room you didn't book."

"I'm sorry. It was a personal call, and I didn't want to talk in the open at my desk."

"Business with Ryan's death?" she asks.

"No. Frankly, it was personal, and you need to back off." Nosey bitch.

"Oh, don't try to be coy. I heard it. You were making a lunch date with someone. Don't get caught running around with a new man so fast. You'll regret the reputation you're building for yourself."

"I appreciate your concern, but this is really not your business. I'm sorry I took your conference room. Now, if you'll excuse me, I'm going back to my desk." I step around her and leave the room.

When I get to my desk, I slam my phone down and let out a pent-up growl. What is wrong with that woman? Why does she think she has a right to talk to me that way? I start working on answering e-mails. I'm typing furiously and smashing the keys when I feel a warm hand on my arm. I look up into Alana's eyes.

"Hey, I'm walking to the cafe for some stout coffee. Wanna come?"

I think about it for a minute. "Sure, I could use the walk and air." I look over to my manager's cubicle, "Dee, want coffee? Alana and I are going to the cafe."

"Oh no, dear, thanks for asking. Be safe," she answers.

Alana and I are silent as we get on the elevators. As soon as we step into the building lobby she looks at me. "What happened?"

I shake my head. "What do you mean? Nothing happened."

"Bullshit. You were tearing that keyboard apart. You're pissed."

"Dragon Lady is giving me shit because I have a lunch date today."

"What? Really? How did she know? Never mind Dragon Lady, fill me in on this lunch date."

"That would require me to fill you in on my run date last night."

She jumps up and down clapping. "Yes! Tell me!"

I grin. "It was amazing! I didn't die. I didn't quit. I didn't keep up either. But, hey, I hung in there."

"Great, kiddo. But that is not the kind of update I was hoping for. Did you shove your tongue down his throat and jump his sweaty bones after?"

I laugh so hard I snort. "Uh no. We ran. He walked me home. After sitting on the porch a while, he left. No fireworks. I did take a chance by giving him my number, though."

"I was hoping for wedding bells or something. But, giving him your number is a start."

I stare at her open-mouthed. "There is something desperately wrong with you. You know that?"

Alana shrugs. "I know."

"He called this morning. I went to the conference room to call him back."

"That's a good sign. He must be interested in a little down and dirty with Rhae."

"Jesus! I don't know about that. What I can say is that he wanted to meet me for lunch today, and I agreed. Want to tag along?"

"No. I'll let you work out your virginal dating approach on your own."

"Thanks."

The barista overhears our conversation and is laughing to herself when we order. I shrug. There's enough self-esteem challenges in my life, I can't care about one more. We discuss the new art hanging in the café while we wait for our drinks.

On the walk back, Alana says, "Now, tell me how Bernice found out about your lunch date."

I shrug. "She had that particular room booked and stood behind me listening while I was on the phone, then yelled at me for taking her room."

"Bitch."

"I know. So that's when you caught me killing my keyboard."

"Right. Ignore her."

"I'm trying, but she is like the voice of my conscience. She keeps bringing up how Ryan is barely dead and that it's inappropriate for me to move on."

"You aren't the one who had an affair and impregnated your mistress and died."

"I know. Still, something about moving on feels wrong. No matter how badly I want to stand on my own and figure out life, it feels like I'm doing something wrong to Ryan."

"It's all in your head. Only you can figure it out or let it go."

Alana hugs me as tight as her little frame can, then sends me back to my desk much refreshed, and in time to make a meeting with a new client.

The rest of the morning passes without incident. Everything goes according to routine and as scheduled. When it comes time for lunch, I'm more than ready for my date with Cade. The idea of seeing him sends me into a tail-spin. I'm excited and nervous at the same time. I bolt out of the elevators and through the front door, a woman on a mission.

I try to walk casually, but as soon as I turn the corner, there he is. He's cool, sitting back with his legs stretched out, ankles crossed in front of him. He's wearing faded blue jeans, a gray T-shirt, work boots, and a ball cap. Between the ball cap being pulled down low and the dark sunglasses, I can't be sure he isn't taking a nap. Just as I'm thinking he might be sleeping behind those glasses, he reaches for his cup and takes a sip. Turning his head in my direction, he smiles and sets his cup down. He stands and takes a few steps in my direction. "Hi," he says simply.

"Hi," I return the greeting, suddenly feeling shy and out of place.

Cade reaches for my hand and leads me to the table. He pulls out my chair and gestures for me to sit. "A nice outside spot with good shade, or we can move inside if that would be better?"

I can't help but smile. "No, outside is perfect."

"What would you like to eat? I'll go in and order for us."

"No, you are not buying my lunch." I shake my head and move to stand.

Cade puts his hand on my shoulder and leans in close. "Friends can buy each other lunch." He smiles, and I am dumbfounded.

"Sure. Okay. I'll have the fried chicken salad. Honey mustard on the side."

"Salad? You're a salad girl. I don't know about this friendship." He makes a face like someone farted.

"Wait until you see that salad. Run along, now, errand boy." I wave him off dismissively. The sarcasm making me feel instantly more comfortable and confident.

He laughs and takes off inside. I feel a beaming smile spread across my face. *What is happening?*

A few minutes later a cup and straw appear on the table before me. "I got you tea. The girl at the counter said she knew you, and that you like unsweet. That right?" I have to branch out. When the people working in a restaurant know your order, it's time to try something new. *File that away for later.*

"Perfect. Thank you."

He takes his seat across from me. "They said they'll bring the food out to us. So, how's your work day going?"

"It's the same every day. Dragon Lady harassing me, Bill running her off and making me laugh. Praying no one asks, 'how are you?' It isn't so bad. I've only been back to work for a few days now. I guess they need time to process my grief since I did all my processing away from there." I open my straw and take a drink of tea. I realize that was a small rant. "I'm sorry. I shouldn't go on and on about stuff like that. How's your day been?"

"Wait and see. That's it. All I do is run errands for the hospice nurse and my grandmother. They stay and watch over my grandfather." He shrugs and turns that smile on me.

"You need to stop doing that."

"Doing what?" His eyebrows draw inward, and he cocks his head to the side. He seems confused.

"Smiling at me like that." I raise my eyebrow.

He laughs again, a little harder. "I'm sorry. Who is the Dragon Lady? She sounds fun."

I grin and fill him on the people in my office: the judgy admin, Dragon Lady, Ms. Jimmie, Bill and Ginger. By the time I finish telling him all about Ginger, he's laughing almost as hard as I was the other day. Finally, a deli server comes out with our food. The tray looks like it's about to give out. He sets down my salad and two small cups of honey mustard. Next is Cade's lunch, if you can call it that. The man must have a hollow leg. He has a large sub sandwich, chips, cup of potato salad, and a cookie.

I don't mean to, but I can't help it—I gawk. "Holy Lord! Where are you going to put all of that?"

"Just watch, baby." As soon as the endearment leaves his lips, he freezes and looks at me. Slowly removing his sunglasses, he reaches out to my hand. "I'm sorry. I didn't mean..." he trails off. "It slipped out."

"It's okay." I cut him off. I dig deep for a genuine smile. The familiar term feels alien coming from him. I try to shake off the uneasiness it causes. "Go ahead. Show me how you handle all that food."

I carefully prepare my salad by cutting through the lettuce to make it bite size and apply the right amount of honey mustard. Cade, on the other hand, digs in enthusiastically. The boy can eat! I'm getting full watching him. In between bites, we talk about our lives. I tell him about the girls and Jillian. He tells me about his parents and grandparents. Inevitably, we get back around to Ryan's death. Cade seems cautious with his questions. It makes me feel bad; I'm not that fragile. So, I take a deep breath and tell him about the accident. When I finish and look up, Cade is staring at me.

"What?"

"I know you said you hate this, but I'm going to say it anyway. I'm sorry." He reaches across the table and takes my hand.

It's unexpected and sort of nice, but I don't hate it coming from him. It's one of the most genuine sentiments I've heard yet. I smile for him—a real smile. "Thank you."

"So, that's the story?"

"Not all of it." I look down, still deciding if I want to tell this part to anyone else.

"What? I mean he's gone. You had the funeral. You are back at work, making new friends." He smiles and winks at me. "What's next?"

I take a deep breath and set my fork down. Taking a drink of my tea to clear my throat, I tell him about Melody. The shock washing over his face is not something I expected.

His shock starts to become anger. "Son of a bitch. I'm sorry. I don't mean to cuss a man I don't know, but how could someone do something like that? Are you okay? Have you talked to her anymore?"

"I don't want to talk to her. I'm as okay as I can be. Maybe better than most would expect." I grin and wink at him. "Can I be honest with you?"

"Of course. We're friends, right?" He's moved onto his cookie, while I can't eat at all.

"First off, wow. You ate everything. Good boy. I wasn't sure you could pull that off. Definitely a hollow leg. Secondly, I don't know what I want my life to be now. I haven't been on my own, ever. I met Ryan when I was seventeen, and we got married when I was twenty. What am I supposed to do? Stay in a house that makes me feel heavy with memories of him I don't want to have anymore?" I shrug and drink more tea before pushing the remainder of my uneaten salad away from me.

I sigh and continue, "This affair makes me think our whole relationship was a sham. I haven't even called my former mother-in-law since the funeral. I'm dealing without really dealing with things. I have no idea what's next. Nothing about my life from before the accident makes me happy. I'm uncomfortable everywhere. Something has to change—that much I know for sure." I stop to breathe, and he's squeezing my hand.

Cade slides his chair closer to mine. He grabs both of my hands and holds them in the space between our knees. He looks into my eyes, and answers my rant, "You can be whoever you want to be. You can go wherever you want to go. You can change whatever it is you want to change. You are not required to deal with anything until you decide you are ready. I think you are more vulnerable than you want to let on. Breathe, Rhae. That's all you have to do." I nod, and the tears welling up in my eyes spill down my cheeks.

"Will you call me when you get home from work?" he asks softly as he uses his thumbs to wipe my tears.

"Yes. But I need your number."

"You have it. Remember, I called you earlier?"

"Duh. Sorry. Sloppy mess over here."

We laugh together, then are smiling and standing as he reaches for me and says, "Come on. Let's take long way to clear your head before you have to be back."

Cade continues to hold my hand as we walk down Main Street. The light around us alternates between sun and shadow because of the tall buildings. I point out some of the other lunch places, and the art gallery. We don't talk about anything particularly important. Just touristy discussion about the buildings we're passing. It doesn't take long to get back around to my building. He seems to contemplate something, and then slowly reaches out and wraps me up in a big hug.

"You are going to okay," he says close to my ear. I shiver. His voice is…is…yummy.

"I am. Definitely. Call you tonight." I pull back and wave as I go into the building.

I float back to my desk. I can't stop thinking about Cade. "I'm back," I call across the cubicle walls to Bill, as per our routine.

"Good to know," he grumps.

"Okay, what's wrong?" I step over to his cube and peer over his wall.

"Dragon Lady saw you out with your new friend. She's been over here four times waiting on you to get back. She keeps talking to me."

"Sorry, Bill. I'll …"

"I knew it!" Uh oh, I'd know that cracked, whiney voice anywhere.

Dragon Lady is standing outside our quad. Oh, and she is fiery. I have to handle this delicately. "I saw you with that man. You do have someone already."

"I don't, Bernice. He's a friend that's in town visiting his grandparents who live down the street from me," I defended. "I knew you would think that. It's why I said it was none of your business."

"God knows the truth, Rhae." She crosses her arms and storms away. Nice, now I'll be the subject of her lunch gossip with judgy admin. Whatever. I am beyond giving a shit about that anymore.

I look at Bill. He shrugs. He doesn't know what to say either. I shrug right back and return to my seat. For a minute, I think about what Bill said earlier. "…Living right…pissing Bernice off…" I smile. Things are right, then.

I do my best to stay busy, but I keep replaying lunch over and over again in my mind. His smile causes my heart to skip beats. Does he get the same feeling from me? I hate this. It is so hard to tell. What if all I feel for him is a school girl crush on a guy who's way out of my league? I haven't dated anyone since I was seventeen. Am I looking for someone to date? Am I just lonely?

The more I think about it, the less I can sit still at my desk. This is ridiculous. I'm not getting any work done. I'm wasting time being here. I head over to my manager's desk. "Hey, Dee, do you mind if I jet out? I'm not feeling right." It's not a lie; although, it could be interpreted differently.

Dee lets me leave without question, and I bolt out of the building with a renewed energy. When I get home, I slam the front door and lock it. I proceed to blast the stereo as loud as possible and pour myself a drink. A couple drinks later, I am dancing in the living room and the sun is setting. A nice shadow is cast across the living room. I spin circles like I used to do when I was a little kid. Spinning and spinning until I feel sick and my fingers are numb.

I fall to the floor and stare at the ceiling while the room spins around me. Around the time I feel brave enough to stand up again, there's a knock on the door. I jump up, probably too quickly and stumble over furniture as I make my way to the door. I rip the door open to find Cade standing on my porch.

"Hello, handsome," I slur in greeting. I lean against the door to keep from falling over.

"Hi. How's it going?"

"Great. I thought I was supposed to call you when I got home. What are you doing here?"

"I got impatient. I thought maybe I could pre-empt the call. I'll go." He turns to leave, and I nearly panic.

"Okay, want to come in?" I nearly fall over.

Cade reaches out to steady me. "Sure, let me help you." I throw my arm over his shoulders. He leads me to the couch and sits me down. "You are drunker than Cooter Brown," he observes.

"No. It's the spinning."

"Spinning?"

"Spinning. You know, hold your arms out and spin as fast as you can, then fall down and watch the room spin. Only, I drank a little before I started doing that, and then, *bam*...you're here."

He laughs. "Ah, okay. How was the rest of your day?"

"Well, Dragon Lady totally accosted me and accused me of having you as a side project before Ryan's death. She has some serious issues. I didn't have the courage to tell her that it was ironic of her to accuse me. Considering."

Cade nods. "Right. What a bitch. I'm sorry. It was because of me, huh? What does she do, stalk you at lunch too?"

"I guess so. I don't really care. I'm not sure I want to stay at this job anymore. I honestly don't know if I want to keep living in this house or even this town."

A look of surprise crosses his face. "Where would you go?"

"I haven't given it much thought beyond just leaving. I have some options. My dad is farther south of here, still in Mississippi. My cousin is in Texas. I think she would let me come stay a while. And we have family in Florida, too."

"Will you stay in touch with me if you decide to take off?"

I nod, but don't answer out loud. I hadn't thought about vocalizing my thoughts on leaving before I did it. Now, I hope I haven't said something wrong. It's true, though. I've been doing nothing but thinking about what to do with my life. Do I really want to stay in a place where I can't even sleep? Every time I get in the bed all I do is think of Ryan. When I walk through my kitchen, all I can think about is Melody's revelations. My job doesn't need me anymore, so there's no hope of finding purpose there. Am I ready to talk about any of that with Cade? My foggy head starts to clear.

"Listen, I need to change. I don't want to sit around in my work clothes. Is that okay?"

He nods. "Of course. I'll sit right here."

I smile and squeeze his hand before I head to my room. Once inside, I strip down and stare at myself in the bathroom mirror. Matching bra and panty sets always make me feel beautiful and like I have my shit together. Always. Even if I really don't. Which, I don't. A couple of twists and turns help me see how good I look in them. Still too much middle, but I do look pretty damn good. Quietly laughing, I rummage through my drawers and put on a pair of pajama pants and a tank. I knot my hair up on top of my head like some kind of Dr. Seuss character and do a quick wash of my face. I head back into the living room when I'm sure I can handle hanging out with Cade.

"Better?" I ask as I pose against the door jamb with my arm stretched high. I hope it looks more like a model move, and not like an awkward ox.

Cade laughs. "Perfect. Now I feel overdressed."

"That's okay; you're hot no matter what you wear." *What did I just say?*

He smiles sweetly and pats the couch seat beside him. An invitation I try to accept without giving away too much of my excitement. We begin talking about nothing and everything all at once. It's like we're connected. If I readjust my position, he does so in a way that allows him to stay within arm's reach of me. We sit in various configurations on the couch and recliner for hours. I find a level of comfort I haven't had for a long time. Talking about the hell in my world doesn't hurt when I'm talking to him. Without warning, Cade's body lets out a grumpy whine.

I jump. "Oh, my God! What was that?"

His cheeks pink a little. "Dude, I'm so freaking hungry right now."

I laugh. "Well then, we must feed you. Do you want me to cook?"

"Wait a minute, you cook?"

I feign offense. "Of course I cook! Let's go see what I have in the kitchen."

We rummage around in my pantry and refrigerator, but the options are slim. He's about to suggest we order out when I stumble across the makings for poppy seed chicken casserole. I hold up a can of chunk white chicken meat. "Got it!"

He scrunches his face and says, "No offense, but canned chicken meat doesn't sound very appealing."

"I'm not offended. You just don't know about the best Sunday School potluck casserole ever." I shrug nonchalantly.

"Best? Casserole? Ever?" He still seems suspicious.

I nod. "Here, take this." Cade holds out his arms and takes the two cans of chicken, and one can of cream of chicken soup. I hustle over to the spice cabinet and locate the poppy seeds, and then dive into the freezer for my bag of frozen peas and carrots. Next, I check the fridge, and sure enough, I barely have enough sour cream. Cade looks a little worried when we get everything lined out on the counter.

"*Oh!* I almost forgot. Go back to the pantry and get the Ritz crackers," I direct while I start opening the chicken. Cade is an obedient helper. He retrieves the crackers and offers to start a pitcher of tea. I'm all too happy to have the help!

Within thirty minutes, I'm taking the casserole out of the oven. The toasty brown cracker crust on top is making my mouth water. Cade looks a bit more interested now. I serve up a healthy portion of casserole for each of us while Cade pours tea. We cop a squat in my living room floor, and I watch as he takes his first bites. The look that crosses his face, changing from fear to complete decadence, makes my day.

"Good, right?"

He's shoveling in another bite, and talking with his mouth full, "Oh, my gah, I can't. What is this gloriousness?"

"See, I told you—best casserole ever."

"Can I have some more? All of it? I need this."

I laugh and take it easy while he gobbles down one plate and goes back for a refill.

Sometime later, sitting on the floor. Cade has his back to the couch with his legs stretched out in front of him. He's moaning as if he's stuffed himself way too much. Without thinking, I lay my head in his lap and look up at him as we talk. I can't help myself. It's late and I'm exhausted. Every now and then, he reaches out and strokes my hair back from my forehead, and it feels natural. Maybe I'm feeling guilty or hopeful about him touching me, but it seems his hand lingers a little longer each time he does it.

I'm not really paying attention too much until he gently tugs the tie out of my hair and fans it out over his lap and onto the floor. This time I'm sure he lingers as he runs his hands through my curls. I close my eyes and listen to him tell me about growing up and visiting here when he was a kid. Cade's voice is like a soothing lullaby. I'm calmed hearing the resonance of his voice in his chest.

I drift off as I listen. I wake when Cade rubs my cheek and asks, "Rhae? You asleep?"

I yawn. "Yeah, I think you petting my hair and talking put me out. It's nice. I haven't been sleeping much lately."

His eyes are soft, and his small smile is apologetic when he says, "Why don't you go ahead and get to bed? I'll see you tomorrow."

"What if I said I don't want you to leave?"

He's stunned into silence. I'm about to play it off and make a sarcastic remark when he says, "If you think the Dragon Lady had a problem with lunch, what would she do with the shameful rumor that I stayed overnight?" He chuckles.

"I don't give a shit. It's not like I offered to sleep with you. I'm just asking you to stay so maybe I can sleep through the night. You make me comfortable." I stretch as I sit up off his lap. Chancing a look at his face, I peek over my shoulder. Conflict. All I see on his face is conflict. "Never mind. I need to get to bed. Maybe you should go." I stand and walk to the front door. When my hand reaches the knob, I sense him behind me. He places a hand on my waist and pulls me back to him. I stand stock still and wait.

"Don't. I'll stay," he whispers.

"You will? Don't do anything you don't want to." I close my eyes. He can't see them anyway.

I feel his breath on my ear when he says, "I want to. I needed a minute to think. To decide."

"Decide what?"

"If I can stay with you…as you sleep. As a friend."

"Oh." Truly my finest moment. "What did you decide?" I'm bracing myself for his answer. I mean, the *friend* thing is hanging in the air, now.

"Let me call my grandma to let her know where I am in case she needs anything. I'll stay until I'm sure you're good and asleep. I won't stay the whole night. Deal?"

I think over it for a moment. "Deal." Getting some sleep is going to be amazing. My heart starts racing as I pull myself out of his arms and make my way to the bedroom. I sit and wait for Cade to come back. When he does, he seems as nervous as I feel. He does his best to put me at ease. Smiling, he comes and sits on the bed. He slips his boots off and scoots back against the headboard. I turn on the TV and move over to him, mimicking the position we had been in on the floor of the living room. My head across his lap.

I take a deep breath. "Something tells me I should feel guilty about this, but it feels too comfortable to think bad about it. Thanks for staying. I can't wait to get a good night's sleep."

He starts stroking my hair again. "I think I would do anything for you. We are friends, right?"

Nodding, I can't help the hurt that consumes me. I guess that is all I am after all. I mean, a minute ago he was standing with his arms around me, whispering in my ear. He seemed like there was something between us. I guess my ability to read guys is really further from accurate than I first thought. I don't know why part of me wanted there to be more right now. Maybe I'm as screwed up as Melody. The standard pitfall of taking kindness from a guy as anything other than what it is–kindness.

Maybe I feel this way because I'm so lonely without Ryan. I close my eyes and try to imagine that Ryan is stroking my hair and flipping through the channels on the TV. I can't see his face clearly anymore. It's like a faded image, but I can feel the warmth I would have had if it were his hands on me. I snuggle a little closer, turning my head into Cade's tummy. He smells so good. His smell is different than Ryan's, but still intoxicating. I pull my knees up to my stomach and wrap my hand in his T-shirt. Cade starts talking to me at some point, but I don't know what he's saying because I fall asleep so fast.

The next morning, I wake in a room full of sunshine. It sure is bright for six-thirty a.m. My mind registers that the sun is wrong for this time of day. *Oh shit!* I sit bolt right up in bed. I grab for my phone on the nightstand, and stare down at the time. *Damn it!* It's after ten a.m.! I look around the room, and Cade is gone. *Of course he is.* He said he would only stay until I was asleep.

Dee is going to roast me. I left early yesterday, and so far, I'm a no show today. This is going to be bad.

I rush through the shower and dress in the first thing I grab out of the closet. A red sleeveless dress. I slip on sandals and run out the door. Hopping in the car, I try to find the balance between driving safely and hurrying at the same time. I all but run through security and make it to my desk, where I'm met with Dee and the Dragon Lady. Lovely. I slow my approach and wait for "the talk." Dee isn't as upset as I thought she should be. Dragon Lady, on the other hand, she wants blood.

"Good of you to join us, Rhae." She glares at me.

"Rhae, did you have an appointment or something this morning? It's not like you to run this late." Dee asks, concerned.

"I would like to discuss this in private, if you don't mind," I state, returning Dragon Lady's glare.

Dee nods. "Bernice, if you'll excuse us. Rhae, let's get a room."

I follow Dee down the hall, purse in one hand, and car keys in the other. She picks a room close to our work area and closes the door behind us. She looks at me compassionately, but her words still feel harsh. "Rhae, you know this is unacceptable. What is going on?"

"I know. I've only been back at work a few days. Listen, I haven't been sleeping at night. Last night I finally got to catch up a little, and I slept through my alarm. I'm so sorry. It won't happen again."

"Well, you know Bernice notices everything. I'm not who you have to worry about right now. She is complaining on both of us. She thinks I'm allowing your behavior. I may not have a choice but to take action."

"I understand. But it's happened once. One time. It shouldn't be that big of a deal."

"I just wanted you to know this could turn out bad for you."

I try to muster up a smile. "I understand. Thank you. I really am sorry." This isn't Dee's fault. Bernice has been out to get either one of us for a long time. It's like she's gunning for one of our jobs. I really have liked working for Dee. She's been so kind to me, and I hate that I screwed up today.

I start working through client e-mails and am able to schedule meetings with prospective clients that are being assigned to me. I grab coffee and check the time on my phone, only to see that I have a text from Cade.

"Good morning. Sleep well?"

I can't help the smile the spreads across my face, and reply, *"I did. Thanks for staying. Still on for our run tonight?"*

"Yes! Looking forward to it."

What could he possibly be looking forward to? I am in trouble.

A Place to Stand

9
Dreams

Ryan and I are sitting at the kitchen table. It is early enough for us to have breakfast in front of us, but late enough that the sun is bursting through the front windows. So much light. I imagine that this is what the light in heaven might look. I stare into his eyes and feel a mixture of love and hate. It swirls in my head and through my body. I don't want to upset him, and I'm just about to ask the questions that are hanging in the back of my mind, when he starts to speak.

"I'm sorry, Rhae. I'm so fucking sorry. I don't know why I did it."

My heart contracts around his words. "Why you did what?"

"The affair with Melody. I don't know why I did that. I love you so much. You are my everything. My world. I don't know how to live without you."

"Well, I hate to break it to you, big boy, but you aren't living. You died. You left me here in this mess. Dealing without you." My feelings turn to anger.

"I know. I'm sorry about that, too. I didn't know that would happen." He turns uncomfortably in his chair. After a few moments of staring out the window, he says, "We should have talked. I should have cleared the air with you before that happened. I didn't know how to talk to you about Melody." He looks at me earnestly, "I fucked up. There's no other way to put it."

Irritated, I stand and take a few steps away from the table before turning on him. "Yes, you did. I need to quit thinking about you. I want to forgive you, so I can live with it. I don't know what I'm supposed to do about your mistress and baby. I feel guilty for being mean to her, but I really have no idea. What do you want me to do?"

"Be her friend. The affair was my fault. Don't hate her."

I gape. "You're kidding me, right? It takes two, Ryan. I mean you didn't make a baby for her all by yourself. She had to participate. She knew you were married. That might actually make her more culpable!" I'm yelling by the time I finish my rant.

"You're bigger than this. You know you don't have to act like a child. Be angry with me but be kind to her. Please. That's all I ask."

"You…" I point at him. "…don't get to ask me for anything. I'm angry at you. No permission necessary. I'm angry that you died. I'm angry about Melody. I'm angry that I hate my job and this house now. I'm going to do something about it though. I don't know what that will be yet, but I'm doing something."

Looking away from me, he nods. "I understand."

I feel hot tears on my face. "I love you, you know it?"

He nods and looks up to meet my gaze. "I know. I love you, too. We had it all, didn't we, baby?"

"We did, until you did a fucktard thing like dying."

He laughs. Oh, I have missed that sound. I smile. We stare at each other for a long time. Finally, he speaks, "Move on, and be happy. Find someone to love you the way I should've loved you."

"I will. I have no choice. You're dead."

I sit up in bed and wipe the tears from my face. My pillow is soaked, and my phone is buzzing. I take a second to compose myself before reaching for it. Cade is calling.

"Hello?"

"Hey there. I was thinking we could hang out today."

The statement takes me back a bit. We have spent the last few weeks either texting or running after work. He's been spending some nights with me to help me sleep, but he always leaves after I'm asleep. I'm feeling better than I've felt since Ryan died. I think about what Ryan said to me in the dream: *"Move on."* Besides, we're just friends. It's Sunday, maybe I could invite Cade over for dinner and call the girls up too.

"Uh, sure. How about dinner tonight? I'm going to invite my sister and a few friends over, too."

"Oh, okay," he says as if I've disappointed him. "Well, we can do that. Would you want to do something else with me today before that?"

That idea spins me for a loop, "Okay, what did you have in mind?"

"It's a surprise. Dress comfortably. I'll pick you up in an hour."

"What time is..." Before I can ask, he hangs up. I huff, a bit frustrated. I hate when people hang up like that. I glance over at the clock and see it is nine-twenty a.m. What is wrong with that boy? I huff again and throw myself into the shower.

That dream about Ryan has me sluggish. My mind won't focus. I'm standing in the shower with the water running over me, but not actually washing yet. My mind has that dream on replay. Over and over again. I study his eyes and his smile. I think about the curiously bright light surrounding him. He wants me to be friends with Melody. Can I even do that? Even if I could, why would I want to?

I turn off the water and get dressed. I decide on sneakers. When in doubt, go with sturdy footwear. Leaving my hair down to dry, I slip a rubber band over my wrist to catch this mess of hair later on. I make my way into the living room, planning to sit and wait for Cade, when the doorbell rings. Right on time. I open the door and my breath catches. I should be used to him by now, but I'm not. Those brown eyes and dark hair always scream trouble, and my body is willing to get into some of that today.

"Hey," I say.

"Hey, you ready?" he asks, excited.

"I don't know. Your enthusiasm scares me. What are we doing?"

"I told you, it's a surprise." His smile broadens as he holds his arm out for me to take.

I reluctantly reach out and take it as he leads me through the door. He gives me just enough time to lock the door before pulling me down the porch steps.

"Woah, someone's a little amped up. Either this is terribly dangerous, or you're afraid I won't like it."

"Neither." He gives me that devilish smile.

"I thought I told you to stop doing that to me."

"I can't." He pauses and keeps pulling me to the truck.

What is up with him? I resign myself to stop asking questions, and vow to not freak out over anything he surprises me with. I climb into his truck while he holds the door and closes it behind me. I buckle in. Cade is in the driver's side and taking off before I know it.

We head down so many winding country roads, that even as a life-long resident of the area, I'm lost. Still, I enjoy the sunshine and wind blowing through the windows. I take in all the smells of freshly harvested fields, cut grass and sunshine. I swear sunshine has a smell, too. The sun is warming my face, and I can feel sweat gathering in the middle of my back. I start to feel self-conscious right about the time Cade to stops the truck. I open my eyes slowly and take in the large shade tree we parked beside.

We are in the middle of a field. Only the shade tree and us. Cade is staring at me. "Do you like it?"

"Like what? It's a shade tree in an empty field." I smirk.

"Exactly. Do you like it?"

I nod and smile. Cade bounces out of the truck and gathers some things from the back before coming around to open my door. He takes my hand as I hop down.

"Nice dismount," he says, jokingly. "This way," he takes my hand and leads me to the far side of the tree.

"How old do you think that tree is? A hundred years?"

"Two hundred."

"No. You pulled that out of your ass."

"No, really. This is land my family owns. The story is that one of my great grandfathers planted this tree for his wife. They have always farmed around the tree."

"Two hundred years, that's more than a great grandfather, but I don't feel like trying to figure out how many. That's really sweet. I love little gestures like that."

"Little gesture? A two-hundred-year-old tree is a commitment. Not a gesture."

"Sorry. Why are we here?" I ask.

"We are here for a picnic." He smiles and shakes a basket at me.

"A little early to eat, isn't it?"

"A picnic is not just about food. But if you're hungry, I packed a few things."

I grin like a goofy school girl as I watch Cade set about spreading a quilt and sliding off his boots. He stuffs his socks inside to keep them safe, then motions for me to join him. I start to, and then I'm met with the memory of Ryan's face in my dreams and I freeze. He wants me to move on. I want to move on. I need to stand on my own. I'm not sure what Cade and I are exactly.

"What are we doing?" I ask.

He stops. "What do you mean? I already told you—it's a picnic. A pic-a-nic, Yogi."

I can tell he's trying to make light of the concern on my face. "No. What are we doing? Are we friends? More than friends? I keep trying to think through what we are, and I can't put a name on it."

His smile fades, and he loses some of the enthusiasm he's had this morning. "What do you want us to be, Rhae?"

Shaking my head, I shrug, "Me? I don't know. I know you can't want to be anything more than friends. But then you do something like staying with me at night, at least until I fall asleep, and then sometimes you do things like plan a surprise pic-a-nic. I don't know what we are doing."

He stands, and steps toward me. "I don't want to pressure you. I just want to spend more time with you and figure out what we're doing, too. I can't get through the day without thinking about you. Sometimes I manage to text you, but all I really want to do is be at your door the minute you get home from work. And what do you mean, you know I can't want anything more than to be your friend?"

I swallow. Oh, he heard that part of my ramble… "I mean, why would you want to be with me? I'm an overweight widow. You may not have noticed, but I'm pretty broken. Why would you want to get involved with me?"

Cade takes my face in his hands and studies my eyes. "Are you crazy? You're amazing. You keep waking up every morning, dealing with the shit storm of a mess your husband left you. I can see how broken you are. But you go to that job you hate and take care of the house you hate. You don't have to know what you're doing or where you're going to keep moving, and you keep moving. As far as being an overweight widow, *who cares?* I see you. The real you. The heart of you. Why do you think I'm so tangled up inside? I want us to be something, but I'm afraid of how broken you are. I don't want to push you too hard too fast. Maybe wanting to be with you is selfish."

I'm crying as I start to see myself through his eyes. It takes me a few minutes to settle my breathing. He wipes the tears from my eyes.

Carefully, he brings his face closer and rests his forehead on mine and says, "Let's just take it one day at a time."

I nod, but I can't speak. He tilts my chin up until I'm forced to look into his eyes, and that's when he kisses me. At first, he is tender. A small kiss on my mouth with no urgency. It is barely a brush. Feather light and sweet. He pulls back to look into my eyes. They're wide and focused on him, but I'm no longer crying. He pulls me to him again and wraps his arms around me in a bear of a hug. He kisses me again. This time he applies more pressure and holds me there. I can tell he is unwilling to let go, and I love the feeling of being in his arms. Cade makes me feel things I thought died with Ryan.

I pull back to stare at him this time. "We can't do this. I need to stand on my own before we declare we are anything. I don't even know what that means yet."

"I know." He smiles as he wipes the remaining moisture from my cheek with his thumb. "That's why I haven't tried to label us. We spend time together. We are friends. We are friends until you're ready for something more."

I've been misreading his patience. "I don't know how long that will be." The statement comes out as a heavy sigh.

"I'll wait. I'll be right here by your side until you know."

"But you don't live here. You're only here until... What happens when it's time for you to leave?"

"Let me worry about that. You worry about finding your feet."

I smile as he guides me to sit on the blanket. We lie back on the quilt, our hands tangled. I enjoy the warmth of the sun on my face and the warmth of Cade's hand covering mine.

"I had a dream this morning," I blurt out.

He takes a deep breath. "Tell me about it."

"It was about Ryan."

Cade takes a deep breath, and I can tell he's bracing himself by the line his mouth has formed. It hasn't occurred to me that he may not want to hear any more about Ryan until now. I ramble through the details of my dream and focus on his reactions. I tell him how dream Ryan was surrounded by heavenly light, asking for my forgiveness and how he wants me to be friends with Melody.

He waits patiently for me to finish and then asks, "What are you going to do?"

"I don't know. Nothing, I suppose. I don't think I can handle being friends with her. Not even if Ryan was still alive. Plus, I haven't told his mother about the baby yet."

"Was the dream in color or monotone?"

I frown. "Why does that matter?" *Weird question.*

"Don't you know anything about dreams? Color or monotone?" he pushes.

"Full color. High-def color. As real as you and me."

He nods. "It's time for you to meet my grandma."

"Uh okay, when?"

"Now."

Before I can process that thought, Cade is packing up our picnic and pulling his socks and boots on.

"We aren't going to eat first?" I ask.

"Nope. This is important," he answers. "You can eat a sandwich on the drive back."

A chuckle escapes as I hurry and put my sneakers back on before he leaves me behind. We load in the truck, and he drives to his grandma's house. As if she knew to expect us, she is standing on the porch when we arrive.

"Well, I'll be! If she isn't the prettiest thing I've seen in ages.

Glory. The Lord has blessed Cade with a woman."

I laugh pretty hard. "I'm Cade's friend, Rhae. Nice to meet you, ma'am."

"Nonsense. My name is Irma; you call me Irma. How did you snare him?"

"I'm sorry? I didn't snare him."

"You did. You're all he talks about. How did it happen?"

"Grandma," Cade starts, "I told you about Rhae. She was running one night, and I tried to be chivalrous when I saw her stop to catch her breath."

"Well, sweet girl, let me get a look at you." She takes my hands as I step up on the porch. She spreads our arms wide and studies me for a minute. Then she reaches up and grabs my face firmly. Her smile is disconcerting. She stares directly into my eyes as she holds me still. She makes several "mmhmm" or "a-ha" sounds as she does. "Well, dear, what were you running from?"

"Who says it wasn't a who?" I ask her. The conversation is taking some strange twists and turns, but as most elderly southern women have a streak of clairvoyance, I remain patient.

Irma smiles and says, "It was a who and a what. You got trouble girl. I can see it."

"Ma'am? I don't know what you're talking about."

"Yes, you do. Indecision is hanging over your head like an albatross. You better get to decidin' before it lands on you and drags you under. Loneliness and unhappiness are the worst."

She turns to Cade. "You are right to bring her to me. You stay here. Come with me, Rhae." She turns to go inside the house and pulls me behind her.

"Ma'am? Where are we going? Why is Cade supposed to stay outside?" I give him a look that hopefully says *help me*. He gets the message but shakes his head silently.

"We have things to talk about. Cade don't need ta hear." She takes me to the back room of the house, past a closed door I assume contains Cade's grandfather. Irma sits down at a small, round table in the middle of the sitting area.

"Sit," she commands. I do as I'm told even though I can't form a rational thought as to what this is about.

"Tell me your story."

"My story?" I ask.

"Your story, child. Start talking." She raises her eyebrows at me expectantly. "And don't let go of my hands." She reaches across the table and holds my hands, then nods.

At first, I don't know where to start, so I start telling her I have two sisters. My mama has passed, but I still have my dad.

"No. Not a biography. Tell me your story, child."

I nod and consider her request. Then I start talking and it spills from me like pouring water from a jug. I'm crying and sniffling. I'm laughing and smiling. I talk for what seems like forever. I finish with the dream I had of Ryan this morning.

When I finish, Irma is nodding, and her eyes are tearing up. "Your story with Ryan isn't finished yet."

"Yes, it is. He's dead. If that doesn't put finished on the story, I don't know what does."

"No. Who you become now is why the story isn't finished. You have decisions to make. You don't realize it, but they are decisions you are refusing to make. That's why your spirit is uneasy. Ryan's spirit senses this as well. This is why he visited your dream this morning. It will not be the last visit you have in a dream."

"Why can't he just rest and leave the damage he's done behind? Leave me alone?" I ask, feeling fresh panic in my voice.

"He wronged you. He can't rest until he makes it right somehow. There are other spirits that are concerned about your well-being. One in particular has been watching over you for quite some time. She's worried. She paces your dreams and your father's dreams."

Panic runs through my brain as I try to think of a spirit that would worry about my dad and me. "Mama? Why would she worry?"

"I don't know. Maybe she knew what was happening with Ryan."

"What can I do? How do I put them at ease?"

"Honey, they will rest when you have peace. Maybe you need to disappear for a little while. Sort out your own mind before trying to move forward as if nothing happened. Do you have somewhere to go to do some thinking without interference from these spirits?"

Immediately, I think of Clea and Stephen in Florida. I nod.

"Okay, hon, you spend the night with Cade and set him at ease that you'll be back. But our discussion here is between us. You sharing this with him will upset him. He will try to fix it for you. That's just who he is. Understand me?"

"I'm not sure I understand anything you've told me. But my mother always told me there were people who could see through the veil. So, I'm trusting what you tell me because if anyone fit the bill my mother told me about, it's you."

"I'm praying for you, baby. You'll find your way. You'll find how to stand on your own, and when you do, you'll have peace."

Irma grabs me with her tiny frame into a monster of a hug. I feel new tears spring to my eyes as I hug her back. I'm not one for signs of affection with people I don't know, but she feels like family. We emerge from the back room, arm in arm, and find Cade sitting in the living room. He pops up as we enter, and bolts over to us.

"Grandma! What did you say to her? She's been crying!"

"I'm okay." I try to soothe him. "She knew what I needed to know. Thank you for letting me meet your grandmother."

"Cade, you know me better than that," Irma admonishes him. "I would never hurt her. She needed my vision. Now, you two get going. I believe you have dinner with some of Rhae's family tonight."

I turned to her surprised. "How did you know..."

She winks at me. "I know lots of things. Now, go!"

Cade drives me home as I get on the phone to Jess, Red, Liz, Alana, and Marie. Yes, Marie. If part of my Mama's worry is over the fuss with Marie and me, I need to sort it out. I ask all of them to bring something for dinner. Pot-lucking seems easiest tonight. I think about what Irma said, so I text Clea, *"I miss you! Can I come visit?"*

The evening is more fun than I thought it could be. The girls are taken with Cade. None of them can believe the secret I've been keeping from them. Of course, everyone bought my "friends only" explanation, except Liz. She saw right through it.

Liz and I are digging in the pantry for more sugar and tea bags when she proclaims, "You are such a liar! You know you want more from that boy than 'friends!'" She air-quotes the word.

"Do you mind keeping it down? He's in the next room, and it's a small house," I plead with her.

"I'll keep it down if you admit his smile is panty-melting."

"Fine. I admit it. The man is delicious, okay! Happy?" I snap at her.

"Perfectly," she smirks, "Now, what are you doing inviting Marie here since you and she aren't really speaking?"

I sigh. "I have to fix things."

"You do. But I thought you said she would have to apologize first?" she asks.

"You know that is too close to right. Plus, I met a lady who sees things, she said Mama's spirit is hovering because she's worried about something. I think this thing with Marie and I has a lot to do with that."

Liz nods her understanding. "So, you are going to apologize?"

"No. I'm going to tell Marie it's water under the bridge, and no apologies are going to happen between either of us. Forgotten."

"Then what?"

I shrug. "I don't know, but it's a place to start."

Liz and I rejoin the group, and Cade's face flushes red when he sees me. Ugh. I think he heard Liz in the kitchen. I smile and shrug covertly. He raises his glass to me.

Jess runs over to hug me. Poor drunk heifer. I love on her for a second and listen to her ramble about Red and Marie. When she's moved on to the next, "I love you, man," I tap my glass to get everyone's attention.

"Okay, bitches! Listen up!" I wait for everyone to quiet down. "I'm going on vacation. Yes, I know I had all that time off with...Ryan...but I'm going on vacation. I'm taking a leave from work. I may stay a week, I may stay a month. Who's taking care of the house for me?"

It is deadly silent as everyone looks around the room. I notice only one face: Cade's. He looks... angry?

"Anyone? Bueller? Hello?"

Jess raises her hand. "Yeah, honey, I got it. I'll come over and air it out and get your mail once a week. Where are you going?"

I smile. "Daytona Beach. I'm going to spend time with Clea and Stephen."

Cade won't even look at me now.

Slowly, everyone resumes their conversations, of which, I fear, is about me. I decide now is as good a time as any. I pull Marie aside for a discussion. She is satisfied with a forgotten approach to our tiff. It feels good to resolve at least one problem on my list.

Shortly after my vacation announcement, people start leaving. I hug necks and promise to call or text. Finally, Cade and I are left standing in the kitchen alone. I'm afraid to see the hurt or anger in his eyes.

Looking down at my hands. I take a deep breath and break the ice, "I'll be back."

"Yep," he says softly.

I look up, "What? I'm going to see family."

He shakes his head, "No. That's fine. You can do that. We aren't anything anyway. I just found out about this trip along with everyone else in your life. Nothing special."

"Oh, please! Stop being such a girl. What does it matter anyway?"

His frustration is palpable when he snaps, "It matters to me. You matter to me." He takes a deep breath before continuing, "Promise you won't stay gone for months. I don't think I can handle that."

His feelings surprise me. I take a minute before I respond, "I promise. I can call you and text you while I'm there."

"There's that. I still can't believe you just up and decided to leave like that, though."

I shrug, "I have to. I need some space and time."

"Why? Can't you figure out how to get through all of this here? With me?" He looks like he is on the edge.

"No, I can't. I've been trying to do that for months now. It's not getting better."

"Okay." He nods. "I understand. Please call. Every morning.

Every night. All the time. I need to hear your voice." He takes a few steps toward me and opens his arms for me.

I step into them and bury my face in his chest "Promise. Every morning and night. I'll call you. But give me some space to figure things out. Okay?"

"Okay," he answers before lifting my chin to kiss me.

His kiss is intense, and his arms slide around my body, one hand landing on my ass and the other twisting into my hair.

"Have I told you that I love your curls?"

I smile. "No, you haven't, sir."

"I do. I absolutely love how they look in the afternoon before our run. They are always wild and frame your face so that you look untamable. Then you always knot them into a bun on the top of your head, but not before one curl escapes. You always twirl it with your finger before tucking it behind your ear. I can't keep my hands out of them when you fall asleep with your head in my lap."

"Mmmm, that's what makes me fall asleep. You start petting my hair and I'm helpless against the pull for sleep."

"Good to know." He kisses me again and then pulls me toward my bedroom.

I dig my heels in the floor as we approach the doorway. "Cade. We can't." All of the evening's revelations, proclamations and promises have me questioning his motives."

"Trust me." I'm not sure he's saying it as a statement or a question. "Trust me," he says again, when he notices the panic on my face. I realize that the answer is yes, I do trust him.

I nod, and he continues to lead me into the room. He picks up my pajamas, which I haphazardly threw on the bed this morning. "Get dressed for bed."

I go to the bathroom to change, and when I return, Cade is settled into the bed, flipping channels on the TV.

"Make yourself at home, then," I say sarcastically.

"Thanks, I will." He flips the covers on my side of the bed back and pats the mattress. "Come to bed, Rhae."

I consider what he wants, and then head over and crawl in bed next to him, giving him a kiss before settling on my side to sleep. Cade slides down to match my position as he spoons up to my back and lays his arm over my waist.

He kisses my cheek. "Sweet dreams, my sweet Rhae. I'll keep the dreams away tonight."

And he does.

10
Vacation

I bask in the warm sun and cool breeze. It's pretty early, so I'm at the beach on my own. Clea had to work for a little while this morning. She took off after our workout, and I came out here. I've been doing this pretty much every day, with and without Clea. We talk most of the time we're together. When I'm alone, I read. Cade texts me every day. Many times a day. He seems to miss me terribly. I know I miss him. Most texts are about us and how I'm doing, and then others are about his grandparents. Irma is in a panic. She believes the time for her husband's death is close.

These days, when my mind drifts, I think of that night before I left. For the first time, he didn't leave. He held me all night. Even when I was sweating from the body heat, I stayed as still as possible. Sleeping with him as was peaceful as promised. I didn't dream of Ryan again. I didn't really dream at all.

The next morning, I explained more about who Clea was and where I would be. I didn't look at Cade while I was talking. I was too afraid of seeing anger, hurt or frustration. I didn't know how he would take it that I would want to hang out with friends and family that tied me to Ryan. When I finished my rambling explanation of guilt, Cade said, "Go. You need this."

He wraps his arms around me and squeezes me into a hug, which we hold for much longer than necessary, neither of us willing to let go. Resting my face against his chest, I let the beat of his heart pound its way into my memory. I would need his warmth, and to have that engrained in my head while I am away. After a few moments, I pull back to look into his eyes and see if he has any doubts about letting me go. He can tell I have anxiety about leaving.

"Hey, I'll be here when you're ready. You're beyond stressed with all that's going on; although, you fight to hide it. I see right through you. And, for the record, you have nothing to feel guilty about. They don't have to leave your life because your husband died." He smiles at me and the warm feeling in my heart spreads to other parts of my body. I groan because it's still too soon for us to become anything else.

"You're doing it again," I observe.

"What?" He looks puzzled.

"That dangerous smile. It's like your thing. You know you can get whatever you want with that smile, don't you?"

"Oh, I don't know. I haven't gotten everything I want." He smirks.

"And what would that be, sir?"

"You."

I have no idea how to answer that. His statement stuns me silent for a few minutes. He takes advantage of it and swoops in for a kiss. He kisses me stupid and then says, "Hey, I know you aren't ready for much more right now. I'm letting you know that when you are ready, I'm ready, too. Okay?"

"Okay." I sigh. "Thank you for understanding. You'll text and call me, right?"

"Yes."

The next morning, I left for Daytona Beach.

Remembering where I am, I stare out over the ocean. This is the most peaceful place on the planet. No one to ask me questions. No one making assumptions. Being here is the closest thing to happiness I have had since Ryan died. I feel like I haven't ever been happy. Not until I got to this beach. I do miss Cade, though.

My time here is pretty low-key. Clea, Stephen, and I usually have dinner then drink wine and watch movies at night. Occasionally we replace our wine with ice cream. Out of guilt for our indulgences, we get up and hit the elliptical machines at six a.m. in the gym provided by their homeowner's association.

Clea pushes me to be better. She loves working out, and when I have her to motivate me, I love it, too. I think the squishy middle I hate is starting to change into a nicer shape. Originally, I thought I would stay a week, but I decide to stay a second week because I really don't want to go home. Just thinking about going back to that house and that job makes me want to sink below the waves of the ocean and never come out.

I heave a sigh and decide I'd like to get in the water for a little bit. I wade out into the ocean and bounce as the waves wash over me. I dip beneath the surface several times to get my hair wet. I love how the ocean feels, but hate getting saltwater in my nose. Unfailingly, I inhale saltwater. I should be better at this by now. Clea swears she'll get me surfing or boogie-boarding before long. I think she's crazily optimistic.

As I bob in the water, I wonder what it would be like to float on the waves like I do in a pool. I float and see where the waves and currents take me. Would I float away into the ocean? Would the waves keep pressing me back to the beach against my will? If I did float out away from land, would I fight it? Surely some type of survival instinct would take over and I would involuntarily swim in. Or would I? What if I died in this ocean today? I think my sisters would miss me, but would I be one less burden in their world? I think so.

I spend a good deal of time letting the thoughts swirl through my mind while I bob in a little over chest-high in the water. I do think about my dad and my friends, too. I recall what Jess said when I was staying at her house after the visitation. They all stayed with me because they thought I was suicidal. Jess said she didn't think I could live without Ryan. That I didn't know how to live without him. Maybe I don't. Seems like dying would be easier than all the struggles of life. Maybe that's what Irma saw in my eyes.

When I start feeling waterlogged and drawn with the salt on my skin, I make my way back to my lounge chair and umbrella. I dry my hands and body, comb through my tangled hair and lie back on the lounger again. I pick up my book and read until I fall asleep. It isn't long until my phone is ringing. I look and see that Jess is calling, again.

"Hey."

"Hey? Really? Okay, well, I got your mail and made sure nothing was broken into at your house. You're welcome. When do you think you're coming home?" Oh, she is in a peachy mood.

"Thank you. I don't know."

"Why does it sound like that is the saddest thing you have ever had to consider? Don't you miss us? Dad?"

"Jess, please, of course I miss you guys. I don't want to be home anymore. I'm all alone. Everything about the house reminds me of Ryan. As soon as I step in the front door, it's like I've lost him and learned about his affair all over again." I take a deep breath and think of how I can make her understand this. "Imagine re-living the worst moments of your life every single day. I experience it every time I make dinner, every time I take a shower, and worse, every time I get in the bed we shared."

"I get it," she interrupts my rant.

"Jess, he dies again every day. I get over it and I'm not so sad when I'm at work, but that's a short reprieve, which is hell too. They are all judgy and sympathetic. I feel like someone is staring holes through me all the time. Plus, there's the Dragon Lady."

"Fuck the Dragon Lady. I'll kick her ass myself." She was fiercely defending me, then she softened. "Honey, I didn't know it was that bad for you. What about Cade? You spend a lot of time with him, don't you? It doesn't help?"

"I don't expect anyone to know that's what this feels like. I bet Dad is the one closest to us that knows. Cade is amazing, but at this point we're just friends. I don't know if I should pursue being something more with him. It seems too soon. I mean, don't I have to wait a year or something to start dating again?"

Jess is silent, I assume thinking through what I said. "So, what are you and Clea doing this afternoon?" Great, a subject change. I got too close to her emotional center. She's worse about closing things off than I am.

"I don't know. She'll get off around lunch time, and then we'll decide."

"Okay, well, call me. Call Dad too. He misses you."

As soon as we hang up, I decide she's right, and I give him a call. Based on the time difference, he should be up drinking coffee, planning his day, or getting back from the lake. Crappies don't stand a chance against the old man. He knows where to find them, and he keeps two freezers at his house stocked with fish filets.

"Hey, baby."

"Hi, Daddy. What no good are you up to?"

"Just sat down with a cup of coffee. Are you still in Florida?"

"Sure am, for a couple more days at least."

"Are you getting a suntan? Tell me you are using sunblock. You don't want skin cancer. You know it hits everyone in our family."

"I use a 100 SPF. No tan for this ghostly pale girl. How's the boat?"

Now, there's a topic he loves talking about—his boats. He goes on to tell me about his latest modification to the frankentoon, which is a pontoon boat he built out of two 1970s models. He tells me about finishing his Boston Whaler. I learn he picked it up used and is refurbishing it. The plan is for it to be a single-person fishing boat. It's is really hard on him to put the frankentoon in and out by himself. Dad goes on to tell me that he wants to have us all out to go tubing soon.

I think about how wonderful it is to hang out on the boat and jump in the lake whenever the feeling strikes me. I smile as he finishes talking about all his projects.

"Daddy, how do you do it?"

"Do what?"

"I feel like Ryan dies over and over again every day. I am so unhappy being in our house. I'm unhappy at work. I don't know how you are so adjusted and able to deal with Mom gone."

"Aw, sugar, listen, I had time to prepare to lose your mom. It wasn't easy, but I was ready. Ryan was a shock. It wasn't supposed to happen; you guys are so young. I get busy with my boats and in the yard when it hits me. I get distracted, and I get better. Is that not working for you?"

I swallow some tears. "No, distraction doesn't work for me. Honestly, I don't want to go home, but I have to for my job."

"What are you saying?"

"I think I need a fresh start. I don't really know what a fresh start would look like, but I know that I need something. Distance. More distraction."

"You know you shouldn't make decisions when you're emotional. Think about your fresh start carefully. You do whatever it is that you need to do, and I'll support you anyway that I can."

I consider telling him about all the things I want to run away from, but I don't. "I love you. You always say the right thing. Thank you."

"I love you, too. I'm fixin' to go fishing with J.D. Call me when you know for sure what you're going to do."

"I will."

We end our call and I sit back, reflecting on our conversation. What would a fresh start be? How far would I need to go? Sell the house? Should I move to a different state? Is Cade the answer? I have no idea what is going on in my head anymore. I only know that I cannot continue to live a life so full of unhappiness.

I pack up my chair, umbrella and beach bag, and head for the car. As I'm throwing my stuff in the trunk, my phone starts ringing again. I fish it out and manage a weak, "Hello," to which I'm greeted with an overly bubbly Clea.

"Hey!"

"Hey, are you off yet?"

"I am. I'm driving home now. Meet me at there, okay? I have a great idea for today."

"Sure thing. I'm on my way there now."

We hang up. I dust as much sand off my rear and feet as I can, but I'm disappointed at how much sticks to me as I get in the car. This is a consistent problem. The floorboards of my car might soon qualify as a beach in their own right. Maybe I should hang a starfish from the rearview to complete the look. I laugh at myself and drive back to Clea's.

I'm just getting out of the car when she pulls up.

"Hey, we need to clean out my car before I take half the beach home to Mississippi with me."

"Yeah, later. Today, we are going to the spa! I am talking hair, main/pedi, massage...waxing." She says waxing like it's a secret, dirty word and waggles her eyebrows at me.

You must be kidding me. "Clea, I don't know. Massages? Waxing? People touching my bare skin? You know how I feel about strange people touching me."

"They aren't touching you, they are massaging you. Professionals, not random strangers. C'mon, please!"

She's going to kill me. "Okay, sure. Let me get a shower, I'm all salty and whatnot."

"Yay!" She is literally jumping up and down clapping her hands. I'm so glad I gave in. She's a perky thing, and it makes her happy to push me out of my normal boundaries.

I shower and dress as instructed. Comfortable. I interpret this to be a tank and yoga pants with flip flops. Clea approves and we head out. Turns out her great idea was sparked by gift certificates her boss had that were about to expire. Full day spa packages including the mani/pedis and massages. The only thing we need to cover is our hair, waxing, and gratuity. Not bad, considering. She always gets the great hookups.

When we arrive, we are escorted to the ladies' lounge area, and given plush bathrobe. We are instructed to change and then meet our salon representative in the foyer. We do as we're told and are escorted into the massage area. I have to mentally talk myself off the ledge. I honestly think my hands may shake clean off the ends of my arms. I'm so nervous it's ridiculous. The massage therapist is very kind, and I like her a lot. She can tell how nervous I am and does a lot to put me at ease.

She leaves the room and I get adjusted on the table as instructed. I'm less nervous now that I know I get to stay mostly covered, well the good bits anyway. After a few minutes, I'm close to falling asleep and wondering why I have never done this before. *Good Lord! This is amazing.* Before I know it, the massage is over, and we are guided to the nail salon.

We sit in large massage chairs while our hands and feet are cleaned, buffed, and moisturized. There is one person working each of my hands while another works my feet. I feel like a queen. Clea and I choose to get matching nail color. Harlot red, as she calls it. We giggle as we are moved to the nail dryers for a few minutes.

Next, we are escorted back to the ladies' lounge where we are served fruit and champagne. I really don't know how to act around all these other ladies. I just do my best not to make a mess. I think I end up drinking too much champagne, though. My head feels bubbly and tingly by the time the stylist from the salon comes to get us for our hair appointments.

My stylist has curly hair like mine—naturally, as it turns out. Her name is Monique, and she is as sweet as can be. I really like her sense of humor. She knows how to handle my curls without turning me into a fuzz ball. I'm excited. I discuss short styles with her and colors. She doesn't recommend any specialized colors that would require lightening. The chemicals used to lighten hair would likely strip my curls in an uneven way, kind of unpredictable. With Clea's urging, I agree to skip on color for today, but I do ask for a short style. Collectively, we decide on an asymmetrical, inverted bob.

Monique sets to work. I am washed, cut and styled in no time. She spends a few minutes explaining how to style it curly, and then decides on flat-ironing it for today. She breaks out the round brush and it is nearly perfectly straight when she gets done blow-drying. Then she sprays a sparse amount of heat protector before breaking out the flat iron. These are tactics I need to commit to memory for future use. I really should take more of an interest in my appearance. I always thought it was okay not to care because I had Ryan. Since I wasn't looking for a man, or a job, why should I care? I realize with the way I'm feeling at the spa, I should care for me.

We end our day in at the waxing stations. We get our eyebrows shaped and then talk with the waxer about getting either a bikini wax or a Brazilian. After I listen to the descriptions about what takes place and what is involved in both, I am absolutely terrified. However, I am also intrigued. I never considered getting waxed with Ryan, and he never mentioned it. I can't help but wonder what Cade would think about a little lady grooming when we finally get that far. If we get that far. Thinking about Cade emboldens me, and I opt for the bikini.

An hour later, Clea and I have completed our afternoon trip to the spa. We have been massaged and pampered until we're literally high on being spoiled. I keep trying to forget how awkward and painful the bikini wax was, but I'm glad I did it. We swing by the grocery store on our way home. Stephen is home from work and apparently starving—based on his phone call to Clea. We pick up chicken, zucchini, and yellow squash to grill. For our appetizers, we decided on baby carrots and garlic hummus. We skip dessert in favor of using those calories on merlot.

Clea and I cook together and then sit down with Stephen to eat on the patio. Clea is pouring the wine, and I decide to kick off our dinner conversation. "Well, I've been giving it some thought. Like I told my dad earlier, it's time for a fresh start. Don't ask me what that means. I don't know yet."

Clea seems to think for a moment. "Didn't you tell me that Ryan had life insurance?"

Shit! "Yeah, a ton of it. I still have the check in my purse. I don't know what to do with it." I forgot I even had it. "Checks don't go bad, do they? Like expire?"

"You probably have six months to get it deposited. Maybe, you should use it to take some time off. Start by quitting your job. Live off the life insurance money for a little while. Travel. Explore. Discover who you are without Ryan. That could be a fresh start."

I think about her words for a little while. I think she's right. I need to know who I am and what I want from life before I make any huge decisions. Experience more of life outside of Bell Hills and the great state of Mississippi. There will always be other jobs, and quitting would eliminate a major segment of unhappiness in one big swoop.

"Clea, my dear, you are a genius. I mean that. You are a lady and a scholar." I hold up my glass of wine in a toasting gesture.

"But, of course, we all know this." She beams.

As we enjoy our evening together and make plans for the coming days, always around her work schedule, my phone starts buzzing.

Clea laughs. "Cade again?"

"Shush it, missy!" Of course, she's right. It's Cade. I nod and stand to leave the room before answering. "Hey!"

"Hey." He sounds like something's wrong. "Uh, I was calling to let you know my grandfather died today."

Jesus. I didn't expect that. What do I even say to him? I know what "I'm sorry" sounded like to me. Still, that's all I want to say to him. I settle for, "I'm coming home. I'll be there tomorrow."

"You don't have to. I know how you might feel being at another funeral."

"That's true, but I need to be there for you and Irma. That's what...friends...do for each other."

"Friends. Right. Okay." Something in his voice sounds wrong. I think to mention it or ask but remind myself it's probably the grief. "When do you think you'll be in?"

"I'll leave tomorrow morning. It is about a thirteen-hour drive. Longer when I'm sleepy. I'll text every time I stop. Cade, are you okay?"

He's silent for a long while. Long enough that I begin to wonder if he hung up. "Okay. Yeah, I'm okay. We knew this was coming, right?"

"We did. But that doesn't make it hurt any less. I'll see you as soon as I can."

"Okay. Bye, Rhae."

Something feels so wrong about the way he ended the call. I can't quite put my finger on it. I return to the dinner table and tell Clea what's going on.

"So, you're leaving?"

"I have to. He would have done it for me, had he known me when Ryan passed."

"Okay. Honey, how does he figure into the fresh start?" she asks gently.

"I don't know yet. I know I feel things for him that I haven't felt for anyone in a while. What that is or what that means, I don't know."

"Does he know how you feel?"

"We've talked. I mean, I know he wants to be more than friends. He's made that crystal clear. I don't know what I can give him back. I should have a piece of me to give him, shouldn't I?"

"Right now, you are still broken in a million pieces. About half of those pieces are starting to form a whole person again. I think, before you know it, you'll have a piece to give him. It takes time."

We spend the remainder of the night packing my things and watching movies. Okay, so we also indulge in some ice cream.

Clea gets up with me at six the following morning. She makes me a bagel and coffee. I smile because she knows me so well. When I finish my bagel, she tops off the to-go cup of coffee for me. We walk out to my car, and she fully lectures me on safety being a woman driving all that way by myself.

I give her the typical, "Yes, Mom," smarmy answer, and then the biggest hug I can. Neither one of us wants to let go. We hug long enough that we start crying.

"Stop it. I'll be back soon. Promise," I say as I try to swallow back my tears a little bit.

Clea sniffles. "I know. I can't wait. Be careful. Call me when you make pit stops, okay?"

"Okay."

"No texting and driving though. That's dangerous."

"Okay."

"Call me when you get home, too."

"Clea, you are a worry wart. Settle down. I'll be fine. Love you."

"Love you more. Talk to you soon." She pushes away from me and takes a couple steps back. I get in the car and buckle my seat belt. I start backing out of the driveway and wave at her.

I hit the interstate an hour later and settle in for a long drive.

I pull into my driveway a little after nine p.m. The drive took longer because I'm so sleepy and I kept stopping for coffee. I made good on my promise, calling Clea at every stop. She always answered the phone as perky as ever. Her perkiness is a gift and a curse. I also called and texted Cade at every stop. He would sometimes respond with an, "Okay," or would not respond at all. It was frustrating. I tried to be forgiving, knowing what he's dealing with.

I leave my stuff in the car and head straight inside the house. I dial Clea one last time as I lock the front door behind me. We talk for a few minutes as I look around. When we hang up, I make my way to the shower. Driving all day has me feeling super-gross. I stand under the water until it runs cold. I let the warmth of the water numb me all the way to my toes. When I get out, I brush through my hair and then wrap it in a towel. I throw on some pajamas and fall into bed.

Laying there, staring at the ceiling, it occurs to me that I might need to let my family and friends know that I'm back. I send one text to my dad and sisters, *"Back home in Mississippi. Love you. Call tomorrow."* The second to my friends, *"Home from vacation. See you on Monday. Big changes are a comin'! Love you."* After I hit send, I realize that I have left Cade out of both messages.

I take a deep breath and start a new text. And then I stare at the screen. I'm thinking through it, but I don't know where to start. God! I have to stop over-analyzing everything. I'm starting to annoy myself with this bullshit. Okay. Here goes. *"I'm back home. Hope you're okay. I miss you."*

I hit send and turn my phone off. I don't want him to text back. Okay, so I want him to text back, but I don't want to read it tonight. My resolve holds for about an hour. When I can't get to sleep, I grab my phone and turn it back on. What the hell is wrong with me? I'm torturing myself. The phone boots up, and I wait for it to find cell signal. When it finally flashes LTE at the top, I have one new text message that loads.

"Missed you. We need to talk."

What? What does that mean? How do I take that? I stare at the phone for a long time. *I. Will. Not. Over-analyze.* Sleep is what I need right now. It has been a long day of driving. Tomorrow is the start to the weekend. Time to get my shit together.

I don't know if it is because I'm so tired, or because of all the changes in my life, but I dream of my mama.

She is beautiful, working in her garden. Flowers and plants as far as the eye can see. She's wearing a T-shirt and a sun hat. She stands and waves at me. I can see the light in her eyes and the big smile she always wore.

I start running toward her, but no matter how fast or how long I run, I can't reach her. She still waves at me, but I just can't get there. Finally, I stop running. I settle for yelling, "I love you!" She looks like she might cry, and then she disappears.

I'm so angry I couldn't reach her. I start to cry. Eventually, I sit up and wipe the tears from my face. I take a few breaths to steady myself. It's only a dream. I repeat the phrase over and over in my mind. Eventually, I calm enough to get out of bed. Mama would have run to me if it was really her. *Wouldn't she?*

Sleeping with my hair in a towel was not one of the management techniques I learned at the spa. During my morning shower, I can't get the imagery of that dream out of my mind. I need to talk to Irma. She can interpret for me, but I don't want to ask her to do anything today. I need to help get them through the visitation and funeral. So many people helped me through Ryan's that I need to pay it forward.

Styling my curls the way Monique taught me, I study it in the mirror and hope Cade will think it is as cute as I do. Giddiness bubbles up in a laugh as I think about showing my new look to him. I quickly remind myself he is going through a hard time, and I can't get bent if he doesn't fawn all over me. I decide on a blue, spaghetti strap sundress, and wedge sandals to wear.

I make my way down to Irma's house and knock on the door. I wait for anyone to answer, but there isn't one. I send Cade a text. *"Hi. I came over to Irma's as soon as I got up this morning. Nobody's home."*

An eerie feeling crawls over my skin, raising goosebumps in its wake. I look around and decide to sit on the porch swing a little while. When it becomes clear that Cade and Irma aren't coming home anytime soon, and with the lack of response to my text, I begin to feel like a fool. I head home.

I spend the remainder of the morning and most of the afternoon washing laundry from my trip and writing out the plan for the fresh start. I need a bank account for the life insurance money, and I need to work through a 401k rollover from work. I need to decide what the plan is after I quit.

The sun is getting low in the sky, so I grab my tea and head out on the front porch. The seasons are changing, and the air has a chill to it now. I sit with a book in my lap, not really reading until it is too dark to see the print anymore. Then it hits me, Cade never called. He never answered my text. He didn't come over. Shaking my head, I gather my empty glass, book, and cell phone and go inside.

I know he's dealing with so much in his life. Death isn't easy on anyone, no matter how they try to seem tough and unaffected. I tell myself he'll call when he's ready. He knows where to find me.

A Place to Stand

11
Alone Again

It is a bright morning. Ryan and I are sitting at the kitchen table. He is staring into my eyes and holding my hand. I can see his light tan, and a smattering of a beard covering his jaw. His light brown hair is growing out.

In the distance, I hear a feminine voice. "Rhae, honey, do you want sorghum on your biscuits?"

What? "Mama? Is that you?" I look around, but all I can see is white light. I can't see anything other than Ryan and the kitchen table. "Mama, where are you?" I shout as I look frantically for her.

"Aww, baby. I'm here. Calm down. I'm making you some biscuits. Sorghum?"

"No. I don't want anything to eat." Panic is filling me from my toes to my head. "Mama, let me help you!"

"The only way to help me is to help yourself. You know what needs to happen. Call your Dad. He can help. Tell Jess and Marie that I love them."

Confused, I turn to Ryan. "Why are you here?"

He shakes his head, "You're holding grudges. I asked you to be Melody's friend. That'll help you let go of the anger you have for me."

"Everyone can kiss my ass! I don't know what I'm supposed to do anymore!"

I feel tears welling up and I wake up. A dream. God, I can't do this. These dreams are killing me. I can't fix it. Why do they all think I can?

Several days have passed. Cade still hasn't called me. I'm completely numb and worthless. I go to work, come home, eat, drink and sleep. I'm a living machine. My routine is a spiral into non-existence. Nothing makes sense. Going out with friends is unappealing. I don't call anyone. I think about the fresh start plan, and then I lose focus. I spend hours thinking through every moment we spent together. Analyzing every conversation for hints of things that I did to piss Cade off. I don't land on any one thing. I briefly consider that he's just dealing with his grandfather's passing. What I can't rationalize is why he wouldn't allow me to help him through it. I need him here.

By the end of the week, I'm more than hurt, more than numb. I'm angry. Nearly a week without a word? Nearly a week! Sucking up my pride, I decide it is high-time to do something. I need to quit my job. It occurs to me that I might hurt Bill or Alana, or maybe Lucy and Julie. Echoes of my private meeting with Irma resonate in my mind. I need to do this now. I need my mama and Ryan to rest and stop showing up in my dreams. I know if Mama is in my dreams, she's in the dreams of Jess, Marie and Dad. They are too proud to admit they believe or that it's possible.

Friday afternoons are when the girls and I usually get together for our Shady Lady lunch. Our time to discuss all things without barriers, borders, shame, or pride. I know that what I'm about to do may shock them, but I need them to know I love them. I need to know they will support me.

I send an e-mail:

Ladies—I don't care what you have going on today. We are going to lunch. I don't care where we go, but I do have requirements. The place must have good food, good music, and a quiet corner where we will not be kicked out for our normal conversational topics. See you in the lobby, regular time.

Alana and Jules stop by my desk and give me a fist pump, and a, "Hell yes." This does nothing to let me know if they have decided where we're going. In the meantime, I spend my morning looking as busy as possible, and accomplishing nothing.

Dee and Bill come in and we exchange pleasantries. I kill time reading old e-mails and sipping coffee. I must be on my third cup when Bill finally says, "Any particular reason you're tanking coffee so fast? Not sleeping?"

"Uh, no. I didn't realize I was doing it. I've got some things to discuss with the girls over lunch. I guess I'm a little nervous."

"That's right. Its ladies' lunch day. Been a while since you guys had one of them. Coffee ain't gonna help nerves. If anything, you'll be shaking by the time lunch rolls around."

"I know. Do you need help with anything this morning?" I might regret asking, but I need busy work.

"Nope. Just running queries."

"Let me know if I can do anything."

I decide I need a big distraction. I pop in my earbuds, load Spotify, and start a radio station from my favorite playlist. I'm checking on some of my client sites from the customer perspective when inspiration hits. Obituaries are published online these days. I don't know Cade's grandfather's name, so I search Cade's. The search engine doesn't hit on anything except an obituary. *Chester Miles, 76, Bell Hills, MS. Army veteran. Survivors: Wife, Irma Miles and grandson, Cade Miles.* I read through to the arrangement announcements. *Shit.* The funeral was yesterday. I had no idea. Sulking had taken all my time and energy. I didn't even notice any extra traffic on our road. I suck. Worst friend ever. I nosedive into self-pity.

"Let's go!"

I look up and see Alana standing by my desk. Oh! Lunch with my girls. "Yeah. Let's go." I grab my purse and throw on my shades. I assume we're walking, but I won't know until we meet up with the others.

Lucy and Jules are waiting in the lobby. They both look ready for a walk. Jules is the first to speak, "We're going to Seven Whiskeys."

I look at her with an eyebrow raised. "We're going to a bar for lunch?"

"We are. The non-smoking dining room downstairs should be nearly empty. The have good music, and decent bar food. What else could we ask for?"

"Fair enough," Lucy answers.

Lucy and Jules walk a few feet ahead of Alana and I. Alana doesn't say much on the walk. When we arrive, we get seated in the dining room Jules described. It's dark and dank. A small bar punctuates the room at the far end. There are blackboards hanging that list the daily specials. I read through them as the others order their drinks and food. When it's my turn, I throw a curve ball.

"Blue Moon on draft, and I'll have the deluxe grilled cheese with fries."

The waitress hovers while the others exchange confused looks. "Blue moon? Draft? You sure?"

"Yes, ma'am. Thank you."

"Rhae, honey, we have to go back to the office. Well, unless you took off and didn't tell us," Alana states the obvious.

I smile. "Nope. I just don't care anymore. I have news for you guys." It's moments like these that make me wish I could freeze time. I mean it's priceless reading their faces. One is concerned. One thinks I've lost my marbles. The other is considering joining me for a beer.

"When I went to Florida, I did some thinking. Life has to change for me. I can't go on pretending things are okay. They aren't. I hate my job and the house. I don't want to go on living where I have always lived. I want to branch out and see things. Do things."

"Where are you going?" Lucy asks, intrigued.

"I don't know yet."

"What money are you going to live on? What about the house?" Jules, the practical one, asks.

"Ryan's life insurance money. And I'm listing the house."

There is a collective sigh from the group, and Alana reaches over to hold my hand. "Honey, we are so glad you're doing this. We've been talking a lot about what's next for you. Honestly, we thought you would crack from the strain. But this is great!"

"Really? You don't think I'm being stupid?"

"Hell no! What does Cade say about all this?"

I look around at all of them and swallow a little pride I didn't know was stuck in my throat. "I haven't heard from him. I drove back from Florida last week because his grandfather died. We texted a bit while I was on vacation, but now nothing. No calls. I don't know what's going on with him. And as far as I'm concerned, it's his loss. I'm going to do things without sitting around waiting for someone else to join me or approve."

"That's my girl!" Alana hugs me.

Lunch is delicious. We talk about Lucy's new man because the sex at the beginning of a relationship is exciting. It's fun to hear what's happening in their lives. There is a book series I'll have to add on my Kindle app later. Jules makes it sound so amazing and definitely sexy. I need a bit of that in my life right now. Hell, a dead husband and a missing would-be friend/boyfriend means I'm not getting any action anytime soon.

After my draft of Blue Moon, I drink water. No sense pushing the limits too far. When we get back to the office, I spend the afternoon sorting through personal items on my desk that I might want to take home. I make quick work of extra papers by taking them down to the recycling bin. Dragon Lady walks by and stares at me but doesn't speak. Add that to the list of shit I won't miss. Maybe she can take my job. I laugh out loud on that one. She is so not qualified to do what I do.

After work, I swing by the liquor store and buy caramel flavored vodka then drive to Jess's house. Liz and Red are usually there on Fridays. I'm hoping for a good ole porch perch before I jump into my plans. Plus, I need to tell them what I'm doing.

When I arrive, Jess has CCR blaring in the house so loud she can't hear me at the door. I let myself in and run straight into Miss Jillian. I hug her tight and sling her up on my hip. We get into the kitchen where Jess is singing into her chili spoon like a microphone. Jillian giggles and breaks Jess's concentration. We all laugh so hard tears fill our eyes. "Bitch!" Jess yells at me between gasps for air.

"I'm sorry. I just came for the porch perch."

"You know you're always welcome for that. Jilly, go wash your hands, so you can eat. What's in the brown bag?"

"You know what's in this bag. You got Coke?"

She nods and keeps cooking. I mix a drink, then head out on the porch to watch the sunset. Connor has wired speakers so that whatever she's playing in the house also plays on the porch. There is no escaping CCR tonight. Ever.

Liz and red join me on the porch a little bit later. Jess brings out bowls of chili. It really is still too hot to eat chili, but none of us complain. Jess makes due with what they've got, and she does a good job with it. I know we need to eat, too. It'll help absorb alcohol.

After dinner and playing around, we are sitting on the porch singing Skynyrd. I drift off to a trance while the girls talk. The bug light is, all of a sudden, the most interesting thing I have ever seen. Jess snaps me back to the conversation. "So, what made you want to join porch night anyway?"

"Ah, well, I'm going to sell the house and quit my job. Wanted to let you ladies know what I'm doing."

"You're what?" she asks, incredulous.

"Selling stuff. Quitting." I drink more vodka. I quit bothering with the Coke as a mixer a few drinks ago. Walking to the kitchen just isn't worth the effort.

"Have you talked to Dad?"

"Not yet. But I'm meeting a real estate agent tomorrow, and I plan to quit on Monday."

"You have no direction, limited income from the life insurance, and now no place to live. What part of that sounds like a good idea? You have lost your mind." Her volume has gone up progressively with each statement, and her face is beet red. Jess is pissed. I didn't expect this reaction.

"All of it!" I yell back for emphasis. I'm nothing if not hardheaded. "You try going to a job that makes you feel useless, walk into a house that reminds you of everything you've lost, and live in the same city with the mistress of your dead husband. You tell me what you would do."

"All right. Stop this," Red speaks up. "Jess, she's doing what she thinks she needs to do. Rhae, she's just looking out for you. No fighting on porch night."

"I'm sorry, honey. I worry you'll end up homeless and broke. Nowhere to go kinda thing," Jess confesses.

"I love you, Jessi-Poo! If I end up homeless, I can always live with you and Connor. Jilly loves me."

We laugh off our tiff and toast my assumptions.

I wake up Saturday morning with a pain in my left cheek. Oh, shit that hurts. My mouth feels like Velcro, and my head is so heavy I'm not sure I can lift it. My eyes are definitely burning out of my head. What the fuck is happening? I scrunch my face up and fight against the urge to move. Everything hurts! Continuing my assessment of the situation, I smell coffee. I'm just mustering the courage to turn my head when someone kicks me in my ass. "Get up, heifer!"

"Ughhhhhh, Jess. Help me. I'm stuck." I try to swallow, but my throat is sandpaper raw.

Jess reaches down and helps peel me off the porch. My cheek is stuck to the panels with my own drool. It is as sticky as duct tape. I think I leave skin on the floor when she finally gets me up. God love her, she passes me my shades and a cup of coffee. I ball up in the corner chair in the last piece of shade on the porch. I sip my coffee carefully as to not burn my tongue. It has been a long, long time since I had a hangover. This is beyond a hangover. This is the hangover a hangover gets.

"How much did I drink? How did I end up sleeping on the porch?"

"Well, you polished off the bottle of vodka you brought, and against my better advice, you let Liz tease you into drinking tequila. You declared you had to pee, and when you stood up, you landed face down on the porch. We were scared to death until we heard you snore. I have to tell ya', we laughed until Red nearly peed herself. Never saw you like that, baby girl."

"Glad I could provide some entertainment," I grouse. "Everything hurts. Even my hair."

"Aw, don't be a spoiled sport. Anyway, we decided it was a good time of year, and we could let you sleep there without worrying about you. We were right. Here you are, just fine."

"I would not say I'm fine. Not even close. More coffee."

"Shower, then more coffee. I left a pair of shorts and a T-shirt on the guest bed. Go."

I do as I'm told because it sounded heavenly. When I finish and emerge from the bedroom, Jess hands me more coffee and ibuprofen. "What time are you meeting the real estate agent?"

"Holy shit, Jess! What time is it?" I hadn't thought about the things on my list today.

"It's almost noon."

"Great. I need to get going. The agent is coming over at one. Thanks for everything."

The agent is at the house when I pull up. She's apparently been here a few minutes because she's walking around taking pictures of the exterior and making notes on things she wants me to do to improve the curb appeal.

After we tour the inside, and let her get pictures and measurements, she tells me what she wants to list the house for. It all sounds good to me.

Feeling like she's just about finished, and before I sign the agent agreement, I fill her in on my one rule, "No low ball offers. Don't even bring them to me. I am pricing the house very reasonably and I do not want low ball offers."

She agrees and is gone. The whole meeting took about forty-five minutes. Now what do I do with my day? I'm not good with downtime because it allows me to dwell on things I shouldn't. I decide to start packing a few things. I won't take the boxes with me, but at least I'll be that far ahead when the house does sell. When I'm finished, I run to the grocery store for some dinner. Because of the prior evening, I decide I've had enough alcohol for one weekend, so I avoid buying the beer that's calling my name.

Saturday night is filled with more of the same dreams. Ryan and Mama lecturing me about grudges, friends, forgiveness, and the sisters. Nothing I've done so far is getting me any relief from my nighttime terrors. After the third such dream in the same night, I sit up and drink coffee while trying to read a book. No wonder I'm doing so much drinking. Without Cade around, it's the only way I'm getting any sleep. Cade. There's an ache in my chest when I think about him or imagine his face.

Sunday is torture. I pack up a couple suitcases in preparation to leave town. I lay out my Monday morning office clothes. Late in the afternoon, I write my resignation letter. Then when I run out of things to do, I sit on the porch swing and watch the sunset. I think about the time I saw Cade in the middle of the oranges and purples that fill the sky. Trying to blow off any feelings I might have for him, I mentally explain away the chills as the weather's continual decline. Temps are dropping, after all. No matter what mental games I try to play with myself, the truth is always there. I miss him.

12
Fresh Start

Monday morning, shortly after I arrive in the office, I craft an e-mail to all of my clients giving them Dee's contact information and informing them I would no longer be working for the company. I walk over to Bill's desk. He's hunched over, squinting at a spreadsheet.

"Bill, I need to talk to you."

"What's up?" He sits back and smiles at me.

"I thought I should tell you first. I'm leaving. Quitting. Resigning."

He seems to process my news for a minute. "I'm proud of you. Ginger is going to miss you a lot."

"Thanks, buddy. Do you want me to write down instructions on how I make the coffee?"

"Would you? Lord knows what kind of coffee I'll turn out, but hey, it's worth a shot."

I grab his legal pad and write up the instructions for using the coffee pot and which brands of coffee I buy. At the end of the note, I write down my cell phone number and my e-mail address. When I look up, Bill is staring down at the paper, and then he grabs me in a bear hug.

"I'm gonna miss you, girl. I'll send you pictures of Ginger…tap dancing on Dragon Lady's face."

We both fall apart laughing. "You do that. I look forward to it!"

Feeling satisfied that I have thought of everything, I walk over to Dee's desk.

"Can I speak with you for a moment?"

She looks up from her computer, then locks the screen, "Sure. Come in."

"I wanted to say thank you for everything, but I have decided that to resign my position." I smile and hand her my resignation letter.

She nods. "Are you sure? We can work through this thing with Bernice. I'll help anyway I can. We really can't afford to lose you." She's sweet to offer.

"It's not the company, or you. It's not even Bernice." I think through Irma's directive and the need for a fresh start again. I can't share any of that with Dee without being outfitted with a white jacket that lets me hug myself. "I love working for you! Thing is, I need to find out what else is out there for me now. You know I'm on my own. I have a little insurance money from Ryan, and I think I just need to spend some time figuring out my life."

Dee looks like she's about to cry. "I understand. I wish you all of the best. We'll miss you so much."

We shake hands and I go to my desk to pack up. When I'm finished, Dee walks me to security where I turn in keys and my ID badge. She grabs me for a swift hug, and I let her. Apparently, I picked the perfect time to do this. As I pull back from Dee's hug, the Dragon Lady is strolling through the lobby.

"What's going on here?" she asks with a fake smile.

"Bernice," Dee begins, "Rhae has decided to leave the company."

"Well, I wish I could say I didn't see it coming, but I did. Best to you, Rhae."

I gave her a sarcastic smile. "Kiss my ass."

"What did you say to me?" Dragon Lady gapes at me, and God help me, Dee starts laughing. She is laughing and covering her mouth to mute the sound, which only makes it worse.

"You seem to be getting slow in your old age. Plus, you seem addled with all the gossip and back biting you've been doing for so long. I'll say it again, slowly. Kiss. My. Ass. Dee, it has been a pleasure to work for you. Thank you for everything." I smile at Dee genuinely, and then I turn to Dragon Lady, who looks absolutely stunned by my small rant. I flip her off and walk to my car. I feel like a million bucks. I stood up to the old Dragon Lady!

Instead of heading straight home, I decide it's time to deposit the life insurance check. The assistant branch manager is available to help me. He walks me through depositing a check that large and going over how long it will take to clear. Then he explains that I should look into investments, so the money can work for me. That's probably the smart approach. I'm not interested in smart today.

On the way home from the bank, I have all my windows rolled down. I'm at a fine cruising speed. The wind is higher today, bringing a change of seasons with it. Fall is ready to give way to winter, and I'm ready to move on from this life. Maybe one of the things I'll do is visit Alaska or take a trip to Canada. Somewhere really cold. Somewhere I can test what it might be like to live in an area that is the polar opposite of North Mississippi.

When I get home, I air out the house by letting in some of the cooler fall air. After cleaning house, and reading for a while, it hits me. If Cade isn't calling me, has he abandoned Irma? Mama raised me better than this. I might have missed the funeral during all this, but I don't need to forsake Irma. I pick my best house plant and dig for a piece of ribbon in my desk drawer. All I can find is green with white polka dots. "It's the thought, right?" I ask of no one. Or maybe somewhere I think I'm asking Mama.

I tie the ribbon on the plant and go for a walk down to Irma's house. I'm not surprised to find the sweet little lady swinging on her porch swing. Stopping at the foot of the porch steps, I look up to her.

"May I?" I ask.

"Of course, baby. Cade runnin' off don't mean you ain't welcome." She smiles and waves me up.

"I'm sorry I've stayed away so long. I wanted to be here." I say, almost ashamed as I hug her neck. I set the plant on the railing of the porch.

"Nonsense! I had enough to deal with anyway. All those casseroles. Why do these women think I need to be fed because my husband died?"

I laugh so hard I have tears in my eyes. "Oh, Mrs. Irma! I know exactly what you mean. We had this discussion back when Ryan died. I'll never understand it."

Irma pats my knee. "Hell, some of them ain't the sharpest tools in the shed, but they mean well. Where you been anyway?"

Sighing, I answer, "I quit my job today."

"What? What are you going to do to pay bills?"

"Ryan left me a little money. I'm going to use it to travel and change my life. You know, be on my own for a while. I think that's part of Cade's reason for disappearing. I don't know if you know, but I was with Ryan since I was a teenager. He was my first boyfriend. My first kiss. My first...everything."

"Sex, honey. Use grown-up words around me."

"Yes, ma'am. I haven't ever been on my own. Something tells me that this is the key. So, I'm going to use the money to find my feet. I'm also selling the house." I can't look at her.

Memories of everything that happened from the day we bought it until now flash through my mind. It wasn't all bad. There wasn't much bad at all, really. Actually, there are really great memories there. The few sad memories are related to our inability to have children. There were a grand total of two pregnancies during our years together. Each ended in miscarriage. It took me months to get over the wasteland of emotions afterward. Finally, I told Ryan I didn't want to be a mother. Logically, it didn't make sense for me to keep trying and hurting myself that way. It was a lie, though. The affair with Melody and her pregnancy confirm that Ryan wasn't the problem. Our infertility was my fault. The reality hurts.

Irma keeps the swing moving, much the way Cade did the first night we met. If she notices my mental absence, she doesn't mention it. After a while, she reaches over and holds my hand. I love the softness of her thin, wrinkly skin. It immediately reminds me of my Granny and Mama. Blinking tears from my eyes, I turn to look at Irma's profile. She's smiling and staring into the distance as if she can see hundreds of miles away.

"Don't give up, Rhae. Your story's not over yet," she says softly.

"I know. It's so hard." I start sobbing. "Sometimes... sometimes, I wish it was over. That there wasn't some puzzle to solve, but peace. Like I want to go to sleep and not wake up. When Cade was here, I felt lighter, like I wanted to keep fighting. Now, I... I can't, I don't... God, I don't know anymore. When he quit calling, something else shattered. I don't know how much more of this I can handle. Look at me, Mrs. Irma. I'm a crying, snotting mess. I never cry. Never have been an emotional person until these past few months."

"Keep fighting, baby. Don't stop fighting for your life. Fight for the peace your Mama's and Ryan's souls need. Solve this for everyone in your life. Find happiness for you and Cade. He has as many cracks and breaks as you do." She stops and swallows. Irma's crying and then she turns to look me square in the eye. "When you see him again, you hug him so tight that all the broken pieces between you stick together. Hold each other up. Get through this together."

I hug her hard enough to see if she can help stick my pieces together right now. She hugs me as hard. Pulling back, I wipe the tears from my cheeks, nod and stand to leave. Sometime later, I wander up the steps to my house. I pour myself numerous drinks. All of which I drink sitting at the kitchen table and staring out the front window. A part of me is willing Cade to walk up the driveway. It doesn't happen, and I run out of booze before long. Carefully pulling myself along the walls, and using the furniture for balance, I manage to lock the front door and head to bed.

Something in me is so desperate for the comfort and assurance of Cade that I text him.

"I know you're broken. I am too. Maybe one day we won't be."

I fall asleep waiting for a response that never comes.

The next morning, I am forced to suck down ibuprofen with orange juice. My head is a total mess. Hangovers don't really happen to me, until lately. I mean, I'm the one who helps the drunks recover. It's never me. I read some e-mail and fart around on Facebook for a little while. Oh look, someone is having eggs for breakfast. Good news, someone is bragging about their new car. Joy, there's a party happening tonight that I'm not invited to. This shit is so depressing.

Rolling my eyes, I get dressed in shorts and sneakers. I head to the shed. I need to work on my to-do list from the real estate agent. I start hoeing the grass that has crept in around my boxwoods. Next, I prune back my roses and crepe myrtles. Not too much on the crepes. No sense in cutting them too far back. I really hate crepe-murder. I work all day on the curb appeal of the house.

Sitting alone inside that evening is worse than all the other nights since Cade left. Maybe even tougher than Ryan dying. While I'm eating soup and flipping through the paper, I decide to call my dad.

"Hey, honey," he answers.

"Hey, Daddy. I'm going to be coming for a visit."

"Okay, when? I'll get the guest bed made up for you. Should I thaw out some fish? Do you want me to go to the grocery store?"

"No, no, Dad. Don't do anything more than you would do for yourself on a daily basis. I'm going to leave here tomorrow. I listed the house with a real estate agent."

"Throwing in the towel or moving forward?"

"Moving forward. I think."

"That's my girl. See you tomorrow. We'll talk all about it when you get here."

"Okay, Daddy. Goodnight."

The next morning, I hold true to my word. I load my bags into the car. I add a few essentials—books—I can't live without. Then I head inside to look around and make sure I haven't forgotten anything, like a phone charger. There's a notepad laying on the counter. I decide to write Cade a letter in case of a crazy chance that he comes by.

Dear Cade,

I'm not sure what went wrong. I'm not sure if you are angry with me, or hurt, or just dealing with losing your grandfather. Irma and I spent some time together yesterday. She is worried about you as much as I am. She has the benefit of her sight letting her know you are okay, whereas I have to take her word for it.

When Ryan died, my soul shattered into a million pieces. The time we spent together let some of those pieces begin to mend. For that, I am grateful. The past weeks without any contact from you has splintered the healed places all over again.

I've listed the house for sale, and I'm starting over. Perhaps, one day, when we're in a better place, we can find each other.

All the best,

Rhae

I fold it in threes and place it in an envelope. I write his name on the outside and tape the envelope to the inside of the storm door.

I lock the front door, and head for my car. I turn the radio up as loud as I can stand. Something has to drown out the temptation to cry. For a few minutes, I stare at the front of my house and gather my strength to leave it. I put the car in reverse and slowly back out of the driveway.

Two hours later, I pull in at my dad's. His crazy dog, Max, meets me at the car. He's so excited to see me that I have to hold him off the door to even get out of the car. Max is licking and jumping all around me until my dad commands, "Get down!" Max runs off like his ass is on fire. Almost everyone knows better than to cross the old man.

Dad comes over to the car and wraps me in a big hug, "How was your drive?"

"Fast." I grin.

Dad shakes his head. "See, that's why I never ride with you."

"Hey, Daddy." I mumble into his chest where he has me almost smothered.

Dad pulls back to look at me. "All right. We have things to discuss. Let's get something to drink."

I walk in behind him. The smell of the house reminds me of my mama. Dinner cooking, Clorox from cleaning the floors, and lemon dusting spray all mix into a smell that says I'm home.

"Who's been bleaching floors and dusting furniture?"

"Jess. She worries. Comes down here once a week or so to clean house. She thinks I'm going to die under a pile of dust bunnies if she doesn't come down. I mean, seriously, am I that much of a mess without your mama?"

"No, sir. That's just Jess. She has to take care of someone all the time. I'm glad she's that way."

"Hell, I am too. I put on pinto beans for supper. Can you make cornbread?"

"You got Mama's mixing bowl?"

He laughs and leaves me to it in the kitchen. We always use the same mixing bowl because Mama didn't measure anything. She taught us to cook by eyeballing the amounts. It is actually a bit more precise if I can use the mixing bowl I grew up with.

I dig around in the cabinets and set about locating the corn meal, salt, butter, eggs and milk. Since Dad's been on his own, we always check the dates on anything we use from the fridge. Luckily nothing's expired. Jess must have run through checking when she was down here cleaning.

After I get the cornbread in the oven, I fall into the couch next to Dad. He immediately mutes the game. "Talk."

I spend a few minutes getting my thoughts together, and then I launch into the reasons that I'm selling the house. None of which is news to my Dad. He's been down this road. I tell him about my dreams. I pick and choose what else to tell him: Melody–no, Cade–yes. He looks surprised about Cade.

He doesn't register an official opinion until after I'm finished. Then it's more of a confession than an opinion. "I've been seeing your Mama here too. Not in my dreams, but like a shadow here and there when I know I am absolutely alone out here."

I'm stunned. I don't know what to say to him. He follows up with, "Don't tell anyone I said that."

I smile and nod my agreement.

A Place to Stand

13
NOLA

    A week passes, and I am feeling stronger than ever. I haven't thought about men or pregnant mistresses or even being lonely. I've heard from the girls and from my friends at work a few times. Everyone is worried, but I'm not. I decide that my next destination is New Orleans. I've never been there, it's only about a six-hour drive, and it sounds like fun to embark on an adventure all on my own.

    Traveling was something I had always wanted to do. Life, however, had other plans. Ryan and I rushed into marriage and jobs so fast that we never took the time. The absence of him in my life has created an opportunity for me. I don't think most people think of someone's death as an opportunity, and I wish this had happened a different way. I wish he was here with me and we were traveling the U.S. together. But God had plans I couldn't prepare for.

    I arrive in New Orleans right around sunset. The sun kisses the tops of buildings and burns like a purple fire in the sky. I almost can't see where the land ends and the water begins as I'm driving across Lake Pontchartrain and am filled with wonder and awe as I process how beautiful the city looks. There are signs of the damage caused by Hurricane Katrina, and I suppose there always will be. A person can't forget the impressions made by something so massive, and a city can't either. All you can do is pick up the pieces and move forward. New Orleans and I are picking up the pieces together, I think.

I park and walk over to Café Du Monde. Beignets are perfect at any time of day, and I can always use some coffee. I settle in on the patio to watch the sunset finish and begin to people watch, which should be considered a sport. I watch families with a stroller walk by as a toddler has a meltdown when their mothers decline to come inside and get the ooey gooey doughy goodness. I see old-time lovers and remember things my mother used to say, "They hold hands to keep from hitting each other." I laugh, but I know she was only kidding. She was with my Dad for forty years. They loved each other every day. Still, I can't help but think about the stories shared by the passersby. Have they been together forever? Did they just meet? I build scenarios in my mind that could rival the strangest stories told by any soap operas.

As the sun continues to set, I notice the crowd changes from the elderly and family mix to more of the younger tourist and party crowd. I decide I need to figure out where I'm staying tonight or for however long I think I will be in town. The girl cleaning tables seems kind, and her friendliness with the customers makes me think she might be the right person to ask. I wave her over and introduce myself. Her name is Mandy, and her accent is striking. We talk about the best places in the city to see different things, and tours I should take. Finally, I feel comfortable enough to let her know I'll be staying in town for a while, and that I'm traveling alone. She suggests I go about a block away to Dauphine Street and stay at the Maison de Luxe.

I leave my car where it is and walk to the hotel. Her recommendation is on-point. The building is old, but not decrepit. The desk clerk is friendly, and we talk about my needs. I bargain for a reduced rate to stay a full two weeks. After I get into my room, all I can do is stand in the window and watch the people below. I'm hypnotized by the lights of the busy streets, and I imagine story after story as I continue to ponder life here. After I inspect the amenities in my room and begin to feel sleepy, I remember I need to go back for my car. The hotel has parking, and I can store the car for the duration of my stay. I heave a sigh and eventually convince myself to go take care of business. I slip my wallet in my back pocket and leave my purse in the room. Reluctantly, I tie my sneakers and head out.

Music is spilling out from the clubs and restaurants I pass on the way back to my car. Mostly jazz, zydeco, and country. There are even musicians in the street. They are extremely talented. Something about the vibe of the street party makes me forget about being tired and about going to get my car moved. It's hard to walk through these streets without feeling a desire to shake my booty. Street vendors are telling fortunes and others are selling miscellaneous souvenirs. I wonder if their wares are voodoo-related or perhaps the key ingredients to a spell you could cast on someone. Perhaps they could give me a spell to help me forget the pain and misery my life has been recently. The reality is they are likely selling knock-off tourist items. They probably source them overseas and sell them as "authentic."

There are hawkers trying to draw people into their clubs. One interesting fellow is dressed in an old black suit with his face painted like a Dia de los Muertos skull. He isn't yelling to get the attention of people walking by. He isn't flattering ugly women to gain their attentions. No, he is quiet. He is dancing to the music coming from the club. I watch him for what seems like an eternity. He never tires or seems exhausted by his dance. Peeking in the doors of the club, I can see the sway of the crowd inside. Their movement is curious. Like a single consciousness moving through all of them. The music they dance to is hypnotic. Without a thought or even a decision crossing my mind, I head toward the entrance. It's as if my body has no power to walk away. It pulls at me from the center of my being, and I need to be a part of it.

I immediately blend in with the crowd and find myself surrounded with people I've never seen. Yet, somehow, we are sharing this moment together. We sway, and I sometimes spin. Hands grab for me and either support me from spinning out of control, or just steady me in the sway. When the song changes, everyone moves back to the tables and bars lining the edges of the dance floor. I feel cold and abandoned without the others. Swallowing my disappointment that this curious moment is over, I go to the bar, order a beer, and settle into a table to watch the crowd. It is sweaty for November, but I suspect that has more to do with the dancing and alcohol than the weather.

The server is a kind, young man. I make quick friends and ask him to keep the beers coming. He nods and does a great job keeping me with a new one as needed. Men and women both smile or nod as they walk by my table to the dance floor. After several beers, I swallow my regret and apprehension, and join the new flow of people to the dance floor. The music has slowed and is even more hypnotic than before. I close my eyes and give myself over to it.

A pair of strong arms slides around my waist from behind and a body begins to sway with me. At first, panic wells up in my throat, but I quickly push it down. This is what the fresh start is about. Exploration. We continue dancing, never changing positions. I sink into the body behind me and it is a firm, strong place to rest. I reach up my right arm up and place my hand on the back of a sweaty neck. A mouth comes near to my ear as I pull on my dance partner. "I love the way you move," he whispers in my ear. His voice is familiar. Before I focus in on the familiarity too much, I take a huge gulp of my beer and set the bottle on a nearby table.

Turning around, I chance a look at my mystery dance partner, and I'm floored. I start blinking rapidly as if something is wrong with my vision. I'm hallucinating. I have had way too much to drink. It can't be. He can't be here. Not now. No. I shake my head and back away from him, bumping into tables and knocking over drinks. I push through the crowd to get to the door. I burst onto the street and breathe in a huge rush of cold air. It is so cold that I get chills.

"This is *not* happening," I scream into the night.

"It is happening. Come back inside." I spin and see him clearly under the street light. Cade. "Come back in, please. Or we can go somewhere else. We need to talk."

"The fuck we do! You need to disappear again. It's too much. What did you do, follow me? You know what I was going through. I let you in, and you destroyed me. Why should I do anything you want?" I'm screaming at him. There are about a million things swimming through my buzzed brain. Bubbas are stopping on the street to watch this play out. They are prepared to help defend me against Cade. There's no reason to, though. He hasn't done anything to hurt me. But their stance is telling.

He shakes his head. "Please, Rhae. Jesus, I didn't mean to hurt you. Please talk to me." He looks contrite, but I just don't know what to do or what to think.

"No!" I'm still screaming. "No," I say calmer, hoping to let the bubbas know it's okay. They get the hint and move along. Cade better know I saved him an ass whooping.

Cade looks like he's going to ask to talk again but drops his head and shakes it. He seems defeated. He approaches me slowly and reaches a hand out to me. Before he can reach me, I spin on my heel and take off toward my hotel. I may not be a fast runner, but I did it. I ran. I reach the elevators and head to my room. I never look back. I don't know if he followed me or not. Did I want him to? No! Of course not. What the hell?

I flop back onto my bed and huff. I lay there staring at the ceiling for a long time. Memories of our dance at the club seep into my mind. I had to know it was him. My drunken fling idea wouldn't let me pay attention to the fact that his body knew mine, and his voice. I lay there, trying to calm my breathing, and eventually close my eyes. *Air in, air out. Air in, air out.* I settle into a rhythm, and eventually fall asleep.

I wake myself up screaming and slap a hand over my mouth as to not get hotel management called. Taking a few deep breaths until I feel like I can trust myself again, I drop the hand covering my mouth. I wince as the sun hits my face like a laser beam. Holy hell! *Ouch!* Oh, that's right, heavy drinking, dancing, Cade. *Shit!* My body and head feel like shit. I get up and shower since I slept in my clothes from the day before. I have to dress in the clothes I slept in because I never did move my car, and all my other clothes are in there. *Shit!* "Nice work, genius!" I say to myself in the mirror. Quickly, I pull my hair into a small ponytail on the back of my head and then put my sneakers back on. I grab my wallet and put my keys in my pocket.

As I step off the elevator into the hotel lobby, I'm frozen in place. Standing by the front windows looking around is Cade. *Shit!* I backtrack to the elevator and start to consider if there are any other exits from the hotel. The clerk notices me and obnoxiously asks, "Is there something you needed Ms. Peters?"

Cade jumps to attention at the mention of my name and starts toward me. *What a bitch!* I hate that clerk. "No. Thank you," I bite back at her. She looks embarrassed, but self-satisfied at the same time. *Bitch.* I look up and Cade is less than two feet away from me. "Hey," I say in a voice that sounds too small. Too quiet.

"Hey," he answers. "Are you okay?"

"I'm sorry? Am I what? Okay? You mean, after you didn't call, didn't text, and stood me up? Oh yeah, fine. Dandy." I'm far more sarcastic than I intend to be. I almost feel bad. But then I think of those weeks of pain and regret, and I can't find it in me to care if I feel bad or not.

"I deserved that," he says, staring down at his feet. "I was hoping you might let me explain."

I don't say anything. Mama once told me not to be afraid of silence. Let the silence stretch and see if anything shakes out of it. It does.

"Can we please go somewhere for breakfast? Let me explain. Please?" he says almost begging.

"This is not what I came to New Orleans for. I'm over you. I'm living my life on my own terms. I do not want to go talk with you, and there really is nothing to talk about. You said all you needed to say back at home when you disappeared."

"Jesus, woman! You are the most stubborn thing I have ever dealt with. Please, for just one meal, talk to me. I'll even buy."

His frustration tickles me, and I can't help but laugh at him. "I have to move my car first," I say without any true expression on my face.

"I'll do it. Tell me where it is and give me the keys."

"Well, I need my luggage brought in too. You gonna do that for me?"

The clerk adds her two cents, "Oh, the bellboy can do that for you." Why is this bitch paying us so much attention? Then I notice she is smiling a little too brightly at Cade.

I turn to her, annoyed, "Really. Thanks." I hand him my keys.

Cade laughs. "Be right back. Don't run off."

"Uh, excuse me. Running off is your move, not mine." I shake my head and make my way over to the lounge and have a seat. What the hell is going on? Why is he even in New Orleans? Let alone sneaking up on me in a club and showing up here this morning. This makes no sense. I don't hear from him for what, two, maybe three weeks? I don't even know. I quit counting. Now he is trying to be all "knight in shining armor."

By the time Cade comes back with my luggage, I'm extra pissy. I nod to the bellboy who comes over to help haul my stuff to the room. Cade waves him off and then takes my hand. "I'll carry it up."

I roll my eyes so hard it hurts and yank my hand out of his. I consent to his offer because I don't want to cause a scene in the hotel lobby. We go to my room in complete silence. I stand at the door to my room. "Give me my luggage. I need to change so we can go have this talk."

"I'll take it in for you," he offers.

I put my hand flat on his chest to stop him, big mistake. The contact with his body makes me weak in the knees. I manage to regain my thoughts and say, "No. You are not welcome in my hotel room."

"Rhae, stop being hard-headed. Let me take this in for you. I'll put it on the bed and leave."

The thought of Cade being near my bed and in my hotel room makes my heart race and my breathing quicken. My brain starts to short-circuit. *Shit!* I'm angry at him. I can't feel this way.

"Put it down and leave," I say and my voice cracks nervously.

He grins, and I feel tingly in all the wrong places. Or maybe they are the right places. That damn white T-shirt and blue jeans does things to me. I open the door and enter the room, holding the door open for Cade. He comes in behind me and heads straight for the bed. I close the door.

Cade turns to look at me and like he might be about to say something but stops. I walk over to him and, with a few inches between us, I breathe in his smell; it's delicious. Just as I remembered. He reaches out and strokes my cheek with the back of his hand, and I drop my chin as he does. Using his finger, he lifts my head, so I look him in the eye.

"I am so angry with you," I blurt out. "I mean I hate you. Really. Hate."

"I know. I'm sorry," he says. He's sincere. My knees are gooey, and I'm leaning toward him.

Cade wraps his arms around me, one hand on the back of my head and the other around my waist. He draws me into a massive hug, but he doesn't squeeze. He holds me there until I melt into him. I hate that I'm so drawn to him. I feel a resurgence of anger, and when I'm about to push him away, he tightens his hold on me. At first, I struggle because I'm at war. My heart wants to stand here with him, and my brain wants me to say, "Fuck you," and run way. As a compromise, I place my hands on his chest and try to push him back a step.

"Cade. Stop. I can't. I can't be here with you like this."

"What? I'm just hugging my friend," he answers innocently.

"Friends. That's right. How could I forget?" Anger swells in my chest, and I push him away even harder. "You don't want me," I spit the words at him.

"Don't fight me, Rhae. You know what I mean. We never said we were..."

"What, Cade? We never made declarations. So, I'm still only a friend? Is that it? Is that what you wanted to talk to me about? Being your friend after you shit on me?"

"No," he says, wounded.

"Then what do you want from me?" I turn my face to see into his eyes again, and he kisses me. A mix of rage and panic fills me, and my body betrays me. I melt into his embrace and kiss him back.

I guess Cade is winning the war in my brain. I knew he would. It was pointless to think it could turn out any other way. Desire surges through my body, and I push up on my tip-toes to close any distance left between us. He reaches down and lifts me in the air as if I weigh nothing. A small squeak escapes my lips, and I wrap my legs around his waist. He holds me for a few minutes as he kisses each of my cheeks and my forehead and then leaves a trail of kisses down to my neck. He buries his face in my breasts and kisses my chest. I'm not sure what kind of sound leaves my mouth, but it is nothing coherent.

Cade laughs. "Did I find something you like?" I can hear the smile in his voice.

"Shut up," I snap. The fact that I've given in to my lust for him is annoying.

He chuckles. "Yes, ma'am."

He drops me on the bed and continues kissing my neck and chest. I throw my head back and arch towards him when he abruptly pulls away.

"C'mon. We need to talk. Let's go." He holds his hand out to me.

"What!" I say, feeling bereft.

"I said we needed to talk. I can't do this until everything is fixed between us. It's not right."

My breathing is still heavy, and I feel like I was just robbed of dessert. I tug on his hand to pull him back on the bed with me. "Yes, you can. We'll talk after." I demand.

The look in his eyes tells me I might be close to winning this battle, but then he shakes his head. "You have been in a dry spell far too long. You know you'll feel shitty if we don't fix this mess first.

Let's go. Brunch is waiting."

I growl. "You owe me big time. You know that, right?"

"I know. I'm good for it." He flashes that devilish grin I love so much.

Reluctantly, I slide off the bed and storm for the door. He always gets his way. Fucker.

Cade and I walk around the corner to a little cafe he suggests. He whispers to the hostess, smiles and takes her hand. We are then led to a table for two in a darker corner of the cafe. In fact, I look around and there is no one else seated in this section.

"Ask for some privacy, did ya?" I ask.

"It's necessary. You might try to kill me. Don't need witnesses."

"You're planning for me to have a violent reaction?"

His expression is serious. "There's a lot to talk about. Coffee?"

I smile because he knows what I need. Cade orders drinks for us, and then we order our food. Half way through our meal, he clears his throat. "Okay, let's get into it."

"Can I finish my food first?" I know when things get really intense, I'll lose my appetite.

"Well, that will delay our return to your hotel room. But if you would like to finish first, we can do that." He smirks.

Heat rushes into my face, and I know he sees it. "Talk. I'll eat."

Cade lets out a bellowing laugh, and then he starts, "I have thought over this conversation for months. Actually, I've been running some of this through my mind since the day we met." He takes a drink of coffee and I shove another bite of Belgian waffle in my mouth. I'm watching him cautiously when he says, "I love the way you eat. In fact, that's the heart of what I need to say to you. I love you."

Did he drop the L-bomb on me? And he waited for my mouth to be full to do it. I keep chewing and trying swallow. My eyes are watering from the effort.

"Are you choking or crying?" he asks, concerned. All I can do is shake my head.

"Never," I manage around all the food in my mouth. After I swallow, I repeat, "Neither. Maybe choking. Go on."

He nods. "I love you. I do. I have spent all this time thinking through the hell that you've been living in since you lost your husband. Not to mention dealing with the shitty secret affair he was keeping from you. Somehow, you still managed to wake up every morning and move forward." He pauses for some coffee. "No one would have blamed you if you wanted to lie down and wallow in it. You have more right to wallow in self-pity than any person I've ever met. I would have let you if you needed it, but you didn't. You are the very definition of a survivor."

He takes a moment before continuing, "When my grandfather passed, I went to my grandmother and demanded she tell me what she saw for you. I needed to know life would move forward for me too. I hoped she would tell me that you and I are destined to be together. All I wanted in that moment was to run to you and fall on my knees and cry and beg for you to have me."

Stunned, I say, "I wanted you to, but I didn't know if it was right. I've been a tangled mess of emotions, and I wasn't sure what I was feeling. I wanted to be wanted, but I didn't know how to handle that."

He shakes his head. "You kept me at such a distance. My grandmother refused to tell me anything. I got so mad at her, but I couldn't walk away. I had promised to help her deal with the funeral and everything with my grandfather's passing. So, I did, but not knowing and being afraid of the fool I would make of myself being around you, I did the hardest thing I have ever done. I stayed away from you."

He reaches across the table and takes my hand, looking deep into my eyes. "After a couple of days, I decided that there was no way for me to come back. If I came back I would be an even bigger fool. At this point, you had stopped trying to call me too. I thought you hated me. I turned into an obsessed stalker. I was driving by your house. I was checking in with Jess and Connor. They were telling me to suck it up and call you, but I couldn't. What would I say?"

I shake my head and then take a steadying sip of coffee before answering his rhetorical question, "You would tell me the truth. You would be that fool. You would apologize and stay with me." I stop when I feel tears welling up in my eyes.

"You're right. I'm an idiot, but I'm learning. After I went to Jess's house, I came back to yours. I ran up the stairs and started to bang on the door. I was committed to doing whatever it would take to get you to talk to me, then I saw an envelope with my name on it."

Oh shit. The letter I left him. "Did you read it?" I asked.

He nods. "I did. I knew I'd hurt you. I'm so sorry. I had to find you. I called Connor, who told me you had been at your dad's. They gave me his number, and I called him."

"*You what?* Oh, he will eat you alive!" I can't imagine what my dad could have said to him. Dad knew I was hurt.

He laughs, "Yeah, he did!"

"God. I'm so sorry." I say, sincerely apologetic.

"No. Don't be sorry. I took the heat. I fucked up. What else could I do? Deny it? That's not who I am. When he finished yelling at me, I apologized for hurting you. He let me finish, and then all he said was 'New Orleans' and hung up on me."

That sounds like my dad. First, he doesn't like using the phone. Second, he doesn't like people hurting his girls. Third, he doesn't say goodbye. He wasn't pissy when he hung up, that's just Dad.

Cade continues, "I jumped in my truck and drove here. I didn't even pack anything. I'm surprised you didn't notice my wrinkled clothes. I've been sleeping in them. Sorry about that, by the way. I probably smell like a barn animal."

We laugh together and all the burden I have been carrying around seems to lift a little bit.

"Anyway, I didn't know how to find you. I got to the city around dark and I wandered around. I walked the quarter and every street I could, hoping I would see you. And I did. It was well after dark, and I saw you come out of the hotel. My heart was hammering when I was sure it was you. You're the most gorgeous creature I have ever laid eyes on. More beautiful than my memory had left me with." Cade reaches up and tucks a curl behind my ear, then places his hand on my cheek.

I turn my face into his hand. "And then?" I ask.

"I thought I might crumble from the inside. I needed to be near you. You'll have to forgive me for not grabbing you immediately. It was so fascinating to me to see you observe the people and the city. You have such a zeal for life, for analyzing everything."

The tears welling up in my eyes start spilling down my cheeks. I hadn't expected to understand how he sees me.

He wipes the tears off my cheeks. "I can see the wheels in your mind turning every time we talk. Every time I see you take in a new situation. It is mind-blowing how you commit details to memory and figure people out in a single moment. It is actually a little overwhelming, too. You intimidate people with how well you read them. That's why I was so insistent you talk to grandma. You remind me of her."

I laugh. "So, you found me. And you've gone full-blown stalker."

"I apologize for the stalker bit, but knowing how pissed you were going to be, I had to approach you carefully. I followed you into the club and took a seat where I could watch you. The way you were dancing was mesmerizing. When I saw you head back to the floor after a break, my resolve was trashed. I had to touch you. I had to be the one to dance with you. The rest is history, as they say."

I sit in stunned silence. The prevalent feeling swirling around my brain is that he came for me. He came to find me. He didn't leave because he was angry or disappointed with me. He didn't leave because he couldn't deal with his grandfather. I had intimidated him into thinking we would never be more than great friends. This is as much my fault as it is his. I shake my head and reach to wipe the tears.

"I can't say it yet. I want to love you. There's nothing in this world that I want more than to love and be loved in return. I just don't have it in me right now. Can we move forward on an *I'll try* basis?" I swallow several times to help alleviate the overwhelming urge to fall apart in this very public place. I really do want to say I love him in return. I chance a look at him and hope lights his face. He drops money on the table, stands, and reaches for my hand. I take it, and he pulls me from my chair.

"I'll take what I can get."

All I can do is nod. Standing in the middle of this little cafe, he kisses me. It's a kiss like none-other we've shared. It is intense, and for the first time in my life, I know what everyone means by "toe-curling." I swear I can feel flames between my legs.

14
Firsts

We walk back to the hotel holding hands. I can help but lay my head on his shoulder every now and then. Being apart from Cade was an agony I couldn't bear. Being back beside him and being more than we were before feels like the greatest gift I've ever been given. As we enter the hotel room, I'm all hands. Grabbing for him. He gets the door closed, and I pull him to me and wrap my arms around him tightly.

"Ugh, Rhae, can't breathe," he wheezes out.

"Sorry. I just needed you to know how much you mean to me." I look up to his eyes and they are alive in a way I haven't noticed before. Like the sun itself shines through him.

"Call your dad and Jess," he says with a smile.

"What? Uh, I had other..." I stammer.

"I know. I have more plans for you too, but I told them I would have you call once I found you and we had our talk. I promised, actually."

I groan. "Really? Okay." I walk over to my purse sitting on the desk and fish out my cell. I call Jess first. All she wanted to know is whether or not I accepted his story and if I was happy to see him. I assure her I am super happy, and everything is fine. I also agree to call her back when I have a moment to go into details without an audience—Cade—around.

The call to my dad was even shorter. I told him Cade had shown up and that we were fine. He answered simply, "That's good. Be happy, baby."

After I hung up with my family, I turned to see Cade had fallen asleep on my bed. He must not have been resting well. Our time apart wasn't hard on just me. It had taken a toll on him as well. Drawing the curtains to darken the room, I decide to let him rest. We have all the time we need now. There's no hurry. We're finally together and everything is on the table. A feeling of satisfaction and a sense of home washes over me.

Gently sitting on the edge of the bed, I bend down and untie my shoes. I take them off and place them under the accent chair. I slide my jeans off, then pull my secret bra maneuver and pull it through the sleeve of my T-shirt. Crawling onto the bed, I snuggle into the nook of his arm and rest my head on his chest. His arm automatically tightens around me, and he kisses the top of my head.

"So tired, baby," he murmurs.

"I know. Rest. We have all the time we need." We succumb to our exhaustion having finally found some kind of peace.

Warmth envelopes me, and I slowly awaken. Cade has covered us with the comforter and is wrapped around me from behind. Endeavoring to be even closer to him, I turn over and snuggle into his chest. He kisses the top of my head, and I sigh contentedly. I kiss the hollow of his throat and work my way up his neck to his mouth. He kisses me tenderly. My mouth parts and we are a mash of sloppy, uncoordinated tongues.

"It's okay," Cade mumbles and pulls back from me. "Relax."

"Sorry," I apologize, feeling reprimanded for my gusto.

"Don't be sorry. We just have to find our rhythm." Cade starts to kiss my neck, and I feel all the tension leave my body as I relax into the mattress and allow him to move down my body. His hands slide down my side and under my shirt. Pushing my shirt out the way on his way up, he kisses across my belly. I am nervous about whether or not he'll think my body is ugly or wrong, but it feels so good that the thought doesn't last long. He reaches my breasts, and I sit up to remove the shirt over my head.

Not one to waste a moment, Cade takes advantage of my temporary distraction to wrap his arms around me and roll us over so I'm on top of him. Straddling his lap, I lean down for another kiss. He holds me close and kisses me deeply. Kissing him could be my new favorite hobby. He uses his lips like an artist painting a masterpiece. He gently teases one moment, and then ravages my lips in the next. Maybe because it's been so long since I've been kissed, but I want to drown in him.

Tangling my hands in his hair to kiss him deeper, I'm trying to eliminate any space there might be between our bodies. His skin is warm, and I can't seem to touch him enough. The fuzz on his chest and belly tickle my skin, and I run my fingers through it. Cade lets out a groan and moves his hands to my hips. I lift so he can slide my panties down and out of the way. Turning us again so that he hovers above me, he kisses me quickly and stands beside the bed. I'm given quite the show as I watch him peel out his trademark jeans and white T-shirt. Dammit, he wears boxer briefs. Who would have known? A big smile forms on my face.

"What are you smiling at?" Cade asks with the corner of his mouth turning up a little bit. I can tell he's fighting a smile of his own. "See anything you like?"

"I was just enjoying the view."

"Really? Do you mind if I lose them?"

"Not at all. Carry on."

He removes the source of my amusement and climbs back into bed with me. He holds me tenderly and explores every inch of my body with his mouth. I'm writhing under his touch, unable to calm my nerves. I steady myself by holding onto his arms. They are strong, and I can feel the definition of every muscle under his skin. As he moves back to my mouth, his hands trace where his mouth has already been. Cade kisses behind my ear as one hand moves to my breast and the other caresses my ass. I arch my back and a groan because I can't contain myself. He continues his multiple assaults on my body, as an orgasm builds deep within me. It has been so long that the approaching feeling of release brings tears to my eyes.

"Shhh, I've got you." He reaches a hand down between my legs and uses his fingers to bring me closer to the edge. It takes only a minute to find release so violently that my body is shaking. I cry out. His mouth is on mine instantly, trying to absorb some of my moans. He kisses me through the duration of my orgasm, and more tears streak down my face. Cade kisses the line of each tear and asks, "You okay?" I barely manage a nod, and he kisses me again.

My desire for him becomes stronger and stronger until I'm holding his shoulders and digging my nails into his back. Urging him closer, I wrap my legs around his waist and squeeze a little. He groans loudly and devours my mouth. Pulling back, he stares into my eyes as he takes me. I feel satisfyingly full, and another orgasm is building already. I relax and allow it to take me again. Cade is moving slowly, and it is a ridiculously great feeling.

Sweat dots his brow. Using all my strength I push him over and onto his back. I move over him and lower myself back onto his erection. We move together as he takes my breasts in his hands. The idea of satisfying him excites me and motivates me to quicken our pace until he let's go. Together, we reach our release. I revel in the face and sounds he makes when he finishes and then collapse on his chest as he holds me. We are breathing roughly, and sweat coats our skin.

"Oh, my God." I pant.

"Yeah, I know," he answers.

"What a wake-up call. You can wake me up like that anytime."

Cade chuckles. "Every day."

I sit up to look at him. "Every day?"

"Every day."

I laugh as I move to cuddle into his side again. "We probably need to find some food. We haven't eaten since brunch. What time is it anyway?"

He looks at his watch. "Uh, it's eleven-thirty."

"A.m. or p.m.?"

"P.m."

"What? We slept all day?"

He chuckles. "Afraid so."

"My God, don't ever put us through this again," I threaten. "We've burned too much energy trying to fix this."

Cade takes the moment seriously. "Never again. I love you too much." We rest lying together for another couple hours. Sometimes we can't help but kiss each other. Sometimes we just lie motionless and talk. Eventually, we both cave and sleep some more.

I'm walking through a field of sunflowers. It is a hot day, there's sweat on the back of my neck. Someone walking on the far side of the field from me, and I call out, "Mama?"

"You make me so proud," she answers.

"I do?"

"Yes, you do."

She is beyond my reach, but I can faintly see her smile. She is brighter than the sun surrounding her. The light is too much for my eyes, and it's hurting to keep my eyes on her.

"I have always been proud of you. I'm afraid I died without telling you enough," she says sadly.

Crying, I yell to her, "I love you. Don't leave me. Promise you'll stay. I can't lose you again."

"I promise. Anytime you need me, I'll be here. I love you more than you could ever know."

I start to shake.

"Are you okay?" Cade rubs my arm gently. "Honey, are you okay? Wake up."

Slowly coming around, I notice that light is filling our room. Sitting up, I wipe my eyes with the heels of my hands.

"Rhae, what is it? Are you okay?"

"I'm fine. I think. It was a dream. I've been having a lot of them lately."

"Not good then?" he asks gently.

"No, it was amazing. I saw my mama. She was telling me how much she loves me and is proud of me. That was part of what Irma and I talked about. How I'm seeing my mama and Ryan in my dreams. Their spirits are lingering. Something about what a mess my life is. Was."

"And now?"

"And now? I don't know. The dream I had makes me think Mama is leaving again. She is satisfied with everything. I can let her go peacefully. It feels like I'm losing her. It's been so long since I felt the sting of losing her." I stop. I don't want to cry.

"Grandma always says spirits come to us when we need them. You needed her after all the hell of losing Ryan, and then when I pulled what I did." He stops and swallows, "God, I'm so sorry I did that. I'm an idiot."

"No. This isn't your fault. I did need her. She needs to be at peace though. I have to get used to the idea of not seeing her anymore."

"Because you're happy?"

I grin. "Yes, silly."

Cade smiles the smile that melts my insides. "And, what is it that you want?"

I shake my head. "Nope. I want a shower and breakfast."

Cade looks disappointed, and I lean over to kiss him before sliding off the bed and heading for the bathroom. Letting the water warm while I gather my towels and toiletries, I stand in front of the mirror and take in my fresh appearance. My skin and eyes are bright. No signs of dark circles. No sign of stress or apprehension. I turn to check the water and run smack-dab into Cade.

"Well, hello there," I say with an exaggerated southern accent.

"Hi," he answers sweetly before wrapping me in his arms. I rise up on my toes, and he kisses me sweetly. He kisses me until my knees nearly buckle and my toes are curling again.

"Wow." I breathe. "Shower?"

"Don't mind if I do." He strips me out of the T-shirt I was using as a cover up until the shower got warm. Of course, being handsome and confident, he's walking around naked. Hey, I won't complain. The scenery is nice. He steps into the water and holds his hand out to help me in. The water is just right, and I stand under the stream with my eyes closed, rinsing away the roller coaster of emotions. Heat from the water lets the happy sink in. At least, that's what I imagine the water doing.

My back is to Cade. He grabs the shampoo and begins to lather my hair. "I love the shorter hair, by the way. I don't think I said anything about it when I saw you yesterday."

"Nope, you didn't mention it. I was so pissed at you that I didn't think to get mad at you for not noticing. It's not the biggest thing that happened in Florida either," I say teasing.

"Really? What else did you do in Florida?" he asks while he

finishes applying conditioner to my hair.

I turn to face him and reach for the body wash. "Well, it was a spa day with Clea. We got massages, mani/pedis, haircuts, and..." I trail off. Heat rushes my face, and Cade grabs my chin to force me to look at him.

"What is it? Why are you blushing?"

"Waxes. We got waxes," I spit it out and pull away from him.

"Really?" he asks and makes a move to look.

I jump, "Cade! Don't! I don't think I want that experience again. Besides, it's growing back."

"Don't be shy. I plan to study every inch of you. Anyway, it doesn't matter to me either way. I love your body anyway I can get it. We will cherish each other from now on. Don't you think?"

"You sound like a girl sometimes," I say jokingly, "but yes, I agree. Too much has shown me that I can't take anything for granted. Ever."

I pull back from him and grab the wash cloth and soap. I wash him, and he finishes by taking care of me. After our shower, Cade steps out first and passes me a couple towels. I wrap one around my head. When I lean back and secure my towel, I notice he is still standing in the bathroom with nothing but a towel around his waist. The view stuns me into silence. A breath catches in my throat.

"What is it?" he asks.

"Nothing. You just...you should get dressed."

"Silly." He steps toward me, kisses the tip of my nose, and returns to the sink to brush his teeth.

I wrap a towel around my body and step out. Joining him at the sink, I stare at our reflection in the mirror. Content doesn't begin to describe this feeling. Recalling the tirades of the Dragon Lady, I find that I don't care about propriety. Being with Cade is right. That's all I need to know.

When we've finished our morning routine, we decide to find breakfast. So, we head back to the cafe that was the scene of our big talk. While I'm shoveling in some eggs and bacon, Cade looks pensive. I stop chewing and drink my coffee.

"Are you okay?" I ask.

Clarity finds his expression. "I'm perfect. Absolutely perfect. I do have something I need to tell you, though."

I turn to look at him sideways, and ask the most ridiculous thing I can think of, "You aren't married, are you?"

His laugh is a huge belly laugh. "God, no. I've waited a lifetime to find someone like you. No one ever came close. No. It's about New Orleans."

"Okay. What could you possibly have to tell me about New Orleans?"

"I live here."

"What? You live here?" I remember he was only *visiting* Irma and his grandfather, but I never thought to ask where he called home.

"It's one of the reasons I was so excited and made such an effort to find you here. It felt like God was hanging one more sign pointing to you. You ran from your home to mine." He is smiling like a Cheshire cat.

"That's...that's...um..." I am at a loss for words.

"Weird, right?"

"Yeah, but kind of great at the same time." I smile.

"After we finish breakfast, I'd like to show you my house."

"Yes! Let's go now!"

We finish in record time and pay the check. He'd left his truck parked near the club where he stalked me. I'm still disturbed by that whole story, but I'm trying to understand what would drive someone to that.

Me. *I* drove him to it.

We make quick work of the walk and soon we're on our way. I can't keep up with all the twists and turns, but on the outskirts of the city, we pull into a neighborhood that seems as ancient as New Orleans itself. The house is beautiful. We are greeted by a wide porch with steps and floorboards painted a dark, shiny green. Flowerbeds full of azaleas are on either side of the steps. They span the width of the house. The railing is the same color as the rest of the house, a titanium white. Brighter than any white I've ever seen. If I didn't know what Cade had been through in the last few months, visiting and helping his grandparents, I would think he had just had it painted.

He leads me up the stairs and grins like a little boy at an amusement park. When up on the porch, I turn to the right and notice a dark green porch swing. I smile thinking of the similarities of his home and his grandparents' house in Bell Hills. He notices the direction I'm looking and says, "I know." He unlocks the door and leads me into the house. It looks newly remodeled. Like new construction. Modern updates everywhere. He doesn't lead me around; he lets me explore on my own. I walk every room on the first floor. The kitchen is massive. In a house this size, and this old, he must have sacrificed another room to make the kitchen this big. I find Cade standing in the foyer, patiently waiting for my exploration to bring me back to him.

"Who's that kitchen for? You don't cook."

"Assumptions, Rhae," he corrects.

"You're right. I mean, wow, you use that kitchen? Sure you didn't build it, so you could get a woman to make you sammiches?"

"I do, actually. That is all for me. I love to cook. Grandma won't let me when I'm at her house. Come on, let me show you the upstairs."

He leads me to the stairs and I look around at all four bedrooms on the second floor. They are fantastic rooms. He has paid attention to the details in two of them. The other two are plain. No pictures, no decor, no colors. The rooms contain only a bed with white linens.

"This house is so much more than I imagined for you, no offense."

"None taken. I did all the work myself. It was abandoned after Katrina. I bought it from the bank. I always wanted to have a family. I built a place for one in the hopes that one day, I would have one."

His idea of having a family gives me pause. "Living on that 'if you build it' philosophy?" I ask.

"Maybe. You're here now, and that's a start."

I smile. "What are you saying?"

He takes both of my hands and moves closer to me. "I want you to live here with me. We can talk about marriage and family and all of that later. Just come to New Orleans and live with me."

My heart is racing. I should say no. This is wrong. I have plans. I was going to travel. Experience life. I can't do that if I jump right into living with him. On the other hand, we've been through so much. I mean, we don't even sleep when we're apart. I need him. He seems to need me. Before I can finish all the lists of reasons I shouldn't do this, I begin to slowly nod. "Yes." I said it because I shouldn't do this. Everything about it is too fast. I don't know if he'll run off on me again. I don't know anything. Maybe that's why I said yes. Embracing the unknown.

"Yes? You will?" His face is lit up like a Christmas tree.

I laugh. "Yes."

He wraps me in a crushing hug and kisses me.

"Cade. Can't breathe. Hang on, I need to check out of the hotel."

"Now? You'll stay now?"

"I will. Wherever you are is my home," I say simply.

Cade practically tackles me. He is all hands, and his mouth is everywhere. He leads me into the master bedroom and we spend the remainder of the morning and most of the afternoon worshipping each other in his luxury king-sized bed.

That evening we drive over to the hotel to retrieve my belongings and pay the bill. The desk clerk looks disappointed when Cade informs her I am checking out. The death stare I level at her keeps her from interacting with him any more than absolutely necessary.

For a moment, I consider that I don't want this to be our life. Girls constantly noticing him and throwing flirtatious smiles and gestures his way. I'm going to end up being that jealous woman and kicking somebody's ass. Ryan's affair has shaken my ability to trust.

Then it occurs to me that Cade doesn't return any of their smiles or gestures. He doesn't notice them. I also notice he can't go a few minutes without touching me in some way. Brushing his hand across my hand, tucking a piece of hair behind my ear, an arm around my waist as we walk into a building or out to the car, or holding my hand everywhere we go. It's like he's afraid I'll run.

We step out on to Dauphine as we leave the hotel. I pull his arm back as he's holding my hand again. He comes to a stop and turns to face me. "You okay?"

"I'm not going anywhere," I reassure him.

"I know."

"You can let go of me and I'll still be right here. There's no need to keep a hand on me at all times. In fact, you might drive me crazy after a few days of that," I joke.

He smiles. "I just can't help but think this is a dream. That if I let you go, I'll wake up and this won't be happening at all. I'll try to give you a little space."

"You think I'm a dream?" I ask, incredulous.

"Well, one of those weird dreams that's great at first and turns all crazy after a while." He has jokes now.

"Oh, I see. So, I need to kick your ass, then?"

He lets out a hearty laugh. I don't. I meant it. On the drive home, we discuss what to do with my house. *Oh my...* Home. With Cade. Not an idea I've settled into yet.

"Well, I was going to sell it, but I had an idea. You might think it's crazy."

"All right, what were you thinking?"

I lay out my idea for him. He looks shocked, but he smiles and nods. "That's perfect. So you. I love it. What do we need to do to make that happen?"

"I don't know. I need to call my real estate agent and see what she says. Maybe call my friend from school who's an attorney. He might have thoughts on what I need to do to make that happen with all the legal stuff."

"So, what about the rest of your vacation?" he asks.

"Well, I still haven't seen New Orleans. I had tour plans and whatnot."

"I see. Well, then, I'll need to put on my tour guide hat. Do you want historic or party? Maybe cemeteries and voodoo queens' graves?"

"All of the above. I want the whole experience."

"Can do, Ms. Rhae."

A Place to Stand

15
Interrupted

We spent the next two weeks doing all the normal tours and shopping. Cade talks about the city like an old friend. He mixes his tour of the city with stories from his college days. Turns out he didn't grow up in New Orleans. For the most part, he grew up in south Mississippi. I finally got to ask about his parents. I learn that his mother took off on him when he was just four years old. His dad raised him as best he could. What made it difficult was his dad worked construction and oil rig jobs. Which meant Cade had to spend huge chunks of time with Irma. It explains so much of their relationship. She raised him.

What is most surprising is that he hasn't ever attempted to find his mother. I start to push for more information, but it is a subject that makes him shut down. It is not open for discussion. At all. This seems to be the only thing he keeps away from me. I do my best to be understanding. I don't like it, but what can I do but wait.

In addition to the regular tours and shopping, Cade takes me for picnics. It is his favorite way to spend the waning afternoons. That time of day between lunch and sunset, when the sky seems to be painted by the very hand of God. Clouds are carefully arranged like finger-paintings against a background of ever changing skies. I look forward to our daily time together on a quilt. The problem is the temperature dropping more and more each day. Eventually we are sitting on a quilt having a picnic wrapped in sweaters and blankets.

One afternoon, I feel the need to point out the end to our outdoor adventures. "You know we can't picnic anymore this year. It is getting too cold."

He looks reluctant to admit defeat but concedes the loss of the season. "What now?" he asks.

I have plenty of ideas, but I start with one that needs to be addressed. "Let's go get my house squared away."

"Have you managed to get everything ready to execute the plan?"

"I think so. The rest we can do while we are in Bell Hills. I have a whole house to pack. Plus, there's all of Ryan's stuff in the attic to deal with. We may need to stay there more than a couple days."

"Have you told your dad and the sisters?"

"No. I don't know where to start on the phone. Somehow, my traipsing around the U.S. like a nomad is better than me living with a man I've only known for a little while. Especially, one that ran off on me once before."

He screws his face up as if he's in pain, "Ouch. Okay. So, we'll do that while we're there."

"I didn't mean to hurt your feelings. It's just a fact." This always happens. I state a fact and people get hurt. It's what happened.

"It's okay. I understand."

"Yeah. I love you. Remember that."

"I do. I love you, too."

We pack up and walk back to his truck at the edge of the field, right where we always leave it. As we approach, someone is leaning against the side of the truck. The closer we get, I can see that it is a woman. She is thin, and her long, wavy, honey brown hair blowing in the wind. I look for Cade beside me to ask if he knows her, but I get the answer when I turn to see he is stock-still five or six feet behind me.

"Cade? Who is that? What's wrong?" I ask as I step back to his side. He doesn't move. His face falls and he looks down at his feet. I ask again, "Who is that?" I feel heat moving into my cheeks and a chill run down my body.

He looks up from his feet to meet my gaze. "Just... whatever she says, don't say anything to her."

"I don't understand."

"Don't talk to her. Don't let her goad you into a fuss. Trust me. Trust us. Please."

Weird. I really don't have a choice. I have to trust him. I take his free hand and nod. "I do trust you. I'll get in the truck and let you talk to her alone. You can explain later." He kisses me quickly, and we walk to the truck hand-in-hand.

Getting a good look at her, I can see that, at one time, she might have been gorgeous. Now? Well, now she is prettier from farther away. I recall the documentaries on TV about meth addiction and realize she has all the markers of that particular demon. Her face has pits that look like acne gone very bad. Her hair lacks any shine or luster. Her eyes are sad, and her cheeks are sunken in too far for what I think her age might be. She is rail thin. Girl needs a good meal.

I take the blanket from Cade and load our things into the truck before getting in myself. Cade's face looks like he has seen a ghost. He almost looks sick or scared. Curiosity is eating me up, but I keep my word. I don't engage this woman. I wait in the truck. I never promised I wouldn't try to read her lips. Actually, might be better if I lower the window a little bit. I roll it all the way down.

"Well, Cade Miles!" she says overly exaggerated as if she's run into him on the quarter.

"Shawna," Cade greets her coldly.

"No kiss for me?" she asks, and I feel sick.

Cade is stone cold. "No. What brings you around today?"

"That's no way to greet your fiancée, Cade. Irma would be so angry for you treating me this way. It's not proper."

"Former fiancée," Cade corrects. "You ended our relationship when you chose the needle over me. Now, why are you here?"

"It's our place. I knew you'd eventually come back, and I need a favor." She slinks closer to him, and it is all I can do not to jump out of the truck and beat her ass. This once I wish Jess or Liz were here to see this shit. Cade takes a step back for every step she takes toward him.

"Aw, baby, don't be that way. I'm better now. I'm off it."

"How stupid do you think I am? I can see you are still on that shit. Now, what do you want?"

"Nothing. Honest. Who's your friend?" She peers around him to the truck. *Shit.* I bet she tries to come talk to me.

"You don't worry about her. What do you want, Shawna? You never show up unless you want something."

She closes in on him and reaches out to stroke his chest. She does her best to look up at him under eyelashes. Oh, she is a pro. "I just, I just need… I need a little bit of money."

"There it is. I knew it. How much?" he asks. The look on his face is hard. It's like he's not human anymore. He's carved from stone.

Trying to work her mojo on him, she whines, "Well, it's for this guy. I mean, he had to come out and fix my front door. I owe him a little money or he's gonna call the parish police."

"Stop it, Shawna. How much?"

"Twenty-five hundred."

Cade laughs. "For a front door? Liar. You're on that shit, and you owe your dealer. Get away from here and don't come back. I ain't giving you a dime." I can hear his voice getting louder. She keeps begging, and eventually realizes he won't give in, so she leaves.

Cade takes a couple minutes to recover. He's standing with his hands on his hips, staring off in the distance. I don't try to talk to him. I do my best to sit patiently and wait. Cade looks absolutely worn out when he climbs in the truck with me. He lays his head on the steering wheel and takes several deep breaths. I don't say a word. I sit in silence and wait for him to talk. I can tell he needs time to process the emotions she stirred up. Eventually, he looks at me and picks my hand up off the seat to hold.

"Thank you. I know you heard a lot of that. I know I need to explain, but can we just go home first?" he asks.

"Of course," I answer. I'm worried about him but try to trust that he'll tell me everything he can. When he can.

He squeezes my hand, and we drive back to the house. Cade remains distant and disconnected as he seems to process things.

When we arrive, something feels off. I can't put my finger on it, but I grab Cade's hand. "Don't get out. Turn the truck around and leave. Something's wrong."

He looks at me and studies the house. "I don't think anything's wrong. Let's go inside."

Before I can protest again, he's out of the truck. Reluctantly, I move to open my own door, and it is shoved closed again. I jump at the sight of the man who slammed the door on me. He's holding a gun. I search for Cade and see him being held by a couple huge guys while a third is punching him. I scream, but it doesn't do any good. The man by my door makes a "shh" motion using his gun across his lips.

I slide my hand to my phone beside me. The guy isn't watching me completely, so I try not to make a noise. Pulling my phone into my lap, I glance down and slide the lock icon open. I hear a thud against the window and look up. The gunman is trying to break the window.

"Bitch! Put the fucking phone down. Ain't no one coming to save the day."

I look around for a way out of this truck. No one is covering the driver's side. I throw my hands up, and show the phone is locked again. I mouth "I'm sorry." I sit quietly and wait. Eventually, he turns to see what's happening with Cade. The men seem like they are trying to bargain with Cade. Too bad you can't bargain with a man who has been beaten and is hanging limply in the support of goons. Cade keeps shaking his head.

While the gunman guarding me isn't paying attention, I slide over and crawl out of the driver's side door. I drop to the ground as quietly as possible, which isn't quiet at all on a gravel driveway. I can't be sure the gunman isn't looking for me, so I do my best to gather my wits and take off running. I think we left the back-porch door unlocked. I might be able to get in and call the police from inside the house. Maybe even grab Cade's hunting rifle and help him. I may not be an ace shooter, but I can make noise and scare them.

I start running, but before I reach the corner of the house, I'm tackled. The gravel cuts into my knees, and then my face slams into it. There is so much pain that I can't remember what I was doing. The man who tackled me is sitting on my back, and he grabs a handful of my hair to pull my face up. I can't see him, but I smell him. He smells sickly sweet, like candy with too much sugar, and there's a musk of cigarette smoke, too.

"Dumb bitch. Where was you headed? You can't help him. You ready to run out on him that fast? Not in for the long haul?"

I don't answer. I focus on being still and not vomiting. He's heavy on my back, and I can barely breathe anyway. He pulls my hair harder.

"Answer me, bitch. Whatcha think you gon' do to help him?"

I don't answer, but I do manage to spit. My mouth is full of a salty, copper-flavored liquid. I think my lip is busted. Apparently, my guard doesn't appreciate my unladylike behavior, and he punches me across the back of my head. I see dark spots and drop my face to the gravel driveway. He grabs my head again and pulls my face toward his. He's even closer than before.

"You sure are nice lookin'. Don't think I've ever seen you 'round these parts before. Think we can have some fun while my boys finish up with Cade there?"

He flips me over and straddles my body, and he slides my shirt up. Panic fills me. I have to get my bearings. Panic won't save me from this asshole. I try to think through the self-defense classes I attended in college. How can I get free? Do I have the strength to overpower him? I have to get myself free. When the asshole grabs my breasts, I lose my mind.

I spit blood in his face. When he recoils, and starts to wipe at his eyes, I roll my body. He's thrown off balance, and I know this is the only chance I'll get. I scramble to my feet and I kick. I land a good one in his stomach and then his face. I'm not sure how many names I call him, but while he writhes on the ground, I run to the back of the house.

Shaking all over, I open the back door and lock it once I'm inside. I can't think about myself. I grab the phone and run to the front window. Cade is still being held. The man who seems to be in charge hits him again. Cade won't last much longer. Out of the corner of my eye, Shawna gets out of the big ass SUV parked to the side. She's screaming at the man hitting Cade.

"Joey, you said you wouldn't hurt him. Stop!"

Things you should think about before getting your dealer over here to pound someone for money, bitch. I look down at the phone and dial. It takes a couple rings, and the operator answers, "911 what's your emergency?"

"My name is Rhae Peters. I'm with Cade Miles. We are at 1311 Forrest..." before I can finish there's a crashing sound at the back of the house. God! That idiot is breaking in. I bolt for the stairs, thinking I can hide from him upstairs. Before I make it that far, he's got me. I drop the phone and it skids into the foyer. I kick and scream, but he's carrying me toward the front door. I manage to land one good kick to his knee.

"Bitch." He growls in my ear. "I can't wait to kill you!"

"Kill me now! If you don't, you are going to pay for this."

"I'd love to see that. I like a woman that'll fight back. Wanna play rough?"

I struggle more, and someone calls out, "Beau, get your ass out here. She can't be that hard to handle." That must be Joey. The man in charge.

I can't help myself. Hell, I don't want to die being weak. "Yeah, Beau. I can't be that hard to handle," I taunt him.

Beau grabs my throat and squeezes. I begin to choke and gasp for air. He pulls me backward through the door and stumbles as we drop down the porch steps. When we reach the bottom, he slings me to the ground. I catch myself on my palms, which immediately begin to ache. I think I've scraped them pretty good. Refusing to go down so easily, I stand and face the situation ahead of me.

The man whistles. "No wonder Beau is a mess. You are a fine lady. Come to me." He crooks his finger, beckoning me.

"Joey, was it? Yeah, you can forget that."

"Aw, cher, you want me to hurt Cade here some more. My boys can oblige."

"Stop! No." Against my better instincts, I walk toward him.

"There's a good girl. Now then, Cade, I want the money and I want it now."

Cade shakes his head. He looks like he can't take one more blow. Blood is everywhere. Tears start streaming down my face. Cade swallows hard, "Fuck off, Joey. You and your crackhead cousin ain't getting shit from me."

Joey is apparently very unhappy with Cade's answer. He grabs me and holds a knife to my neck. "If that's the way you want it, I'll just cut this bitch's throat. By the way, bitch, what is your name?"

Cade pulls against the goons holding him. Beau is still standing by the porch. "Yeah Joey! Show that bitch the time of her life, man."

"Answer me, girl. What's your name? I will cut your throat."

"Rhae."

"Well, Rhae, say goodbye to lover boy. May angels greet you, baby." Joey increases the pressure of the knife on my neck. Shawna is screaming. Cade is struggling and is completely out of strength. Finally, he answers, "Joey! Leave her alone. You can have it."

"That's a good boy. But I'm afraid that, for this one, the price just doubled. I want five thousand."

"Fine. Fine. Whatever you..."

Sirens fill the air. Lights are flashing all the way down the street. Shawna screams and runs for the SUV. I guess self-preservation trumps all. The goons drop Cade and run. Beau has a big lead on the others. I think he's the kind of chickenshit punk that runs at the first sign of trouble. Joey is the last. He points to Cade. "This is far from over."

Cade collapses into a heap on the ground. I take a few steps to get to him and fall beside him. I crawl the rest of the way and pull him into my lap. He groans. I start to cry even harder. He's going to die. I'm going to sit here with his head in my lap and watch him die. "Please hold on. Don't die. I can't lose you." I'm pleading with him. He can't hear me because he is unconscious and barely breathing. "It'll be okay. You're gonna be okay." I repeat over and over until the EMTs arrive.

Everything around me turns to chaos. The police are asking me questions while the EMTs work on Cade. I don't pay attention to the questions they ask me. I nod or say yes or no while watching him. The officer puts his hand on my arm. "Rhae, honey, don't look. Let them help him. He's in good hands. Talk to me." He leads me to the other side of the truck where I can't see anything.

He asks me to tell him what happened. Holding a wad of gauze to my face, covering the scrapes, I start talking. I tell him what happened with Shawna this afternoon. I tell him how the men jumped Cade as soon as we got home. How Beau held me hostage in the truck. Then how I tried to get away and was nearly raped.

"Do you think you can identify them all?"

"I know I can. I can even describe the car they left in."

"Well, I know who Joey is. Shawna and Joey have done this kind of thing before. They are cousins or something. We'll get them. Don't you worry." He is reassuring, but I'm anxious to see Cade. I turn to walk over and check on him. They have him in the back of the ambulance and are leaving. I yell for them to stop. I want to go with him, so I start running.

"Woah! Wait!" The officer yells at me. I give up running and start crying again. "I'll give you a ride. You need to be checked out at the hospital anyway." The police officer loads me in the front seat of the car and hands me my purse. I guess he got it out of Cade's truck. We ride to the hospital in near total silence. When we arrive, I say, "Thank you officer..."

He smiles, and says, "It's Fournier. Officer Jonathan Fournier."

"Thank You officer Fournier. For everything." I step out of the car and make my way into the emergency department. I hear the sounds of doctors and nurses working franticly as I approach the desk. The clerk says she doesn't know anything yet. Officer Fournier informs the clerk that I need to be checked as well. I'm escorted to a bed behind a thin blue curtain.

Several hours later the clerk informs me, "Ms. Peters? Cade would like to see you now."

I stand. "Where is he?" I ask.

She takes me to the back of the emergency department. He is in a bed propped up. I step in the room and stop on the edge of the doorway. As I do, he turns his head to look at me. "Hi, beautiful."

I move to his side and take his hand. "Hey." I can't help it, I start crying again.

"Woah, woah, woah, I'm okay. Just bruised. They are going to keep me a little while. I need to heal up and make sure I don't have a concussion. I'm going to be fine."

"Sure you are. I had to stand there with a gun in my face watching you get kicked all over the yard. Who was that?" I'm trying to tame my anger.

He looks down. "Shawna's cousin. He's also her dealer. She owes him money and told him I was an easy mark. That I would give them whatever to keep them from killing her. They were waiting on me because I refused to give the money to her. This is what they do."

"I told Officer Fournier about Shawna. He said he knows what's up with them, and he will get them."

"You can trust Jonathan when he says that. He's a good guy."

"You know him?"

"Yeah, we went to college together. My best pal. Always the DD."

I nod and lay my head on his hand as I sit in the chair by his bed.

"Get some rest, Rhae. We'll be out of here soon. Did they check you out?"

"Yeah. I'm fine. Just a few scrapes."

He seems agitated, "What did they do to you?"

I shake my head. "Nothing. I'm fine. Nothing happened to me." I think I almost have him convinced when I start crying. "Really, I'm fine."

"I will kill him for putting his hands on you. Do you hear me? I. Will. Kill. Him."

"No. Let the police handle it. I'm okay. I fought back really hard. They only managed to rough me up."

"It's okay. They will. They will handle it. It's okay." It's a mantra. I'm not sure if he means it to make me feel better or himself. He rubs the back of my head as I rest it on his bed. "Rest, baby."

Eventually, I move over to the chair by the window and curl up to sleep. Cade has been in and out with the pain meds they give him. Sometime during the night, a nurse covers me with a blanket. I snuggle deeper into the chair.

In the morning light, I wake up to voices in the room. I sit up, wipe my eyes and stretch.

"There she is," Cade says.

I look around and see that the police officer that brought me to the hospital is sitting on the end of Cade's hospital bed. I put my feet on the floor and prepare to stand up. Everything aches from sleeping in the chair, though.

"Good morning, Ms. Peters."

"Good morning Officer Fournier."

"Jonathan. You call me Jonathan."

"Okay, Jonathan. If you call me Rhae. Did you get them?"

"I did." He smiles broadly. "Caught them at their apartment near the quarter. We got them for assault, possession with intent to distribute, weapons charges, and a number of felony probation violations. They should be arraigned today. We have enough to put them under the jail for a good long while."

Relief washes over me. "Thank you. Thank you so much." I walk over and hug him. I think I take him by surprise because it takes a second before he hugs me back.

"That's enough. Let go of my girl," Cade says, laughing from his bed.

I turn to face him. "Your girl, huh?"

"My girl."

A Place to Stand

16
Home

Cade is released from the hospital. He is sore, and it will take a while for his bruised ribs to heal. Jonathan gives us a ride home. He helps Cade get up the steps into the house and settles him in a chair before leaving. I offered him dinner, but he needed to get home to his wife.

We are quiet as we go about making dinner that evening. I push him to tell me about Shawna and how, if no girl ever measured up, why does he have a psycho ex-fiancée.

"I thought she could be the one. I wanted her to be. I thought we could figure out having a family and working through life. We had a place near the quarter, and she and I moved in fast. Shawna had some previous problems, but somewhere in my mind I was convinced, probably because of her promises, that she was over it and better," he explains.

"What do you mean by 'problems?'" I think I know, but I have to ask anyway.

He shrugs. "As a teenager, she was in and out of a local metal health facility. She had drug problems. Everything from weed to meth. She's done it all. Again, I thought she was a stronger person for it. She had me convinced it was behind her. It wasn't. After a couple years together, we were engaged. I came home from work one day and she was buzzing." He waves his hands. "You know, bouncing from topic to topic as she talked to me. She was like a bullet ricocheting off every surface."

He walks into the kitchen and takes a seat at the breakfast bar. "She was cooking and cleaning and happier than I had ever seen her. When I got her to tell me what she was so over the top about, she told me we were having a baby."

My mind spins out of control. This revelation makes my chest hurt. I'm not breathing well when I ask, "You have a baby with her?"

He shakes his head. "No. At the time, all I knew was that I had to make sure our wedding happened soon. I made a list of everything we needed before the baby was born. I worked extra hours. I found the house and started renovations as I could afford them. I had planned to surprise her when it was finished. The more I worked, the further apart we seemed to grow. One day I came home from work, and she was passed out in the floor of the kitchen. I scooped her up and drove her to the ER."

His face falls as he goes on, "That's when my world fell apart. Shawna had been using again. She had overdosed, and that's what made her pass out. Since she was pregnant, they ran all kinds of tests on the baby. Come to find out the baby didn't have a heartbeat. They kept her a couple days in the hospital to help her sober up a little bit, so they could tell her about the baby and perform a D&C. I didn't know what to say to her. I know the vows weren't taken yet, but to me they were just as serious in the situation. 'For better or worse, in sickness and health.' I wanted to be there for her. I wanted to give her another chance. I tried."

My heart breaks for him at the same time I feel relieved. It's a sick feeling. "You tried to fix her, didn't you?"

He nods. "But I was angry with her. I resented her. The more I thought about it, I couldn't stay with her. She chose drugs over our unborn baby. What would have happened if she hadn't overdosed? Would my baby have been born addicted? How would we have handled that? I went into her hospital room and offered to help her through rehab. She went crazy, screaming at me and causing such a scene that the hospital staff asked me to leave. I did. But the next day, and several days after, I went back over and over and over again. I begged her to get help and we would continue our life together. I never realized that it was a battle I couldn't win.

I sit on his lap and wrap my arms around his neck. "You can't fix everyone. Hell, sometimes I wonder if anyone can be fixed if they don't want it for themselves," I muse.

He nuzzles my neck, and says, "The relationship I thought we had was never what she thought we had. Everything I thought we were, thought we had ahead of us, was gone. Our future. Gone."

I consider everything he's telling me. I have been so wrapped up in my own shitty situation that I never once thought about what Irma meant when she told me he was a broken as me. On the one hand, I think we shouldn't be together. Two people as broken as we are can't possibly be any good for each other. Can we?

He looks away from me, distant. "I'm sorry I never told you any of this. I didn't want to burden you with all you are already dealing with."

"We all have shit we're dealing with. I can't judge you for dealing with yours in your own way. She'll figure out her life eventually. Once she gets out of jail," I say sarcastically.

After a long kiss, we pick back up on our discussion about Bell Hills and what needs to happen there. Eventually, we head to bed like an old couple. He holds me, and I hold him. I nearly lost him, and I just can't seem to let go. What if I had lost him? The thought causes a pain in my chest. It was really close. I do my best not to think about it. It's absolutely insane to think that I would love him and lose him so close to losing Ryan. I would check in to the local mental hospital if that had happened. It would have ended me.

Over the next few days, we talk about our trip back to Bell Hills. We decide on an early morning trip to North Mississippi. We should get back in time to let us meet with the agent for my house the same day. When Friday morning rolls around, I wake Cade up and get him in the shower while I make travel cups of coffee and a picnic, so we don't have to stop to eat anywhere. After Cade gets out of the shower, I hop in. Before long, we are ready to hit the road.

Cade refuses to let me drive, which thoroughly pisses me off. I'm not sure he realizes how much I love to drive. I suppress my irritation by sipping on my coffee. Smiling, I reach over and hold his hand which is resting on the seat beside him. The distance between us feels too great. I move the things between us to the floorboard and slide over. Cade moves his arm at the same time, making room for me to snuggle into his side, and I do. I rest my head on his chest as we ride in silence. For once, instead of watching the sunset together, we watch the sunrise over the interstate.

The trip is quicker than I expected. This may be because I missed most of it. I ran out of coffee, and that, mixed with the rhythmic motion of the truck and pounding of Cade's heart under my ear, must have lulled me to sleep. He never made an attempt to wake me up. He just let me sleep for the whole trip. I wake as we pull into my driveway. My house looks so tiny compared to Cade's. A twinge of regret pulls at my chest when I look at it as something I'm leaving behind.

"Ready?" Cade asks as if reading my mind.

"As I'll ever be."

We go inside the house and I look around. Having cleaned so much out, there is still so much to do. There is a laundry list of things to be done, people to see, and goodbyes to be said. Cade sits on the couch and pats the space beside him. I assume my place in the crook of his arm.

"I want to go see Irma," I say after a while.

He smiles down at me and kisses my forehead. "We can do that."

We decide to walk. It's chilly, but not unbearable today. A walk will do us some good after the long car ride. As we approach the steps to the porch, Irma bursts through the door.

"Get up here, girl!"

I bound up the steps and right into her arms. She is a petite woman but seems to swallow me in a hug as fierce as Cade's. "I missed you, Mrs. Irma."

"Child, you call me Irma. I missed you too, baby. Are things better?"

I nod. "Better than I could have ever imagined."

She smiles and holds my face for a few minutes, forcing me to look her in the eyes. When she seems satisfied I am telling her the truth, she releases me and turns to Cade, who is standing awkwardly a few feet away from us. His face is turned to the floor, and he is shifting on his feet.

Irma walks over to him purposefully and smacks his arm as hard as possible across the back of his head. I jump, and I'm about to rush over, but something stops me. I know better than to step in the middle of someone being handed their ass.

"What is wrong with you? You were raised better than that." She rants on, and there are only pieces that I catch in her rapid-fire tirade. Bits of "know better" and "didn't even call" and "actin' like a fool" and so on. Finally, she reaches the end of her anger and grabs his face, making him look into her eyes. When he does, I notice they are both crying.

"I'm sorry, Grandmama. I didn't mean to do it either. I made a decision, and it spiraled from there. I promise I won't do anything like that again."

Her face softens. "Oh, honey. I don't want you to do better for me. Do better for you. For Rhae."

He smiles and hugs his grandmother, lifting her off the ground in his enthusiasm.

She starts squirming and fussing, "Dammit! Put me down, boy!

Have you lost your mind?" He sets her down and wipes the tears from her face. "Well, let's not stand around freezing to death. Get in the house."

Irma makes us fresh coffee as we bide time around her dining room table. When she sits with us, she reaches out and takes my hand and then Cade's.

"I saw this," she begins. "I knew you needed each other. You were both broken and didn't know how badly. Rhae had to find her own way to see that you were where she needed to be. Her home. Cade, you had to grieve your grandfather and wait patiently on Rhae. Neither of you are fixed yet, but I can see the lines mending."

Pride beams through me. I squeeze her hand and nod. "Patience has never been a strong suit for me."

"No ma'am it has not. Your mama and I spoke about that recently."

"What? What do you mean? You spoke to my mama?" That doesn't make sense. Mama is only in my dreams. Well, Dad's and mine.

"Honey, I see things you don't see. I have been visiting with your mama since Ryan died. Before you were ever involved with Cade. I knew what was happening to you."

I nod, and tears tickle my cheeks. When did I become such a crybaby? This is the most annoying part of allowing someone in. I get emotional, and dammit if it isn't like a leaky faucet. *Drip, drip, drip.*

Cade looks puzzled when he asks, "Grandma, why did you keep everything from me? Why didn't you clue me into what you knew? I could have avoided all the heartache I put her through."

"Had to figure it out on your own. Just because I know things, doesn't mean I need to involve myself. Was bad enough I told Rhae that I knew about her dreams. Ryan and her mama meandering through her head every night. If I didn't let you figure it out, it wouldn't mean so much to be with her now. Would it?" Oh, she is good. She has him pegged so well.

We finish our coffee, and I fill Irma in on my plan for the house. She smiles, and of course, tells us that she knew I would do this. I can't help but side with Cade on thinking knowing what she knew would have been helpful during this whole ordeal. Bottom line: I know she's right. We would have said she was crazy if she told us. Hell, I still think she's a little nuts, but in the best kind of way.

My cell rings and it's the real estate agent. She's on her way. Cade and I love on Irma little bit more, and then we head for the house. The agent is already there as we arrive. Standing with her is a man I've never met before. After some brief introductions, I learn the man is an attorney who works with my agent, Mr. Austin.

My agent starts, "I hope you don't mind, but with this type of request, there is quite a bit of paperwork to have done. I already had the house inspected, and it passed with flying colors. Mr. Austin has drawn up the closing paperwork. You can sign them now, and, per your request, we will let you deliver the papers to Ms. Richards. Make sure she signs them in front of a notary."

"Thank you so much. I appreciate your proactive approach. I think this is all perfect. Thank you, Mr. Austin. You have been most helpful." I offer him my hand to shake.

Mr. Austin shakes my hand. "Can I ask you a question?"

"Of course."

"Why would you pay off your house, only to sign the deed over to someone unrelated to you? It is the most bizarre case I have ever worked."

"I don't really know how to answer that. There is a long story behind the notion. Suffice it to say, I'm gratefully paying it forward to someone who may or may not deserve good things." I turn to face Cade as I finish. He is beaming and squeezes my hand. He still hasn't gotten past the need to touch me all the time.

"I guess I'll never understand that sentiment. But I wish you well, Ms. Peters."

I shake his hand again. Cade and I stand on the porch as we watch the car pull away.

"Think you can go through with this?" he asks.

"I know I can. No big deal. Total peace," I answer confidently. "Can I borrow your truck?"

"Of course, but it'll cost you."

"Oh yeah, what's the going rate?"

Cade places his hands on either side of my face and leans in. He kisses me. It isn't insistent, or urgent. There's nothing but the tender pressure of his lips on mine. We stay there for a minute. When he releases my mouth, he touches his forehead to mine. I keep my eyes closed. "Be careful," he whispers.

"I will. Back soon."

I take Cade's truck and head for Lakeview. My first stop is to Ryan's mother's house. We haven't spoken since the funeral. I bring her boxes of Ryan's things, and then tell her about Melody and the baby. It is one of the hardest conversations I've ever had. She becomes overwhelmed with sadness and joy. When she reaches the point of acceptance, I tell her my plans for the house. I invite her to a dinner I'm planning tomorrow.

Next, I drive toward the community college. Making the necessary turns, I notice that I'm driving on Cypress. I haven't driven on this road since Ryan's accident. Approaching the city limits sign marking the divide between Bell Hills and Lakeview, my breath catches. There are deep ruts off the side of the road. There is grass growing in the ruts, but they are still clear. I slow down and pull off the road.

I walk around the front of the truck and stand in the ruts. My eyes trace them to where they disappear. I can feel what happened here. My sixth sense tells me this is where Ryan wrecked. Standing in the middle of the ditch on the side of the road, I begin to shake and cry. My hand flies to my mouth, covering it, trying to dampen the sounds emanating from me. I fall to my knees and close my eyes. This is it. Where my life changed. Where Ryan's life ended. I stay there, frozen, until the tears pass. When they do, I am a snotty mess, and I can feel the swelling rising around my eyes.

Am I mourning Ryan or the loss of what I thought was a perfect life? Mourning Ryan was how I have spent the last several months of my life. Isn't it? Maybe it's shock from seeing the evidence I turned a blind eye to for so long. I didn't want to see his body, or his Jeep. I certainly never wanted to see this.

"Get up!" I say out loud to myself. "Get the fuck off the ground. It's over. You have a new life to live." Somewhere deep within, I find the strength to stand. I get in Cade's truck and clean up my face in his rearview mirror. It's bad, but not as bad as I thought. I spend a few minutes catching my breath and steadying myself. When I'm ready, I pull back on to the road and finish my drive to Lakeview.

When I pull into the parking lot of the college, I realize I'm not sure where to find Melody. I park the truck in a spot and decide to try the administration building to see if they will help me find her. I walk into the building and stop at the information desk. The girl working the desk has her back to me as she's filing a stack of paperwork. I clear my throat to get her attention, and she spins around.

The first thing I notice is her protruding belly. I'm speechless as I look from her belly to her face. A hollowness starts to fill my chest. I'm stunned at the feeling. Silently, I pray that maybe God will give me one of my own in the future. I tell myself it just wasn't meant to be for Ryan and me. It wasn't the right time.

I'm positive this is the girl who came to my house. It's Melody. I never expected to walk into the first building on campus and find her. The shock of the moment throws me off my game. The look on her face is one of fear mixed with anger; maybe embarrassment.

"Hey," I say as I walk closer to her.

She looks confused. "Hey. What are you doing here?"

"Look, I know you don't owe me anything, but I would like to talk to you. Are you working? When do you get a break?"

"You talked to me when you didn't owe me anything. So, it's only fair for me to return the favor." She rubs her belly and sighs. "I get off in half an hour. I'll meet you at the union building."

"Deal." I smile and head over to the union.

I find a table in a secluded corner of the room and settle in to wait. Nearly an hour later she comes waddling into the room. I mean, that poor girl is carrying a large baby. Larger than I think her frame should be carrying. Poor girl doesn't walk; she waddles. I make a mental note not to say anything about that though. The last thing I want to do is upset her.

She takes a seat across from me and starts, "What brings you here?"

"I was a real bitch the last time we spoke. The first thing I need to do is apologize to you. I'm sorry for that. I won't make excuses about the state of mind I was in or the hell my life had become. I was raised better than that."

"You were a bitch," she says and smiles at me. "But you had every reason to treat me that way. I wasn't thinking clearly either. I bear at least fifty percent of the responsibility for the affair with Ryan."

I don't feel like re-hashing the same things. "Let's move forward," I say. "I have been thinking a lot lately. Actually, trying to figure out some things about what needs to happen so that I can move on. I need to let him go, and I need to forgive him. I can't forgive him while I'm still angry. The anger has to go first. It has been eating at me and keeping me unhappy."

"Okay," she says timidly.

I try to smile. "When Ryan died, he had a life insurance policy through his job. It was substantial."

"How lovely for you," she says with a twisted smirk.

"Stay with me here. My original plan was to quit my job and travel for a year or so. Living like a nomad sounded interesting. I deposited the money in the bank and quit my job the same day. I even made a trip to New Orleans."

Melody leans forward and puts her elbows on the table. "Was it everything people say it is? Magical? Haunted?" She's genuinely curious.

I smile. "Both. What happened there was a defining moment for me. I decided to get rid of my house and move there." I don't mention Cade right now. "Ryan and I didn't owe much on it. We bought it for a steal and fixed it up over the years. So, I used some of the money he left me and paid it off."

I reach down into my bag and pull out the stack of paperwork my lawyer friend prepared. I slide them toward her.

"I have already signed these papers, but we need to go find a notary to witness your signature." I stop and give her a few minutes to read through the top page.

Melody's hand covers her mouth and tears fill her eyes. She looks from the papers to me and back to the papers. "This isn't real. You are not giving me a house."

I nod and smile. "I am. I have no need for it now. Ryan and I shared it. Even if I wasn't moving to New Orleans, I wouldn't stay there. I can't. The pain for me is overwhelming when I'm there. I want you and the baby to have it. Give that baby a good start."

She is sobbing now. "I don't know what to say."

"Don't say anything. Well, do say you know a notary where we can get your signature on the papers. Then we need to work out a moving schedule." I reach out to hold her hand. "This wasn't all your fault, and this way Ryan can still sort of provide for the baby."

Melody rises from her chair and comes over to hug me. She swallows hard and wipes the tears from her face. "I know a notary. We have to go back to the administration building and see the registrar." And we do.

I'm so emotionally spent that I physically hurt by the time I get home to Cade. The sun is setting and casting shadows across the house. Cade meets me on the porch and takes my purse, helping me to the bed. I flop unattractively and just lay there. He sits beside me and rubs my arm in soothing circles.

"Can I help?" he asks.

"No. It went way better than I thought it would, and she cried. A lot. My brain is fried from all of this."

He kisses my forehead. "I know. It's all gravy from here. Want dinner?"

I shake my head. "No. I can't eat. I need a shower, the bed, and you." Cade obliges my requests and tucks me into bed.

I guess it was the stress of the previous day and the long drive from New Orleans, but I sleep until well into the afternoon the next day. Surfacing, I recognize the laughter of my sister in the other room. Curiosity gets the better of me, and I reluctantly throw my legs out of the bed. My body protests as I stand. It feels good to stretch and wake up my muscles. I pad over to the door and close it, so I can get dressed. When I finish brushing my teeth, I go into the living room.

Jess, Connor, Cade, and Jillian are all sitting there. Jillian is curled up in Cade's lap, and she is bright red.

"What's up?" I ask. Everyone turns to look at me. Jess stands and comes over to hug me.

"Thought I wouldn't get to see you again. Dad made it sound like you were running away forever."

I hug her back. "Not forever. Just long enough to figure out my life."

"And the results are?" she asks.

"Perfect." I make eye contact with Cade when I answer. He smiles and slides Jillian out of his lap. She runs to me and jumps in my arms.

"Aunt Rhae!" She has grown at least a foot since I last saw her.

"Hey, Jillybean. How are you, sweet girl?"

"Mama won't let me have any coffee."

"Someone is going to step on that bottom lip if you leave it out like that. You listen to your mama. She knows what she's talking about. Growing girls don't need coffee." I give her a stern look. That is until Jess turns to go into the kitchen. Then I smile at Jillian and say, "I'll sneak you a sip."

Jillian is so excited she squeezes my neck and kisses my cheek. "I love you, Aunt Rhae. You're the best!" I set her down and walk over to the recliner where Cade is sitting. He opens his arms, and I sit on his lap and nuzzle into his neck.

"Sleep good?" he asks while rubbing my back.

"Yeah. What's the plan today?" I ask.

"Well, first," Jess starts, "you need to get your grown ass off that man and make a list of everything that needs to happen to get you moved. I can't lie, I'm jealous as hell that you are moving to N'awlins."

I sit up and look at Cade. "You told them?"

He shrugs. "We got close when I went trying to find you, plus we are going to need some help."

I nod. "I know. I'm really glad you called them."

Connor jumps in with plans for trailers and trucks. Logistics makes my head spin. Cade echoes the sentiments and expounds on ideas that Connor has. Jess motions with her head for me to follow her out on the back porch. I grab Jillian's hand and the three of us slip outside while the boys get more and more animated in their discussion. You would think those two had been hanging out on a daily basis or something. They act like old friends.

Out on the porch, Jess sends Jillian to play in the yard. We sit at the table and face each other. Jess looks pensive, and ready to pounce.

"Go ahead. Ask," I say.

"What do you mean? Ask what?" she feigns confusion.

"You know you want to ask. You are about to bounce out of your skin. Ask," I say again.

"Okay, well, maybe there are a few things I might want to ask about. I mean, you're okay with me asking?"

"Why wouldn't I be? Ask away."

"Well, first, what the hell happened? You're moving to N'awlins with him? It's like Ryan all over again when you were a teenager."

I sigh and shake my head. "It is not like Ryan at all. I'm much older and wiser. I know what I'm doing. I really can't explain what's going on with us. When we ran into each other in New Orleans…" I attempt to cover for Cade's stalker mission to find me. "I just knew."

"Knew what? You aren't getting married, are you?"

"God, no! I have no desire to get married again. We are going to live together. What I knew was that he didn't intend to hurt me. We had a long talk and I understand what was going on in his head a little better, that's all."

"You already jumped into bed with him!" she exclaims.

"Shhh! Keep it down. They are probably at the door listening to us. Jumped is a bit ambitious since we're both recovering from that bullshit with his ex."

"Still won't talk about sex," she mocks.

"Actually, you're right. It was amazing. My hotel room, the shower, his house, a field in the middle of nowhere, all amazing."

"Now you're talkin', sister. Tell me more about the shower. God, that man is delicious, and that smile… Tell me! Tell me!"

I grin. "Oh, so do you want me to tell you about this thing he did with his tongue while we were in the shower?"

"I'm going to die! Yes! Tell me!"

"Sorry, can't. No kiss and tell for me. Just suffice to say, we have closed that gap, and we work well together on that level."

She swats at me, "Bitch! I'm calling Liz. I can't believe you won't tell me. I can live vicariously through you, and you won't share."

"Uh, hello, Connor?" I ask.

"I wouldn't trade him for the world, but you are having a brand-new romance. I want to share the details. Maybe get a thrill by proxy."

We both laugh, and it feels good to relax with her in a way I haven't in a long time.

"Call Liz. Red too. They can help us with all this packing and planning."

She looks surprised, "Okay, will do." She goes in the house and starts making phone calls. I head down the porch steps and play with Jillian, who is inspecting an ant hill at the base of the old oak tree. I squat beside her quietly and watch her poke the hill with a stick.

After a few minutes, she looks up at me and says, "I love Mr. Cade. Him is handsome. Him loves you, Aunt Rhae. Can I call him uncle?"

I smile and tuck a stray piece of hair behind her ear. "You can call him whatever you want to call him, honey. He's not really an uncle, but if you feel better calling him that, you can. He is pretty handsome, isn't he?"

Her cheeks stain red and she starts giggling. "What is it, baby?" I ask, laughing with her. She doesn't answer me, she just points, and I have to turn around to see what she's pointing at. When I do, I see Cade standing behind me, a bright smile on his face.

"Handsome, huh?"

"She has a crush on you," I say dismissively and gesture to Jilly.

He nods. "Ah ha. What about you? Do you have a crush on me?"

I shake my head. "Nah. You're too pretty for my tastes."

We both laugh, and he scoops up a waiting Jillian into his arms and carries her in the house. Jess has been busy making more coffee and pulling my calendar off the wall, so we can write on it as we discuss the moving plan.

That evening we spend approximately twenty minutes discussing the necessary moving items. Mostly we drink, dance, sing, and engage in general foolishness. Liz and Red get in a fuss over something. Jess and Connor put Jilly to bed in my room and slow dance in my living room. I sit back with Cade and take in all the people I love being here with me.

17 Moving Day

Moving day is upon us. I still haven't really told the girls what I plan to do with my house. They assume I've sold it. I'm not afraid to tell them. It's more that I want to leave Melody with a support structure. I need to find the right way to tell them. Cade has been a complete saint through the whole process. Crazy. They'll all think I'm insane for giving my late husband's mistress my house. Fact is, barring the death of Ryan, I've been blessed beyond anything I could ever deserve. She screwed up, but I need to pass my blessings on to someone I think could appreciate it, and I'm certain she comes from good people. They will help her take care of the place.

Tomorrow, everyone will be here to load the truck to send Cade and I off back to New Orleans. I didn't even have to go rent the truck. Cade is taking care of that, too. Back to the comfort of making lists, I sit down at the table with a cup of coffee. I think through the storage places on the property. I'm going to leave the mower and yard stuff for Melody. I just need to get the rest of Ryan's stuff out of the attic and pack my bedroom. Then I think a dinner tonight with everyone will be the perfect send off and time to drop the bomb on them.

"Morning," Cade says as he enters the kitchen. I watch him pour a cup of coffee. He walks over to where I'm sitting, kissing me on the forehead as he takes the seat beside me. "List making?"

"Yeah. It gives me a sense of control. Although, I'm pretty sure this is going to be rather chaotic."

"We'll get through it. Did you call her?" he asks.

"No. I need to do that," I say, standing to leave the room. Cade grabs my hand and tugs me back to him. I stumble and fall into his lap. He wraps me in his arms and cradles me against his chest.

"It'll work out the way it's supposed to," he whispers in my ear.

"I know."

He holds me for a few more minutes and then releases me so I can go make the phone calls to get tonight rolling. I call my family, Alana, Lucy, and Jules. Everyone agrees to meet at my house for dinner at seven. I am beyond excited to have everyone in the same room. My next phone call is to Melody. I ask her to come at seven-thirty. This should give me some time to explain to everyone what the plan is. Nerves make me sick to my stomach thinking about it. They won't understand, but I need them to hear why I'm doing this. The house is hers no matter what they say. I just need to convince them to accept her and support her the way they would me. That's the most important part.

When I finish calling everyone, I start working on packing the bedroom and bathroom. Everything I pick up is a trigger. Before I know it, I have three boxes packed, but I'm crying with every step. I am such a baby. Ugly crying for what? I sit on the edge of the bed and hold a glass frog Ryan gave me when we first started dating. I stare at it and rub my hands over it. It is smooth and cold. The memory of the night he gave it to me is a fond one. As I sniffle, I think my memories are a curse. Lifting my arm, I prepare to throw it and smash it against the wall when a hand catches my arm. Cade.

"Woah, baby. Don't do that!"

"Why not? It's mine to smash if I want." I'm a little surlier than expected. Crying makes me angry.

"You'll regret it. Leave it here for Melody, but don't smash it," he says gently. I know he's right, and that pisses me off more.

"Whatever. Fine." I stand and wrap the frog in a piece of newspaper. Placing it in the box, I notice Cade is sitting still, staring at me. "What?"

"Nothing. C'mere," he holds his arms open for me. I roll my eyes because, even though I'm pissed, hurt, and have more to do than I think I can finish today, I go to him. Standing between his legs, he wraps his arms around my waist and rests his head on my belly. I try to resist his attempts to soothe me, but before I can put up much of a fight, my hands are running through his hair. He squeezes me closer to him. Falling back on the bed, he pulls hard around my waist, so I land on top of him, letting out an uncharacteristic squeak.

Balancing myself, I pull my knees up to the bed, straddling him and staring into his beautiful eyes. He's grinning from ear-to-ear. "How about a little tension breaker?" he asks innocently. Actually, not so innocently. The smile that follows the statement clues me into his intentions.

"What did you have in mind?" I ask, attempting to be flirty. I'm such a failure at these kinds of nuances.

Cade reaches up to grab the back of my neck and pull me in for a kiss. I can feel him stir beneath me, and his intentions are blatantly clear. I hesitate for a moment when I think I hear a knock on the front door. Pulling back, I mumble, "Was that the door?"

"Who cares?" he's grabbing for me again. There it is again. That was definitely a knock on the door.

"Someone's here." I push off him and run my fingers through my hair as I run to answer the door. Before I can get to it, the door opens.

"Rhae, baby!" Irma greets me.

"Irma, how are you?" I hug her and motion for her to come in. Cade stumbles out of the bedroom with a couple boxes in his arms.

"Grandma. What are you doing here?" he asks.

"I came to see if there's anything I can do to help you pack up the house. Looks like you two got tangled up while you were packing."

Heat floods my face, and I look down to see that my clothes are in place. She has a sixth sense for busting Cade. It has nothing to do with anyone looking guilty. I shake my head as Irma lets out a laugh as boisterous as Cade's.

"Grandma. Please. Don't make Rhae blush."

Irma turns to look at me. "Too late!"

We all have a good laugh. I slip away to make some fresh coffee. Irma joins me as I'm scooping the coffee grounds into the filter. "So, who bought the house?" Irma asks.

"I suspect you've already seen what I'm doing with the house," I say.

"You're right. I wanted to see if you would tell me." She smiles and offers me a hug. I take it. She squeezes me and then looks up at me. "You sure you good with doing this?"

I consider her question. "It feels like closure. I'm feeling, I don't know, peaceful about it, I guess. Like, for the first time, I'm doing something right."

She stares intently into my eyes, and then looks past me. I look behind me and there's no one there. She nods, smiles, and then turns back to me. "You are doing the right thing. It doesn't matter if no one understands the reasons. It is the right thing."

"Who were you looking at?" the idea that I'm asking about ghosts or spirits hanging out in my kitchen, eavesdropping on our conversation, is mind-boggling. Irma doesn't answer me. She shakes her head and *tsks* me. I knew better than to ask. I haven't had Ryan or Mama in my dreams for a while now. I thought they had moved on. I guess they did move on from hanging out in my subconscious, but not from watching over me. The thought is strangely comforting.

"Can I ask a favor, Irma?"

"Sure thing, sweet-pea."

"Will you watch over Melody? She's going to have a new baby, and she's trying to finish school. Poor girl still works two jobs on top of all that. She'll need you."

Irma looks like she is mulling over my request. "Of course I will. I'm gonna be a grandma to that baby. You watch." She smiles, and I see a twinkle in her eyes. She means it. She really will insert herself in the life of the new baby and Melody.

The three of us spend the afternoon packing the last of the stuff in my house. Cade drags everything out of the attic. I decide to leave every box labeled "Ryan" for Melody to go through and do with as she chooses. About the time we wrap up packing, people start arriving. I'm regretful because I didn't get to shower before they got here. Cade hugs everyone as they come through the door, and I introduce them all to Irma. I leave out the part about her ability to read them. It's pretty clear when she takes to loving on Jess and admonishing Liz. Lord only knows what she saw of Liz to make her fuss. But in true Liz fashion, she pays attention and takes everything Irma says to heart.

The best part of introducing everyone was when I got to introduce my friends from work to my sisters. Alana, Lucy, and Jules are such a perfect complement to my family. Ryan's mom pulls into the driveway right before my Dad, who has brought a bottle of champagne with him.

"It's a celebration, right?" he says with bright eyes and a broad smile.

"Yes, it is," I answer. "Did you bring bourbon for yourself?"

"Yes, I did." He winks and pulls another bottle from inside his jacket.

I laugh and hug him. Hard. I love him so much. We have gotten over our communication issues. Really, there were never any issues. Our communication patterns don't fit the pattern Jess has with him, but it doesn't make ours wrong. We give each other what we need when we need it.

Cade helps me herd everyone into the living room. He stands by my side with his arm around my waist.

"First, I wanted to thank you all for coming tonight. I can't imagine a better send off. Well, maybe better if I could get you all to come to New Orleans with us. But I know that moving down there with Cade is a new life for me. A life that I need."

The group gives me a round of applause and "woo hoos." Cade squeezes me when he notices I'm blushing and nerves are making me shake a little bit.

"As you know, when Ryan died, I got the worst surprise I could imagine. Hell, I couldn't have even imagined what I found out. I shared with you all that he had been having an affair. His pregnant mistress showed up at the house to meet me after he died. I won't lie or candy-coat it: I was a straight-up bitch to her. While most of you will agree that I have every right to treat her that way for what she did with my husband, the guilt of doing that has been eating at me. Coming to see me had to be one of the hardest things to do. I gave her judgement. I yelled at her and kicked her out of my house.

"When I decided to move to New Orleans, I was faced with another decision. What to do with the house? As you know Ryan and I refurbished this house. It was as much his as it is mine. With the money I got from Ryan's life insurance, I was able to pay it off. So, I did something you all may not understand or agree with. I signed the house over to Melody as a gift."

I stop and let the news sink in. Liz and Red look astounded. Alana, Jules, and Lucy have watery eyes. Jess nods and holds Dad's hand. Irma is the first to speak, "That's our girl."

The corners of my mouth turn up into a small smile as I survey the faces of the others in the room. Ryan's mother smiles and says, "That's what Ryan and your mama would have wanted you to do. I'm proud of you."

Everyone takes turns weighing in their support of my decision. The pride that fills my chest squeezes as each one speaks. "There's more," I interrupt, and look over at Cade for support. He nods. "I need you to be a support structure for her. Babysit, drop in, mow the grass, invite her to dinner... just... include her. She comes from good people. I think that's a bigger gift than the house."

"Do you know us at all?" Liz asks. "Of course we'll include her. She is one of us now."

I beam. "Great. I'm glad to hear it." I look over at the clock on the mantle. "She'll be here any minute."

Everyone looks a little surprised, but the buzz of discussion goes on as if it really isn't a big deal that I've invited her over. I shrug and shake my head. This could not be going better if I dreamed it. Honestly, I thought they might be okay with the house, but not being a part of her life. Goes to show you that people can surprise you. In a good way.

Melody arrives right on time. Cade answers the door and leads her to the living room where she is hugged by each member of my family and friends. The ladies rub her belly and talk about due dates. At first, she looks shocked but then settles in. Jess, Liz and Alana take the lead talking about giving her a shower and helping her move. Red brings her a glass of tea and offers to help babysit when little-bit arrives. Ryan's mom is timid and a little shy with Melody, but they are talking like old friends before long.

Dad moves over by me to get out of the way.

"Hey, kid."

"Hey, Daddy."

"You done good. You know that?"

"I think I do."

"I'm proud of you. I know your mama always was, and I think she is even more today."

Tears threaten, as I lean into his side. "Thanks, Dad. You sure you like Cade enough to let me move off with him?"

He looks over me to smile at Cade who is busying the food to grill. "Yep. That's a good one right there."

I squeeze him in a hug and take in all the activity in my house.

Dinner is uneventful. In fact, I don't have to do much talking at all. The girls take over cooking, serving, conversations, and eventually cleaning. I walk Melody out at the end of the night. I feel like I need to talk to her one-on-one for minute.

"Sorry about ambushing you with my family," I start.

"Nonsense. They are all amazing. I can't believe they accepted me like that. Thank you for including me."

"Would you do something for me?"

"Anything."

"Look after Irma for us. We are going to be about six hours away. We may not be able to get to her quickly if something happens. It would sure help to know that someone is here."

"I'm honored you would ask. It's funny because she asked if the baby could call her Grandma. She wants to babysit for me when I have to go to school or work."

"I think you two will be good for each other. Thank you."

I hug her and help her into the car. I don't know if we'll ever be friends, but the closure on this chapter of my life is complete.

The next day, everyone comes to the house to help load the truck. We are all standing around waiting for Cade to bring the truck. Red is frustrated because there's been a cold snap, and we are freezing.

I'm just about to go in the house and start fresh coffee when I hear a honk and see a truck pulling in the driveway. The truck is white with a blue logo on the side. I step off the porch to get a good look at the logo because it doesn't seem like any rental truck logo I've seen before.

The logo reads: MILES CONSTRUCTON, NEW ORLEANS, LA. I stop and stare for a few minutes. Cade hops out of the driver's seat and walks over to me. "Got the truck!"

"I see that. Mind explaining *where* you got the truck?" I'm stunned.

"Well, that's something I never got around to telling you. I picked up the truck from my office in Memphis this morning."

My mind seems fuzzy, definitely not enough coffee. "Your office? You own Miles Construction?"

He nods. "Opened right after Katrina. I helped repair houses from New Orleans to Jackson and do general construction all the way up to Nashville."

"Shut the fuck up."

He laughs. "What?"

"Why didn't you tell me?"

"What was I going to say? Plus, you love me for me, not my company or money. It's not like I'm some cushy office executive. I work with my men on job sites. I'm very hands on."

"Well, I knew that. You are always hands on." I smirk.

"Is this a problem for you?" he asks.

"Not if it's not a problem for you. I may just laze about the house now. No reason for me to find a job in spite of spending all my money to pay off the house."

"Oh, I don't know, maybe you could be my home office administrator and webmaster?"

"You have really lost your mind." I reach up and check him for fever.

"You don't think we can work together?" he asks.

I think for a moment. "We work well together." I smile and steal a quick kiss. Cade grabs me and hauls me up off my feet, kissing me silly and spinning me around in circles. I laugh. It is a light laugh that makes me feel alive.

He sets me down and smiles like he can't ever get enough of me. I know I can't get enough of him. I never thought we would be here. I turn to see my whole family standing on the porch. They are smiling approvingly. I know they love him too.

I don't know what the future holds, but I'm sure of one thing: I have found my feet. I have found a place to stand.

About the Author

Meg Farrell was born and raised in Mississippi where she and her husband, Jason, still make their home. The Farrells have three children and a host of other non-human lifeforms.

Most of the time Meg can be found running between softball fields, hockey rinks, band concerts, and choir performances. Meg is an avid reader and enjoys books from nearly every genre.

In February 2016, Meg received an award from the readers of the DeSoto Times Tribune naming her as DeSoto County Mississippi's Best Author 2015.

Meg's books are available on Amazon for purchase as a paperback or e-book.

Learn more about Meg and how to connect with her on social media by going to http://www.farrellwrites.com.

A Place to Stand

Mea Farrell

Other Books by Meg

Short Story

Contemporary Romance

Children's Humor

Made in the USA
Columbia, SC
06 August 2018